STAR CHILD

By Leonard Petracci

A story of superpowers

Dedication

To my family, friends, and online community - without them, this would not be possible.

Poets say science takes away from the beauty of the stars - mere globs of gas atoms. I too can see the stars on a desert night, and feel them. But do I see less or more?

-Richard Feynman

For more stories by Leonard Petracci, or to find out when book 2 of Star Child will be released, sign up for his mailing list on Amazon.

Contact Leonard at

LeonardPetracci@gmail.com

INTRODUCTION

Superpowers are based on the topography of where someone is born.

Chapter 1

It was an accident, of course.

My birth, my being in space, and well, I suppose I was an accident as well. An accident from the director of engineering screwing the fat janitor after hours when the rest of the shuttle team had retired; the odds that my mother had been able to hide her baby bump for nine months, the chances that she had been a nurse before being selected from the program and knew how to give birth herself, in a maintenance closet, mere days before the mission was to return to earth. Keeping me hidden was difficult in the small confines of the ship, but the other hundred and fifty crew members had been too busy to pay a mere maid much attention. After all, many insisted that it had not been worthwhile to bring her along, that a maid had been a waste of tax dollars. I suppose that makes me a waste of tax dollars as well.

But there were those that spoke to her unique abilities as a maid. For she had been born deep in the snow of the north, during the first blizzard of winter, that like the first snowfall, she could smooth over any differences in her environment and make it appear uniform. As a maid, it meant that she had an extraordinary sense of cleanliness. As a mother, it meant she could ensure I was overlooked, that my crying was muffled, and later in life, that I appeared no different from anyone else.

Star Child, she had called me as she smuggled me back into the atmosphere, tucked deep in her suit like a kangaroo would carry her young. Star Child, she whispered to me when the project disbanded, and she took me to the inner city apartment where I spent my early life. Star Child, she reprimanded whenever I started pushing and pulling at the equilibrium of our apartment, when she would arrive home from work and all the furniture would be clustered at the center of the room, pulled together by a force point.

"When will I go to school?" I asked her when I was eight, watching the uniformed children marching up the street through the wrought-iron gates of the academy, one of them flicking flames across his fingers like a coin while another left footprints of frost in the grass.

"You already go to school, Star Child," she said. "And your teachers say you've been learning your numbers well, and your reading has been progressing."

"Not *that* school," I had said, pulling a face. "I want to go to the academy. The special school, for the others like me!" I held up a fist, and items on the desk in front of me flew towards it, pens and papers and pencils that stuck out like quivering quills out of my skin.

"Star Child, listen and stop that at once," she said, her eyes level with mine. "There *are* no others like you. Those children; they are all classified, they are all known. You are *not* like them, you never will be. And they can't know, do you understand me?"

"I guess," I answered with a huff, watching as one of the children cracked a joke and the others laughed. "But I don't like my school. Everyone there knows we can't be like them, that we can't be special."

"Star Child, you *are* special. One day, they'll know that too. But not now - if they knew, they wouldn't take you to the academy. They'd take you somewhere else, somewhere terrible."

And as I grew older, I realized that she was right. That when our neighbor started developing powers, a police squad showed up at her front door and classified her on the spot. That they left her with a tattoo on her shoulder, a tattoo of a lightning bolt, symbolizing the storm during which she had been born. Just like the tattoo of a snowflake on my mother's shoulder, colored dull grey, to indicate a low threat potential.

So instead of going to the academy, I created an academy of my own, in my room. Mother made me turn the lights out at ten, so during the day, I collected light outside, keeping it in one of the dark holes I could create when I closed my fist hard enough, and letting it loose at night to read books I had stolen from the library. From the section for the special children, that I could only access if the librarians were distracted.

But distractions came easy to me.

As I grew older, the city streets became more populated with the blue uniforms of police. The academy became increasingly harder to attend, and the gifted girl next door disappeared one night without a note. Mother stopped letting me outside after dark, and the lines for the soup kitchens grew longer. The skies grew darker, the voices accustomed to speaking in whispers, and the television news seemingly had less and less to report. It was as if there was a blanket thrown upon us, but no one dared look to see who had thrown it.

But I would. And when I did, I realized the earth needed a Star Child.

Chapter 2

"Why can't anyone else know?" I asked my mother after school when I was thirteen. "Is something wrong with me?"

"Quite the opposite, Star Child. Let me tell you a story, the story of my early career in medicine," she responded as she set dinner down on the table. My stomach grumbled – I had skipped school lunch that day, preferring to deposit it in the waste bin rather than my mouth. Though he tried his hardest, our school chef had little control of his own powers, weak as they were. He claimed he was from Rome, one of the cities that produced the greatest chef power types, and that our meal was Chicken Parmesan, but neither of those statements held much merit. As I started shoveling food into my mouth, my mother continued to speak, her chair squeaking as she shifted.

"Before you were born, I was a nurse, specializing in the delivery of children. This was back in the north, near my home. But unless your power has a direct medical property, hospitals fear the effect it can have on children, so I was eventually removed from service. But by that time, I'd seen enough to make me want to leave.

"Not everyone is lucky enough to have powers, Star Child. But those who are, their power is altered, depending upon where they are born. Think of it like the seasoning in the meal you are eating – the food holds energy, but with the right spices, it can become enhanced. Similarly, a location can make a power *pop*. And people are willing to pay dearly for the locations.

"The fee my hospital charged was three times my personal salary per child. If there were twins, the couple was stuck with double the bill. And if there were no powers, the bill was still due. This particular hospital was high in the northern mountains, in an area statistically proven to produce the best powers of snow, ice, and weather. If your child had a power, here they would be the strongest. And if they didn't, well, I've heard too many stories of children entering orphanages after the parents wasted a fortune.

"The name of every child born in our hospital was placed on a list submitted to the police, who tracked them for the next two decades. Should a child commit a petty crime and have their name on the list, it was the same as committing a felony since these children were considered high risk. Unless you were still wealthy, of course. And it was strange, those names identified as having strong powers but belonging to a lower class, it seemed like they *always* committed a crime, without fail. That the police just happened to be waiting, watching them for when it happened. Ready to take them in and to send them to rehabilitation camps, where they would enter the military or the guard, after several years of conditioning, to sacrifice their lives on the front lines. And the more powerful you were, the more likely you were to be classified as a delinquent.

"So listen to me, Star Child. The hospital I worked at was a level three facility out of five. Level twos are even more dangerous, and level ones require a massive fortune to even step in the door. And as you know, having a baby in an unauthorized location is a crime punishable by death. Where you were born, that would be off the scales, a level zero location. Fortunately, you've been overlooked, but my power can only do so much. They'd use you or kill you, as a weapon or as a precaution. And you are destined for neither fate. You were fortunate enough that the space program that employed me ended early, due to solar flare activity, otherwise you would already be in the hands of the government. So you listen to me, and you tell no one, do you understand?"

"Yes," I answered, sighing as I finished my plate, and her hand rested heavily upon my shoulder. And that night, when I retired for sleep, I pulled out the first book I had ever stolen from underneath my bed. Opening my palm, I called forth the small black orb from where I had kept it hidden, in a small pocket just above my wrist. Not an actual pocket, but almost like the void under my tongue, or behind my ear. A place where it almost felt as if I had turned the space inside out, and could reach inside with my pinky.

Taking the orb, I unwrapped it slowly, letting the light trapped within escape in a small beam. Over time, it would grow smaller, until eventually with a flash, it would collapse, and I would have to make a new one during the day.

A Directory of Known Powers, the book was titled. *Capabilities and Locations.*

Introduction:

Little is known about what, precisely, determines the chance that a child will develop any abilities. Conversely, the factors playing into the type of power innate in a child are well studied and well documented within the pages of this directory.

There are many dimensions in which a child's power can be analyzed, but for simplicity, the following shall be mentioned due to their high correlation with observable outcomes: locations, power strength, and power type. Other minor effects include genetics, location and passion of conception, and diet during pregnancy. Environmental factors at the time of birth are also known to play a role in power development, though less documentation exists to confirm claims.

Yawning, I flipped through the pages to the pictures section, where a compilation of artists had depicted powers in use. Some were copies of pictures over a hundred years old, documenting powers that had not been seen in so long they were rumored to be myth. Others had so many occurrences that I skipped them, having seen them so often in real life, they now bored me.

Entry 348, Speaking in Tongues, read the title, while the picture showed a girl surrounded by people of all ethnicities, their ears tilted towards her.

Description: A condition in which languages no longer bond speech. Those born with this power have the ability to converse in multiple languages at the same time to multiple audiences.

Strength: Typically a lower level, measured by number and variety of languages that can be spoken, and whether the power can be extended to the written word. Owners of this power are also susceptible to side effects of Silver Tongue (see entry 427) and Pied Piper (see entry 201), which can increase the power by an order of magnitude.

Location: Documented cases occur in hospitals near border regions or in countries with multiple spoken languages.

I flipped backwards to an earlier entry and read another, yawning again as I felt sleep coming soon.

Entry 56, Diamond Exterior. This picture was of a glinting man, half his skin sparkling, the other half normal flesh.

Description: The ability to change portions of the body to rock or diamond, often razor sharp.

Strength: Typically a medium to high power level. Power is measured by mobility after transformation, as well as ability to change objects outside of their own body. Nearly indestructible and difficult to contain, those with strong abilities of this power are weighted extremely high.

Location: Documented cases occur in volcanic regions, with high frequencies at Magmar hospitals (LVL 1), located just above active Hawaiian volcanos. Prior to civilization, it is documented that entire islands once held this ability.

With a small *pop,* my reading orb exploded, illuminating my room like a camera flash for a split second before immersing me in darkness. I frowned – I was just getting to the section where hospitals of all levels were listed, but I'd only stored one orb today, as I had used most of mine reading the night before.

I lay back on my pillow as I drifted to sleep, dreaming about the academy despite my mother's words. Where I could maybe even see some of the rarer powers, where I'd be able to share my secret. Just like the other special children.

But before I had the chance to apply, when they accepted admissions entering higher education, the academy moved.

Chapter 3

"You know, you would have to be an *idiot* to be caught here," said the voice behind me, and I nearly fell out of the tree branch where I perched.

I'd been skipping school, *again*, a regular occurrence now that I was fifteen - this time, during a career fair where parents of the children arrived to show us *opportunities* for our futures. Jim, the short kid with glasses held together by tape so old it had started to dry rot, had turned a bright red when his father pulled the garbage truck into the school lot like a massive show-and-tell.

"You see here," said his father, his new school-provided name tag reading *Jim* already tarnished with a fleck of grease, "ev'ry day, we cart the trash away. That trash goes to the Calorie Exchanger teams, typically born near peat swamp regions, who convert what they can to petrol. Which keeps the lights on, kiddos. So next time you think of garbage, remember what you throw away *always* has value."

The class nodded, several staring towards the next location we would be herded to by Mrs. Whip, a low level Distraction Attenuator. Of course, she had never received any training for a power so minimal, but she was a Saturant, so she didn't have to - for Saturants, powers were involuntary. They simply flowed from the wielder like a type of charisma that could only be slightly enhanced with focus.

Turning right, I saw the Secretary Career location was next, and as we walked over, one of the parent's head snapped up as his face twitched.

"Kids! Oh, kids, futures! You have futures," he said, and his eyes jumped rapidly between each of us, yet never seemed to focus properly on any of our faces. This was Jessica's father, and she forced an encouraging smile as he entered a silence too many seconds long to be acceptable, his face strained as he fought for his next words. "Oh yes, futures! As a secretary, you are one of the most well, most well, most well paid out of all…"

He stopped, entering another silence, and Jessica spoke up, biting her lip.

"Go on, Daddy, out of all the Regulars," she prompted, and his face lit up, having found another train of thought as he continued, blinking several times in rapid succession.

"Like anyone would take that job," whispered Stephen from next to me, one of the children Mrs. Whip's effect seemed have no effect on, and who lived in an apartment several doors down from my own. "Working for the Specials, writing down every word at their important meetings, then having appointments with a Memory Drain at the end of each month to make sure you don't retain any information. By the looks of this one, he must work for someone *really* important. I bet they memory drain him every day."

I shook my head as Jessica prompted her father again and found myself losing interest, my eyes wandering to the fence at the edge of school property. Behind us, Mrs. Whip was quietly laughing as she spoke to Mr. Lynch, the muscular gym teacher who sometimes drove her home after school, and his eyes were practically glued to her own.

"I'm heading to use the restroom," I said to Stephen as I felt my focus falter again, Mrs. Whip's tinkling laugh sounding behind us as other members of the class shuffled their feet. "I'll probably just join the class behind us so I don't miss anything. If anyone asks, let them know that."

"Hey, you can fool them, but you can't fool me," he answered with a wink. "I'd join ya, but Mum said I won't get dinner if she catches me skipping again."

So I made my way to the restrooms, and from the restrooms out the shattered window in one of the back classrooms that had been on the school repair list since last September. And I walked to something more interesting, something I could only see when I skipped my own lessons around this time.

The academy, at recess. Where I had found the perfect spot, high up in a heavily leaved rhododendron tree, where I could just barely see through the vegetation to the children my age playing over the fence. Placing a few well-aimed force points toward the outer edges of the tree, I pulled the branches apart just enough to make a small window, just enough for me to have a clear look.

Powers, as I could tell from my position, were not to be used at recess under threat of punishment. But it was similar to the busy intersection outside my apartment, viewable from my window – if you watched long enough, *something* would happen. And I'd spent hours in that tree, waiting, nearly always to be rewarded.

Just last week, a skirmish had broken out over a hotly contested game of whiffle ball, the two teams shouting about whether or not the ball had landed across the foul ball line. From my position, I could hear Anthony, the right fielder, being accused.

"He used his powers again, and that's *cheating*!" shouted a girl with the bat still in her hand, who made the ground tremor just noticeably when she stomped. "We should use a heavier ball so he can't just blow it out of bounds."

"Did not!" retorted Anthony, a reed of a boy who stood six inches taller than anyone else on the team. "You just can't hit straight, what with the earth never being flat underneath you. Wendy Waddles, everyone calls you, because you can't keep your feet straight!"

Wendy's jaw tightened as she approached Anthony, and I saw Anthony was indeed correct - slight depressions or footprints were left in the dirt where she stomped, dirt that should be hard packed over years of use.

"You take that back!" she hissed. "Or I'll, or I'll—"

"Or you'll *what*?" he teased, sticking out his tongue.

"Or I'll do this!" she shouted and stomped as hard as she could where his foot had been an instant before he moved it, fluttering backwards like a piece of paper caught in the wind. Wendy shrieked as her foot crashed through the dirt until her right leg was submerged up to her knee, her eyes flashing with anger.

"Get back here!" she shouted, trying to yank her foot out as teachers rushed to subdue the fight. "Before I come after you!"

"Doesn't look like you can waddle anywhere, Wendy!" he taunted back.

From my position, I saw both students were reprimanded with detention slips. It took the teachers forty-five minutes to dig Wendy out, the time significantly lengthened when she stomped her other foot in frustration and now had both jammed deep in dirt.

And today, I watched closely, trying to determine what would happen next. Too closely, as the voice behind me nearly made me jump out of the tree to the ground thirty feet below.

"I'm no Telepath, so I don't know," said the voice again as I searched the branches, trying to find the source, "but I'd say you probably *are* an idiot. You should be in school. I wonder what the punishment is for skipping? For us, it's three detentions. What's your name?"

Then I found her, floating just outside the branches, a mass of brunette hair with two brown eyes that squinted towards me. With nothing holding her up, except for her nose looking down on me, and her voice thick with mockery.

"Essie," I choked, attempting to recover.

And I swallowed, realizing that she wore the same uniform as those playing at recess.

Chapter 4

"Essie?" she sniffed, hovering. "That's a *girl's* name, you don't look like a *girl* to me."

"That's because it's S-C," I said, slowly reaching out to remove each of the force points, letting the tree branches collapse back in around me. "Like JD or EJ."

"Well, Essie or SC, it certainly doesn't explain what you are doing in this tree," she retorted and noticed the branches moving. "Hey?! Are you doing that? Are you a Special?"

"No, I'm absolutely not," I said hurriedly. "Just a nosy Regular, and now, I'll be on my way, thank you. Just, erm, got lost."

"You absolutely *are*!" she said, trailing me from the outside of the tree as I started to climb down, realizing I knew her as one of the girls that frequented hopscotch and jump rope on the other end of the playground. With her abilities, I bet she cheated too. "And this isn't the first time I've seen you up here. I tend to keep my eyes on the sky. This is just the first time my teacher turned her back long enough for me to look!"

"Nope, definitely first time I've been here, Arial!" I repeated, now practically falling from the tree in my haste, cursing as I realized my slip-up.

"You know my name! You've been *spying* on me, on us, listening to us? Who do you think you are? Stop, stop right there or I'll report you in before you make it down the block. I'm sure the police would want to know why you aren't in school!"

I froze, clinging to the branch halfway down, considering my options.

I could set a force point above her, one that would drag her upwards and away while I escaped. But it would likely do more harm than good – creating a force point was kind of like kneading dough, or playing with putty. It was as if I was pushing into that area of space, contorting it, stretching it downwards, and letting objects fall in. The problem, however, was that anything nearby would be attracted to it, not just her. It would draw far more attention to me than she ever could by calling the police, and she might be able to fly away before she could be sucked in.

I frowned, thinking quickly as she questioned me again, her voice hard.

"I said, *what* are you doing here?" she repeated, whizzing in closer, sticking her head inside the leaves, a branch tearing her sleeve. "Now look what you've made me do! Mother is going to be irate."

"I'm, well, I've only just arrived a few days ago," I said, an idea taking root in my brain, "But I'm trying to determine if the academy is worthy for someone like me. My parents sent me here, you see, to live with my aunt, since schools aren't the best where I'm from. Since, well, they don't *exist* where I'm from."

"Don't exist?" she asked, craning her neck forward. "What do you mean, don't exist? Schools are everywhere."

"Not when your parents are researchers in the Arctic!" I said, thrusting out my chest. "But I suppose you wouldn't know anything about that, would you, city girl?"

"I wouldn't, and you wouldn't either. Because it's obviously a lie," she snorted, inspecting the tear in her sleeve, trying to press the fabric near her elbow back together.

"Hmm, a lie? You're right, I did lie. I *am* a Special, from farther north than you've ever seen, where it's light outside for entire days at a time."

"Oh yeah? What type are you, then?"

"A Boreal," I stated, brushing a piece of bark off my shirt. "But I doubt someone from around *here* would be familiar with those."

"A Boreal!" she exclaimed, eyes wide. "Of *course* I know what those are. I saw one when I was young! The city booked him out for an entire night. I've never *seen* a show like it! It was as if the sky came alive with colors!"

"I suppose if you aren't used to it, it might seem pretty amazing," I responded and started climbing down the tree again, giving her a sideways glance. "Guess I'm just used to it by now."

"Hold it, I'm not done with you," she said. "Prove it. Boreals are incredibly rare, and I'd know if one entered the city. We'd *all* know."

"Rare, but not powerful. I don't need any sort of permits, I couldn't hurt a fly. There's no reason for me to enter announced."

"Either way, prove it, or I'm still calling the police."

"If you wanted a private show, you should have just asked," I drawled and held up a hand palm up towards her. "I'll need to keep it small, though, and you'll have to keep it a secret. No one is supposed to know I'm here yet, since I don't start school until next week."

Slowly, I coaxed one of the black orbs out from above my wrist, peeling away several strands of light from it while keeping the sphere hidden behind my hand. Light played around the inside of the enclosure, sparkling against the leaves, and Arial's mouth fell open as strands of it danced in vibrating streams, like tiny arcs of fire.

"Do more colors," she breathed, transfixed, practically perched in the tree now instead of floating. "It's beautiful."

"Can't, not yet at least. That's why my parents sent me to school, to train me. And I wanted to see if this school was capable. I'm not so sure, if they can't keep track of all their students."

"Oh, they are, they are! My father knows, he can tell your parents all about it. He would love to meet you too. He loves seeing the rarer types. You should come over for dinner and show him! Here, take this," she said, fetching a pen and paper from her side. "This is my address. I'd love to introduce him to you."

"We'll see. I still have a few other schools to inspect," I answered. "Can't make my decision until I've considered all my options."

"A Boreal, here," she said to herself. "He would be so pleased, and he'd be happy with me for bringing you. No, don't even look at the other schools. Enroll here."

"We'll see," I repeated and jumped the rest of the way to the ground. "I don't want to promise anything yet."

In the distance, over the fence, I heard a whistle and saw Arial turn back towards the school.

"I must be going, recess is over, but keep this address!" she insisted and pushed the paper into my palm. "Anytime, you are welcome for dinner. *Anytime*, SC."

"Anytime," I answered casually, starting to walk away as she flew back over the fence. I kept a slow wandering pace weaving up the street, letting my feet shuffle along as I peered into shop windows with my hands in my pockets.

Then I turned a corner at the end of the block, lost a direct line of sight with the academy, and ran.

Chapter 5

"What are you doing home so early," demanded my mother as I entered the apartment, my breath still coming in quick gasps.

"It was career day at school, so there was early dismissal," I lied as she raised an eyebrow.

"Star Child," she reprimanded, "there is only so much I can do to keep you hidden. The more you act up, the more attention you draw to yourself, and the more difficult it will be for both of us. Go on, fetch your homework - it's too late for you to return to school now, but I won't see that mind of yours go to waste."

Then she turned to the sink and continued the dishes, shaking her head. After cleaning the sweat off, I returned to the kitchen, opening my books on the table, positioning myself near a window where sunlight streamed inside. Placing my index finger in the webbing under my thumb, I flicked my nail against the skin, concentrating as I imagined pulling the *space* in that region together, tying it into a swift knot with my mind. Then, in my palm, a black orb formed and started to absorb the sunlight, growing slightly larger with each passing minute.

In that time, our apartment was quiet save for the tinkling of dishware as I fell into the book, practicing the mathematical equations on the pages for a quiz the next day. The air was near still, the air conditioning turned off either from being broken or to save money, as each week it seemed to alternate between the two. And occasionally, I caught the sound of my mother humming an old tune softly, one that I recognized but could not quite identify, fading in and out of my perception as she moved.

But then, the three knocks on the door nearly started me out of my seat.

These were not neighborly knocks, like those when Stephen's mother visited to borrow the salt, or even strained knocks like when our landlord came to collect the rent, and my mother sent me to raid the couch cushions for spare change while she rummaged together the last dollar. No, these were sharp, quick raps, staccato bursts that didn't wait for my mother to reach the door before opening it.

"Police," stated the square-faced man at the front of the trio as he stepped into our kitchen uninvited, a younger man to his left and a middle-aged woman to his right. "We're looking for a Ms. Alcmene; do you know her?"

"Speaking," said my mother and forced a smile. "May I ask why you have entered my kitchen, and whether I can offer you any refreshments?"

Cold washed over me as my breath caught in my throat, and the trio squinted at my mother. Somehow they knew, somehow they had found me from spying on the academy. But how? That Arial must have told them or trailed me back. I thought I had been careful, but it must not have been careful enough.

I stared as the head policeman looked about the kitchen, his eyes gliding over me as my mother's wrinkles deepened and a vein throbbed her temple, but still managed to smile.

"Yes, you live alone, then? Good," he said, and pulled out a stack of papers, consulting them. "You *are* the Ms. Alcmene that served as a delivery nurse and exhibit Snuffer powers, correct?"

"Yes, yes," my mother responded, wiping dishwater off her hands. "A weak form of powers, nothing to be noticed."

"Nothing to be noticed indeed," came the reply. "If I recall, that's the exact purpose of a Snuffer. It's written here that you are measured to be one of the stronger Snuffers, not that that means much. Regardless, your unique services to the state are requested, Ms. Alcmene. You'll be coming with us at once. We've seen to it that your rent has been paid, that your crucial belongings will be transported. Come along."

"And if I choose not to come?" she inquired, leaning back against the counter. "I already served the state once, quite some time ago."

"Ms.," he said as the woman behind him reached to the handcuffs on her belt, "don't make me change this request into an order."

"What?" I shouted, pounding my fist on the table. "You can't do that!"

A bead of sweat trickled down my mother's neck and the muscles around her smile tightened. For a second, the lead officer's brow creased, and he looked her over once more in annoyance, tilting his head in slight confusion.

"Ms., there is no time to mumble, and I suggest you show us the respect of enunciating your words. Are you coming of your own volition?"

"The hell she's not!" I shouted, springing up from the table as my mother's vein looked like it was about to burst, and she shouted, her voice filled with strain, her face directed at the policeman but her voice at me.

"Shut up and leave! You owe me that!"

I froze, watching as the slap from the officer caught my mother square across the jaw with the back of a gloved hand, knocking her hard against the cabinet.

"The state owes you *nothing*," he hissed as the woman turned my mother around to fasten the handcuffs behind her back, forcing my mother's face to meet mine as it was flattened against the cabinet.

Leave, she mouthed, her eyes pleading, her lip bleeding as I felt myself preparing to cast a force point stronger than I had ever done before, to crush the officers together while we escaped. But her eyes began to water, and she whispered once more as they started to pull her away, and I found myself paralyzed by her command.

"No, leave."

The police left the door open, and I watched them enter the squad car from the window. I heard the officer's final words as I memorized his face, just before the car pulled away.

"We've found a far better use for you than a maid, Ms. Alcmene. And I suggest you cooperate. You're still far enough from Special to be considered a Regular, and I do have witnesses of you putting up a fight. In these circumstances, an accidental fatality would hold up well in the court of law."

Chapter 6

For thirty minutes, I sat at the kitchen table, staring at where the police car had been moments before. It had started raining before they peeled away, so that a shadow of dry ground was left where the car had been, but now steadily faded away with each passing drop.

In my hand, I flicked the black orb back and forth across my palm, letting it roll in rings around the center. The light for it to absorb was now minimal, but rain danced in through the open window, often changing course to disappear into the shadowy mass. I shuddered as I remembered the policeman's slap as I cursed under my breath for listening to my mother.

The sphere was growing heavier now as it absorbed more water, and as my thoughts turned as dark as its surface.

I should have done something. I should have stopped them. I know I *could* have stopped them. I could have saved her. And with her powers, they would never have seen me coming.

It would have been over in an instant.

With a roar, I threw the sphere against the kitchen wall, shaking as the dark mass crashed into the cabinet, then *through* the cabinet and the concrete wall behind with a sound like rushing water. Forks and knives jumped upwards to meet it from the counter top like bugs to a light, disintegrating as they meshed with the darkness, some of them falling back to the ground, stretched and distorted like hot plastic. And where the orb passed through the wall, it left a hole the size of a bowling ball unlike any I had ever seen – the wood of the cabinet *flowing* forwards to meet it instead of snapping off in chunks, expanding inwards to follow the orb's trajectory as it continued into the next apartment, and the next, and then next. I stared through the hole, open mouthed as I saw rain pouring through the other side just as the orb broke through the outer brick layer, and sparks falling from electrical wires.

Then there was a flash of light so bright it left stars in my vision, and I felt the explosion before I heard it as the orb collapsed in upon itself. The wave hit me in the chest, knocking me backwards as I felt what I could only describe as *ripples* flowing in the space around me, waves that I sensed in the same way I could sense the orbs themselves.

"Lance, what the *shit* did you do this time?" I heard our neighbor scream at her husband through the wall, while car alarms started to screech in the street and a child wailed in chorus with them. Through the hole, I could see that the orb had passed clean through an oven, absorbing the metal and the half cooked dinner alike along its path, and a face now filled the space where the meatloaf had been.

Stephen's wide eyes met mine as he stared, face white, holding a book with a semicircular hole melted into its outer edge, the pages morphed into solid pulp from where they had touched the orb.

"What the—" he started as Lance's wife launched into a tirade about how her mother had warned her that he was nothing but trouble, and that they *never* should have left her house outside the city. But then I broke eye contact with Stephen and left through the still open door, taking the steps two at a time to the street where a small crowd had already gathered and stared up at the sky, where no trace was left of the sphere except for the hole leaving the building through brick, the clay puckered outwards as if it had been fired that way long ago.

"Never seen anything like it," an old man was mumbling to his wife, both holding hands on the other end of the street, while their granddaughter pulled at his shirt.

"What do you think it was, Papa? What type of Special could do *that*?" she asked, thrusting a fist in the air and mimicking the explosion. "Ka-Powww! Where were they born? In a thunderstorm?"

"How many years ago was that hurricane, Matilda?" the old man said to his wife, putting a quieting hand on his granddaughter's head. "The category five, was that ten years ago? Maybe it was something from *that*, the one that made them reconstruct the entire block. Ain't no way a normal storm did this."

With my head down, I wove through them, the rain wetting my shoulders and my hair sticking to my temples. And I thought about what to do next, what I *had* to do next.

I had to find my mother, and I had to save her. To do that, I would have to know where to look, to find someone who might know where the police had taken her. A Special who might know.

And once I had found them, I would have to be able to control my power well enough to be sure I wouldn't hurt my mother as we escaped, and to be able to fight them. I'd have to learn, and for that, I'd have to attend the academy while keeping my true intentions secret.

Biting my lip, I shivered in the cold, my thoughts racing far ahead of my footsteps. Wishing that there was an entry in the Directory about myself, one I could consult, and understand my limitations.

By now, I'd been traveling down Twelfth Street for a mile straight from my apartment, and turned a left onto a new block, one with three-story houses instead of hulking buildings, the yards increasing in size with each side street, several maintained to hold exotic floral arrangements by teams of dedicated Climate Controllers and Green Thumbs. None of the cars here had rust or dents, and the driveway to my apartment had more potholes than the entire mile of street.

I watched the addresses on the mailboxes as they ticked upwards, then turned into a drive with a fountain in the lawn, the water following intricate webbed patterns that would be impossible by physics alone to form a family crest suspended in midair, and crossed the grass to the front door. I raised the knocker and rapped on the door, wincing as I remembered the last time I had heard knocking.

In moments, the heavy oak slab swung inwards, and a face peered out at me in the rain, the expression filled with excitement.

"Daddy, Daddy," shouted Arial, jumping into the air with excitement and forgetting to come down. "The Boreal, he's here! I *told* you that I didn't make him up!"

Chapter 7

Arial ushered me inside to the foyer, where her mother spotted me and rushed to the master bathroom, returning with a stack of colored towels.

"You poor thing," she tutted, wrapping me once before I had a chance to move, then sponging me off with the end of another towel, the fabric so soft that I doubted its very substance. "You must not have been expecting the rain. Why on earth did you not call a taxi?"

"In the north, we do not experience rain except once a year, and that as cold as ice," I lied, feigning ignorance and knowing that my lack of pocket money would arouse suspicion. "Why would you not take the rain?"

"I have heard they are strange up there," said Arial, and her mother glared.

"Arial, it's called *culture,* and you should learn to respect it," she scolded. "Now, you've arrived just in time for dinner. First course is coming out as soon as Emma, our chef, finishes. She's French, darling, with a certificate to prove it. Lorraine, to be precise, born in '76. A *fantastic* year."

Already, I could smell the aromas testifying to Emma's powers, scents of spices that I had not known existed, yet my watering mouth knew would burst into explosions of flavor. Beaming, Arial led me into the dining room, the table already set with more utensils than I knew how to handle, and with more decoration food than typically filled my entire pantry. Arial seated me in the guest chair, then claimed the spot next to me, leaning forward in expectation for not the food, but for the coming conversation.

"So," said the man already across the table, his fingers steepled in front of him as he studied me, not a single strand out of alignment in his dark parted hair, "Arial has told me you're a Boreal. How intriguing. I do take an interest to the rarer powers such as those you possess."

"Why, why thank you," I answered, offering a quick smile. "I am fortunate - both for my abilities and for your hospitality."

"Fortunate indeed, for your ability," he responded as Emma waltzed behind us, bearing cups of soup garnished with blooming flowers that she placed before us, her movements so graceful I thought she had skipped me until I looked down. "Born in the northern hospitals - your parents must be quite wealthy for a chance at a Boreal son."

"Yes, erm, indeed," I mimicked, wondering why the letters were missing in my soup, and whether Emma had forgotten them. "Most wealthy, of course. Just like you, wealthy. Which is why they sent me here, to board at the academy, since the schools up there are open to anyone."

"An interesting choice, here of all places," said Arial's father, staring at my shirt, which had a patch over one elbow and a stretched collar. "And yet your clothing choice is quite... unique."

"I've only just arrived, and these are my traveling clothes," I said, "My belongings were misplaced; they should arrive soon."

"Yet your aunt did not see it fit to—"

"Artie," interrupted Arial's mother, "let the boy eat without being berated. Had he been wearing his proper attire, it would only have been ruined in the rain."

"Yes, I'm sure they would have been soiled," he remarked after a minute of silence as we finished our soup. and Emma carted away the bowls. "Tell me, boy - SC, is it? What a curious name, unlike any I have known. Tell me, did your parents phone ahead to the academy or perform any research? I'm afraid you shan't be allowed in."

"Father, a Boreal would *definitely* be allowed in!" protested Arial, her fingertips pinching the edge of the table.

"I have the ability and the strength of it!" I added, but he raised a hand.

"Power is not the issue here, nor rarity. Take Arial, with the power of flight, a common power, yet she was admitted with no qualms. A power from an accidental airplane birth on the way to the hospital, a level one in the Amazon rainforest, with a down payment more than this house."

Beside me, Arial was quiet and still as her father continued, and Emma placed his entree before him.

"No, SC, I'm afraid you can't attend because the school is closing. Had your parents done their research, as any parents should before mailing their son halfway around the globe, I'm sure they would have learned that as well. They would know that due to a gerrymandered district, it is being converted into a rehabilitation facility. I doubt you would have interest in attending there, whether or not you qualify. I've started the process of pulling Arial out, but many of the other children on scholarship will finish their schooling at the facilities there, or they'd have to repay their debt to the city."

He raised his knife and sliced into his braised chicken, expertly removing the meat from the bone, though his eyes never moved off of me.

"But enough talk about the academy, SC. I'm sure we can find accommodations for you elsewhere, with a power as *special* yours. In all my years studying the rarities, I've only come across five or six Boreals. Come, treat us to a show, and I'll inform you how you compare."

He smiled, baring his teeth as he took the first bite, chewing slowly as I felt the blood start to drain from my face. Arial had been simple to trick; she'd only seen one Boreal and from a distance. But her father – her father would not be so easy to fool.

I imagined creating the force point on the table, pushing space downwards to pull her family in with all the food, wrapped in the tablecloth like the filling of one of Emma's pastries. It wouldn't hurt them, I was sure, at least not bad. And it would give me time to escape.

"Go on," Arial's father whispered, eyes glinting, and I felt the other inhabitants of the table lean in as the air stilled. "Or would you care to admit you are something far more common, if anything at all?"

I exhaled and chose my target, a tray of softened butter at the center. And just as I collected my will, the shrill ringing of a telephone interrupted from the kitchen.

Their three heads snapped towards the kitchen as the butter on the tray morphed into a symmetrical ball, pulled together by the point as I released it an instant later before it could cause more damage, the water in the tall glasses around the table sloshing back and forth *just* enough to be noticed.

"For you!" cried Emma, rushing forward with the phone and handing it to Arial's father, who listened to a voice on the other end. Then his expression tightened and he sprang up from the table, wiping his mouth with an embroidered napkin, and shouldering a coat from the rack.

"An emergency has been reported on Twelfth Street," he said to his wife. "There has been an unregistered power sighting, and word is already getting to me an hour late. Something unlike anything I have heard of, that requires my immediate attention. Something *rare.*"

With long strides, he reached the doorway, thrusting it open, and turned back, letting the wind and rain billow past him into the house. Turning back, he spoke one last sentence, letting the sarcasm drip from his voice.

"SC, the next time we meet, I'm sure we would all be *delighted* to see your true abilities."

Then the door slammed, and he raced into the night.

Chapter 8

Arial sniffed, poking at her plate with a fork, ignoring Emma as she placed a miniature dessert at her elbow. The last course consisted of a crepe shaped like a butterfly, the wings streaked with patterns of strawberry, blueberry, chocolate, and balsamic that melded so well with batter that the dish appeared alive. And it nearly was - as a perfectly timed scoop of ice cream melted in the rigid center, the wings drooped down from their upright position as if it was ready to take flight, and two cherry stem antennae perked upwards.

"Oh, Emma, you've outdone yourself," complimented Arial's mother, her speech as forced as wading into cold water. "The dessert, and the *butter* as well! It fits the flow of the table so much better in that shape - I found the rectangular edges otherwise to be quite jarring. The little wave patterns on the surface are so intricate!"

Emma raised an eyebrow as she looked at the butter, tilting her head in confusion as she set down the plate, the back of her hand brushing against Arial's father's drinking glass that had been left on edge of the table. It toppled, the stem cracking in two as it smashed into the floor, and Emma immediately bent over to fetch the pieces.

"Pardon, my apologies," she exclaimed with a quick bow, wiping the water from the table with a fresh cloth. "Fortunately, there is little mess, but I will sweep for any stray shards."

"No need, Emma, no need," hushed Arial's mother, plucking the two pieces from the chef's hands. Then she placed them back on top of each other, stroking an index finger down the glass, the material flowing back together until it was seamless once more. A streak of gray flashed through her hair as she set it back on the table as if brand new. "Just give it a thorough wash."

My breath caught in my throat as Emma took back the unblemished glass, and Arial's mother smiled at me.

"Please excuse my powers at the table," she said with a nod. "Uncouth as it is, they do serve their purpose. It will be our secret."

"You're a Mender," I breathed, and she released a tinkling laugh, throwing a lock of her curled hair behind her shoulder.

"Oh me? Yes, I am, dear. Not the most powerful of types—"

"But exceptionally rare," I finished as mild annoyance crossed her face from me interrupting her performance. And rare she was despite the simplicity of the power, and though Menders were one of the few power types that could be born *anywhere* in the world, their conditions at birth were what made them unique.

For Menders, it was a requirement that the child be born on the brink of death, often mistaken for a stillborn. Brought into the world broken so that child had to be restored to life, its cold body coaxed warm once more, its first breath occurring *just* at the inflection point of mortality. Those cases were common enough in hospitals, children saved by particularly adept medical staff, placed crying into their sobbing mother's arms. But what was *not* common was the last requirement for a Mender to develop - that the doctor that delivered them perish within the same day.

"He was old," said Arial's mother, guessing my thoughts, "and went peacefully in his sleep later that night. And not a day goes by that I don't thank him for his gift."

Then she stood, the grey streak in her hair slowly fading to match the brown of the other strands, and addressed her daughter.

"Arial, it's time for your schoolwork and your friend to depart. Walk him out, but don't leave the yard - though the rain appears to have let up, it's getting dark."

"Yes, Mother," mumbled Arial, leaving her dishes for Emma and treading towards the door. For someone who could leap into the air with the slightest twitch of her toes, her posture slumped as if gravity had laid an extra hand upon her, and she kept her face pointed ahead as she led me outside.

And when the door shut behind us, it wasn't raindrops that splashed against the front porch.

"Nothing's ever good enough for him!" she whispered, her lip trembling and she turned her eyes away from mine, two more tears streaming down her face. "That's why I brought you here, SC. I thought he might be proud of me."

"Arial," I started, unsure what to say as she shook, "it's going to be okay. Your mother seems nice."

"No, no it's not," she sobbed. "Mother won't stop him when he gets like that. And now, my school is shutting down, and he's taking me from my friends. He didn't even *believe* you were a Boreal! If only you had a chance to show him before he left."

"If only," I answered as she steadied her breathing and wiped away her tears, her sleeve still ripped from earlier that day. "Arial, why didn't your mother fix your sleeve like she fixed the glass?"

"It's not good for her," she answered, blinking to dry her eyes, "so Father won't permit it. You saw how her hair turned grey? Each time she fixes something, she has to recover. But she can't *stand* seeing anything broken, so it always makes her angry until it's fixed."

"I'm sorry," I answered, looking to the patch on my sleeve that my own mother had mended physically, Arial's tears nearly contagious as I wondered where she might be now.

"It's not your fault. And I don't care *what* he says, wherever I go to school next, you are more than welcome to come. I've seen your powers, I know you'll get in. Or better yet, I'll refuse to leave!"

"Where do you think you'll be going? I'd like to go to one of the ones better known for fighting."

"*Fighting*." She laughed through sniffles, her face starting to return to its normal complexion. "We don't *fight*. That's what the rehabilitation facilities are for, training the soldiers and policemen. The north really must be so different, or maybe that's why your schools are as terrible as you say."

"Wait, what *do* you do, then?" I said. "What else do they teach you to do with your powers?"

"Our powers? We only use those an hour each day, and just theory even then. It's more reading and math and history. What exactly did you think we did? It's a school, not a boot camp."

"Well, erm, come to think of it, I wasn't sure. I just assumed if it was a Special school you would do Special lessons."

Arial tilted her head, squinting her eyes at me, barely visible in the darkness.

"The north really is odd," she said, just as her mother shouted from inside, and she turned to leave. "But really, come to school with me. I promise you'll like it!"

"Of course!" I lied as she opened the door back inside. "And, Arial, one more question. Your father, what's his power? What's he do?"

"He works with the city in their Special registration department, helping identify Specials that are here without proper documentation," she said, her expression darkening as I mentioned him once more. "He's a Hunter. Once he's felt a Special's power, he can track the individual down from it, almost like a scent it leaves behind. And bye, SC, see you soon! At school!"

Then she left, and I swallowed, looking back towards Twelfth Street. Where a hole was still fresh in my apartment wall, and Ariel's father would be investigating.

Seeking the scent of a Special that *definitely* had no documentation.

Chapter 9

I'd grown up poor, but never so poor to live without a home.

My mother's track record made finding work difficult - she'd been fired as a nurse, and blacklisted from any additional opportunities at the space program by the engineering director trying to cover the potential scandal. Whenever she found work, employers were pleased with her efforts, but the career ladder for maids is short and being a single mother meant she had little time to pursue other opportunities. But no matter how small that week's paycheck, dinner always found a way onto the table. And though there may have been holes in the plaster, a roof was always over my head.

Tonight, my first night without her, was also the first on the street.

Her voice echoed in my head as I walked away from Arial's home, considering trying to return to my own apartment and sneak a night in my own bed, the night growing cold and rain threatening to soak me once more.

They can't know, do you understand me? my mother's voice echoed in my mind.

But by now, anyone inspecting the area was likely gone - crimes occurred often in my portion of the city, and police rarely stayed longer than a few minutes if there was no one present to handcuff. I'd at least check to see if the crowd was still there, or if see if there was someone who might lend me their couch for the night. And I promised myself I would be careful.

I frowned and walked quickly, my hands in my pockets, remembering the Directory's description of Hunters and reviewing it as I came closer to my door, only able to bring the synopsis to mind.

Those with the ability to track the powers of others, their own power level determined by the distance of their senses, ranging from several feet to several miles. After study, it has been determined that Hunters cannot sense individuals themselves, but rather levels of power activity.

Since Arial's father had not been present when I used my power, the danger should be minimal - and just to be sure, I would refrain from using it unless I was certain I was safe. Yet part of me wondered what exactly would happen if he *did* find me. Stern as he was, he held a admiration of the rarer powers, and mine was more rare than anyone's I had ever known. Maybe he'd help me, or at least provide me with food, shelter, and education while I searched for my mother. Once he realized the true nature of my power, maybe he would be eager to help.

As I thought, I cut through a park that had degenerated to wildlife from years of neglect and ran alongside my apartment building, my shoes sloshing through puddles and scraggly trees reaching high into the sky from both sides of the gravel path. The benches I passed were occupied with homeless men and women claiming them like personal territory, glaring as I passed, the wind carrying the sound of their chattering teeth. From the underbrush, I heard rustling and I took care to stick as close as possible to the center of the path, jumping as a chipmunk streaked under my feet. An owl hooted at my back, and I felt the hair on my neck stand up as I neared the exit and saw the blue lights reflected off the mist.

Crouching so the hedges ahead concealed me, I crept forward, thankful that park maintenance budget had been slashed for so long that the last time the lights had been replaced was before I had been born. And wedging myself between two particularly large bushes, with my breath stilled and careful to be as quiet as possible, I suppressed a gasp as I glimpsed my apartment.

Three police cars were parked at the entrance of the building, forming a trapezoidal barrier on the sidewalk with a gap on the right side, two officers manually admitting the other occupants of the apartment after checking identification. Three more officers were posted at each corner of the building, and four surrounded a small group of people with Arial's father at the head, his jaw clenched as he surveyed them. There was Lance and his wife, her expression accusatory while he wore his best bathrobe for the occasion, plus two other sets of neighbors that had occasionally stopped by to ask my mother for aid in mending a garment or removing stains. And at the front of the crowd was Stephen and his mother, Stephen's face white from more than the cold.

"I'm going to ask again," said The Hunter, the edge in his voice carrying into the park from thirty feet away, the crowd bristling as he spoke. "There was a woman and a child in room 662 where the event occurred, most of you have confirmed that much. Although *some* of you," He glared at Lance, who seemed to be missing the beer that was a natural extension of his hand, "can't even recall that much. We need a description of the child; even a simple one will suffice. This is for your own safety, as this could potentially be a situation that could put all of your lives in danger. You there at the front, you stated that he was in your class. What was his hair color?"

Stephen shuffled his feet, his forehead creased in thought, shaking his head as he answered.

"I, I don't know," he said on the verge of tears. "He was my best friend, but when I think about it, I can't remember. I mean, I remember *him,* and I always recognized him, but the details just seem blurry, like I just never really paid attention to them. I know he *had* hair, at least, I think. Maybe brown?"

"Am I to presume he was balding at fifteen?" sneered Arial's father, his voice incredulous, and Stephen flinched back. "Are there no details, nothing from any of you? The boy - that much you have agreed on, that it was a boy - lived there for several years. How is a physical description beyond you?"

"Investigator," said one of the officers to Arial's father, his badge flashing as he turned, his uniform stretched to cover bulging muscles, "you've been at it over a half an hour. We'll dispatch some of our own to question tomorrow, but it's getting late, and we're getting nowhere. We'll check internally to see if we have anything on activity at the apartment as well."

"Fine," hissed Arial's father, his eyes flashing, "You're all dismissed, and each of you will have a follow up. If you are acting to protect him, know that you are standing in the way of the law and will be punished. Roland," he said, confronting the officer that had spoken up, "how close are they?"

"Nearly here," the officer responded. "They received a call on the other end of the city before you arrived, false alarm."

"Wonderful, just wonderful - your team is yet again showing their adeptness for situations such as these. Have they at least found anything inside?"

"Nothing, no pictures, no description. We know his size from his clothes and shoes, we have samples of his handwriting, and his fingerprints, but that's it. Have you…" started the officer, and shifted as he asked the question, rolling his shoulders in discomfort. "Have you sensed anything?"

"Nothing," Arial's father answered. "The entire apartment's muddled. I can't pick up anything distinct. Nothing tangible to lock on to, no clear scent. It's as if no one with powers has occupied it in years. Roland, I want this block monitored every minute of the night and day. I cannot stress to you how important it is that we catch this one alive. We don't have time for another repeat of last time, understood?"

In the distance, a siren wailed, growing louder as Arial's father walked to the side of the building and waved the new vehicle over, a fire truck staffed with a tired crew near the end of their shift. Too far away for me to hear, he gestured, Officer Roland nodding beside him as one of the firemen lowered the bucket for The Hunter to step inside. Then they raised it up the side of the building, elevating him to the hole in the wall high above where my dark sphere had torn through the brick. The Hunter raised his hands to the hole, his fingers brushing the morphed edge, his eyes shut, the artery in his neck visible from even where I stood. Then they lowered the bucket and he walked with Officer Roland back to his car, passing only a dozen feet in front of me.

"It's faint, just enough to sense, but I've got the bastard. Be ready to go at a moment's notice - the next time I sense him using his power, we'll ambush him before he has a chance to escape. With this little to go on, he'll be close. Remember, alive. By how much doesn't matter."

"I'm not going to kill a child, Art."

"That's what you said last time too," came the retort.

They departed, each moving in separate directions, Arial's father towards his home and Roland deeper into the city. And waiting until several minutes after they left, I backed into the park once more, knowing I would sleep in the cold.

If I slept at all.

Chapter 10

"Are you hiding too?" the voice rasped from behind my ear, so close I could feel hot breath on the back of my neck. I jumped and yelped, whipping around as I fell into brambles alongside the hedge, threadlike scratches running up my forearm. Above me, the figure of one of the park's homeless smiled with a nearly full collection of teeth, his gaunt face leaning forward as he studied me.

"Hell, you scared me!" I exclaimed, still trying to back away, thorns digging into my back.

He cocked his head, his straggling hair drifting over his shoulder, and spoke in an excited voice.

"True, that's true! But are you hiding like me?"

"No, I'm not hiding," I said, my feet finding purchase on the ground as I stood up, thankful he had not approached closer but was content to watch me. "I was just going home."

"False!" he exclaimed, wagging a finger. "I know, oh yes I do! True, false, true, false! I always know which!" Then he leaned in, looking left and right before whispering behind his hand to ensure none of the others could hear him, "That's why they don't like me, that's why they tried to get rid of me. That's why I hide. Because I *always* know, and I *always* tell."

"Who tried to get rid of you?" I asked, inching to the right for a path around him, but he sidestepped in front of me, giggling.

"*Them*! But it didn't work. I escaped! Hah, they didn't get me!" he exclaimed, hopping from foot to foot in excitement, then raised an eyebrow as he pointed to his head. "False. Except here. They got me a little bit here, didn't they? I still think of them every night, oh their voices, their beautiful voices. Singing beautiful lies, lies I can still hear bouncing around. Is that why you are hiding? Because they're trying to get you too? You can hide with me. I know all the good places."

"No, thank you," I said, noticing we had attracted the attention of several other figures that were approaching, keeping watch from the darker shadows, as the hair pricked up on my neck. "It's fine, I really don't need to hide."

"False! Oh *so* false!" he shouted to the sky, practically howling the words like a wolf to the moon. "That's what I thought ten years ago too. I was excited - first graduating class, see? The trial batch. I even kept the ring!" He extended his arm towards me, bruises and dirt covering nearly every inch of skin, showing off a silver band on his finger, and concern crossed his face, "I didn't earn the ring, though. I never graduated. But promise you won't tell, will you?"

"I promise I won't," I answered as he exhaled a breath of relief and I thought of potential areas to place force points should the dark shapes move forward to attack, cursing as I realized that would be a dead giveaway of my position to Ariel's father, who was only minutes away.

"True, I think. That you won't."

"Yes, true. But I need to leave now, okay?" I said and started walking along the inside of the hedge as he trotted next to me.

"True."

"It's been nice talking to you, really." I was nearing the edge of the park, where it opened into street lights, and quickened my pace.

"False. False, false, that's false!" he said, matching my steps, his breathing ragged. Then he came to a dead halt as I stepped onto pavement, and he waited at the border of the park.

"They'll take you if they find you, if you're worth it," he said, keeping his face in the dark, his voice strained. "They'll take you where they took me. To rehabilitation. But don't leave the park, they never found me in the park for all ten years. True. They gave up long ago, looking for me, looking for Mikey."

"A rehabilitation facility!" I realized, turning back to face him as he flinched. "That's where they took you? You escaped there? Did they teach you to fight?"

"True, all true," he whispered, stepping backwards, his eyes wide and hands starting to shake. "Oh, I hear them now, the voices. The *singing*. Back to the park for Mikey, back before the outside pulled me away, back to the bottom. Back to hide, true, no more fighting. No matter how beautiful the voices, I'll never go back. Beautiful lies. False lies."

Then he meshed with the darkness until only the whites of his eyes were visible, staring out in the street. And he placed his fingers into his ears, shaking his head as if trying dislodge something, screaming so loud his voice echoed back from the alleyways, stirring dogs to bark as he drew out the word as long as he could.

"False!"

I rushed away, my feet beating against the pavement as he retreated into the park, angry voices sounding in retaliation as inhabitants were awakened in their homes. I was too close to my apartment to risk the attention in streetlight, and I only slowed several blocks later, thinking of where to go next. And knowing that I had stumbled upon an enormous problem.

Had I been attacked in the park, I would have been defenseless without revealing myself. And without full knowledge of a Hunter's skill, risking the use of *any* amount of my powers meant I could be tracked, then found. That meant I couldn't train to fight without being discovered. And without knowing how to fight, without knowing how to use my powers, saving my mother would be impossible.

To learn about myself, I had to know more about Arial's father first. I had to know his limitations, the ways I could evade his power, if any existed at all. And for that, I had to return to the same place that I had stolen the *Directory*.

The special section of the library.

I missed the light from my orbs as I navigated the dark streets, hiding behind trash cans and within alleyways whenever cars passed, waiting until a count of thirty to move once more if they were police. By the time I reached the library's stone steps, my feet were dragging rather than walking and my eyelids sinking under the weight of the day. So I walked around to the back, rain starting to fall once more from above, thunder sounding far in the distance. And I found a reading bench, one meant for sitting upon on sunny days, but served as an umbrella as I fell asleep underneath, the frigid stone biting into my shoulder blades. Knowing that if I cast a force point to my right and my left, I could pull the cold water away from puddling at my side. And choosing to shiver instead.

Chapter 11

The building door opened when sunlight breached the sky, the aged librarian struggling to climb each of the steps, her cane tapping against the hard stone. By then I was awake and rested - not well rested, but recharged enough to venture out from under my bench, thankful that blue sky showed overhead and that the wind was still. And when I saw her climbing the steps, I realized my chance.

The library itself was closed for another half hour as she performed the duties necessary prior to allowing the public inside. For that hour, her hawk-like surveillance of the shelves from behind the central desk would be disrupted - instead, she would be sorting files as I had seen her finishing on those days I had arrived *just* on open. Which meant that any activity from me, so long as it was quiet enough, would go unnoticed.

So as she let the door fall shut behind her, I raced up the steps on tiptoe, careful not to alert her ears, which were far less acute than her eyes. And just before the door shut, I caught it with my index finger, preventing the lock from clicking back into place. I counted to ten, my finger pinched in the door, casting a wary glance towards the street, which was still asleep at this time of the morning. Then I slipped inside, careful to shut the door softly as I treaded through the familiar hall and spotted the librarian with her head down, the enormous bags underneath her eyes visible even from my distance.

I'd heard she was a Narcolept, though I'd never confirmed it - and either way, she certainly bore the look. For though they never slept, Narcolepts were plagued with the perpetual symptoms of a restless night, a source of near constant yawns and long blinks. Typically, they flocked to universities and academia, especially since many trade professions wouldn't even consider hiring one due to the risk of an inattentive worker, though they also peppered the top positions of business and law firms alike. From what I could recall, they were born in locations with near constant sources of noise, near airports and train hubs that ran through the night, and city centers that, like them, never slept.

I crept along the side wall as she faced the other direction, making my way to the shelves towards the end of the library typically monitored by the second librarian who arrived later in the day. Back there, it was still dark, the stacks of books in slumber, many of the volumes covered in dust and unused even during the peak hours. Considering only members of the academies had access, traffic flow was always low, the Specials paying a premium to keep the descriptions of their powers behind the barrier except for those like themselves.

The Directory still under my bed was merely an overview of the knowledge held in these shelves, each of the tomes diving into specific types of Specials and theories behind powers. Some were filled with pages upon pages of raw data, geographic locations, chronological dates, and groupings of powers. Others were far more speculative and outdated, though often there was still a glimmer of truth in the chapters. And today, I walked to the section marked "H," tags underneath each collection of books labelled.

Hawthorn's Distinctions Among Power Classes

Healers

Then, there was what I was looking for. Five books under the tag *Hunters* that I pulled down from the shelf and skimmed in the darkness. Only ten pages long was *A Complete List of Hunter Birth Locations,* and I placed that back on the shelf. Next was *Hunters in History,* and I took it to a small table, casting a look at the clock. Fifteen minutes until opening now, and I skimmed the pages, searching for clues. Most the information concerned figures throughout the centuries, often kept by kings and queens to track unfaithful subjects, and in the turn of the twentieth century, employed by debt collectors seeking to exact money from wealthy clients. Casinos kept them in their employ, and the vast majority had trouble sensing any sort of powers more than a hundred yards away.

And there, underneath, was a description written by one of the more successful collectors, detailing his abilities in tracking down his client's targets.

Imagine you are in a crowded room, one filled with hundreds of guests. You are holding your own conversation, but there are dozens of others in your immediate vicinity. With concentration, you can focus on one of them and discern what they are saying. Or, you can listen for a particular word, a keyword in all the conversations in the room. And when you hear it, you pinpoint where that word came from. That word is the target, and when it is spoken is the usage of powers. First, you have to know what the word sounds like, you have to be looking for it, that's the seed. Then you have to wait for it to be spoken, where it lingers for some time. And you strike.

I frowned and turned the page, continuing to read as it mentioned some of the major criminals that Hunters had eventually tracked down and placed behind bars. There were names I recognized, particularly those who were given life-long sentences, and those that were from far before my own birth. And then there was an account from the criminal Demasti, who had led a squad of three Hunters across the entire country in a string of robberies over ten years before they finally caught him emptying a vault. After four years, he was released in return for his crucial information on how he kept out the Hunters at bay, only to return to jail six years after that for a murder case.

To escape, it read, *you have to know your enemy. The Hunters, they find prey by singling them out from among the many. Typically, the many are quiet. So I made sure no matter where I went, the many were loud. So loud, they drowned out my own scent. And there, the Hunters couldn't single me out, their senses were overloaded. And that, that's how I got away. Is that what you wanted to hear? Can I go now?*

I closed the book and turned to the clock. The library would be opening in just a minute, so I tucked the book under my elbow and returned the way I had come, passing the bewildered library assistant as she passed me on the stairs. I had found what I needed.

And I knew where I had to go.

Chapter 12

Before I acted, I had to test Arial's father's powers, to see if he could sense me as he claimed.

I decided on a large park, near the edge of the city, approximately a mile away from Arial's house. There were dozens of entry and exit points, so I could escape even if the situation became out of control. And more importantly, there was a parking garage at the edge, five stories tall, with the top exposed to open air. From that vantage point, I'd be able to watch the entire park below, but it would be near impossible to be spotted. And to prevent The Hunter from attaining a stronger sense of my powers, I chose a large pond for my location, with no boats or watercraft nearby.

If he wanted a better scent, he would have to swim for it.

I stood on the shoreline, my shoes sinking a half inch into mud, the field behind me deserted save for a few walkers on the far end, a collection of trees separating me from them and ensuring privacy. There was a light breeze coming from their direction, just enough for me to catch snippets of conversations, but not enough to understand any of them.

Taking a deep breath, I flicked a dark sphere into existence in my right hand, feeding it sunlight as it grew. It was the first I had created since the one that crashed through the apartment building, and I stared at it curiously, focusing on how I kept the sphere alive. I realized that I was actively pushing the space at its center down, and the reason the last one had exploded was that it had been too far away for me to maintain. That I kept the spheres alive, and without me, they couldn't survive.

In my hand, the sphere grew heavier, and I aimed towards the center of the pond, knowing that was about as far as I could throw accurately. Then I launched it, watching as the water reached upwards to meet it as it fell, a hole in the pond left static where it fell through. And I started to run, tucking a second sphere away above my wrist and making a beeline through the forest to the parking garage, turning back halfway to see the pond.

There, directly underneath where I had thrown it, water was swirling in a whirlpool the size of my old apartment, pulling in lily pads and floating twigs from the outer edges. And just before I turned back to focus on my escape, the sphere destabilized and exploded.

A column of water and mist shot upwards, creating the equivalent of a tsunami for an ecosystem that small, raining down water, dirt, and bewildered frogs into the field beyond. The walkers at the far end shrieked as they were soaked, their clothes dripping as they scrambled away, pointing towards the pond where bubbles still gave the surface the appearance of boiling.

By now, I had reached the garage and took the steps two at a time to the top, panting once I reached five stories. And I crouched behind a trash can at the edge to watch the scene below.

Flashing blue lights converged on the scene in minutes, eight cars coming from all corners of the city, and the figure of Arial's father stepped out of the first one to run the short distance from parking lot to pond, stopping at the edge just where I had stood. He walked the circumference, eyes at the center, and turned to shout at a cop that had just arrived, her chest rising and falling quickly from the exertion of the run. She stepped forwards, holding her hands in front of her, and pushing them apart as the water of the pond reacted, splitting down the center at her command. The Hunter stepped in the gap between the two walls of water, walking forwards towards the center where a crater had formed in the bottom on the pond, scooping out a portion of mud and holding it up to his face. Then he nodded, leaving the pond as the woman let the walls collapse and the water rushed together at the middle.

As he had inspected the pond, a dozen policemen combed the park and now brought five children before him, all male and roughly my size. After a quick glance, he shook his head, then they returned to their parents just a few feet away, their faces crossed with concern. Then he pointed towards the several areas of thick forest, one of them where I had run, and the police dispatched to comb through vegetation.

I sighed in relief when they returned with nothing, and cursed as I realized that my plan with the pond had failed - that he now had a stronger scent of me to target. But there was another part of my plan that had been successful - in the pocket of space above my wrist, there still was a black sphere that I had tucked away. And that even in eyeshot, Arial's father was unable to sense it. The power required to keep it alive must have been too minimal for his notice. Creating one and exploding one took far more effort.

I watched as they departed, and climbed down after a half hour, making my way to a location far more familiar to me. The tree by the academy, where I climbed once more in its branches, and overlooked the empty recess field. I called a new sphere to life, feeding it light and leaves, watching it grow larger and feeling it grow heavier, but keeping it smaller than the last. And I tossed it into the school yard, the place where I had watched dozens of students exercising their powers in high concentration, relinquishing my hold on it before it hit the ground, the flash nearly blinding me as the sound shook the school door. This one was nowhere near as loud as the one that had exploded outside my apartment, and the enclosure around the recess field contained the sound well instead of letting it reverberate in the alleys in the surrounding area.

The door opened, and a teacher stuck her head out, her eyes squinting against the sun, looking left and right. Then I heard her voice as she walked back inside, and a student protesting.

"*Samuel*, I don't know *what* you did this time, or *how* you disrupted class, but you march down to the principal's *now*!"

I smiled, knowing Samuel as a student with a knack for pyrotechnics, and an even bigger knack for trouble.

Then the door shut and I waited, my ears pricked for sirens that never came even after a half hour, and climbed down from the tree. I walked in front of the academy as I departed, watching as two workers painted over the name on the front sign in broad strokes and started adding new letters where the old ones had been.

Chapter 13

I took the bus twelve miles north of the city center, spending near all the money I had left on a ticket. Considering I had started with nothing as valuable as paper money, exhausting it had not been difficult, especially considering the cost of the meager late lunch I had bought from a vending machine at the station.

I frowned as we bumped along the road, the occasional pothole nearly throwing me from my seat, a wide berth from the other passengers formed around me from what I assumed was the smell I had accumulated over the past day. As I stared out the window, the buildings became more and more sparse, greater sections of forests and fields filling the gaps between them, and my memory recognizing less of the landmarks that flashed by. Part of me wondered if it might be wiser just to stay outside the city, to learn the extent of my powers away from The Hunter, and to return when I was stronger. But I shook my head - though I would be stronger, I still would not know how to fight, and I would miss any clues about my mother's disappearance that might surface. Then there was the matter of food and water, plus shelter. And if events did not go according to plan, I reasoned, I could always scrounge up enough coins from the cracks in the sidewalk to return here.

Near the end of the route I stepped off, waving at the driver as he scrunched his nose, choosing the stop for a long-abandoned superstore with a parking lot that extended around the back. Taking a shopping cart with three wheels and rust that flaked away like red snow, I pushed it around the back, checking for signs of human life and finding none. Chains circled the doors of the entrances and exits, and a modest collection of hubcaps were piled under an overhang, long abandoned by their owner, that I placed into the cart. Above, the sun had started to set behind me, still high enough in the sky for a few hours of light but dragging the temperature with it in its descent.

When I reached behind the superstore, it too was deserted save for the tread marks of cars that came to spin doughnuts in the abandoned lot. Leaving the cart at the center, I placed the hub caps around it and retreated twenty feet away, closing my eyes as I envisioned what I would have to do. That I would have to place the force point directly above the cart like a magnet, to focus it as close as I could so it gripped it tight, and move it quickly enough to prevent disturbing the hub caps.

Concentrating, I pushed the space above the cart with my power, forcing it downwards as the three wheels left the ground. But before I had the chance to swing the force point upwards, the hubcaps spun on their axes and leapt upwards, sailing past the point to scatter across the lot as I released it. I sighed and reached out to place a point in front of the nearest hubcap, scraping it along the concrete back to where it had started, careful to keep the force weak enough that the cart wouldn't tip. Then I repeated it for the second cap, and the third, sweat beading down my forehead as I focused, keeping the actions delicate, unlike the punch of generating dark spheres. And when all the caps were in place, I tried to lift the cart again, swearing as the hub caps scattered once more, and resetting them back in the center through several minutes of effort.

The next time, I thought about the way that I bent the space above the cart - earlier, it had been like a salad bowl, the edges gradually flowing away from a depressed region in the center. And I focused on tightening the bowl into a cone, only letting the tip graze the handle of the cart, and laughing as the back two wheels of the cart rose into the air. My jaw tightened as I focused on continuing to pull it upwards, the exertion of keeping the force point bundled tight together far more draining than simply pushing the space inwards, the feeling similar to the first time I had gripped a pencil to form letters and felt the muscles in my hand cramp. I released the cart after it had risen ten feet, letting bounce back to the concrete as it lost another wheel that wobbled away in a long semi-circle. Then I repeated the action until it grew more comfortable, dragging the cart left and right, and spinning it in a circle, the rusted joints breaking apart when I dropped it the last time.

Taking a breath, I raised both my hands, constructing points above two adjacent hubcaps, raising them in the air and circling them around each other, my forehead wrinkling as the loops grew tighter and faster. Once, in one of the short time periods where we had more money, my mother had enrolled me in a week's work of piano lessons - and now, commanding two force points felt the same as trying to command my fingers to play different notes at the same time, as if I were splitting my thoughts into two interacting parts. Possible, but far more difficult than controlling just one.

Then I turned, flinging the hubcaps over my shoulder towards the abandoned store, smashing them through a panel of windows high above the ground and losing control of the hubcaps as they became too distant, only to hear them ricochet around the insides of the store. I nodded, looking to the cart and the caps, knowing that I lacked the finesse to control them to the best of my ability. But for now, this was all I needed - and perhaps a lack of control would play out in my favor for the next stage of my plan.

The bus ride home was shorter than the one out of the city, since I stopped five miles north of the center, at a gas station that had bars over its windows and flickering lights on the inside. My stomach rumbled - it had been a full day since the meal at Arial's, a day full of activity with little sustenance along the way. Now it would be time to fill up on the rows of snacks, hoping that if I consumed enough of them it would at least *feel* like I had eaten something nutritious.

I opened the door, navigating the grimy tiles that had once been white in a prior decade, approaching the rickety racks holding foods higher in calories than nature had ever intended. Reaching forward, I grabbed a bag of chips, one with a particularly noisy wrapper. And I opened it.

"Hey, you!" shouted the owner from behind the counter, his eyes drifting away from the magazines as he pointed a chubby finger at me. "What the Hell do you think you're doing?"

"Eating dinner," I responded, spraying fragments of salt and vinegar his direction, and jamming an entire candy bar in my mouth.

"You gotta pay for that first!" he yelled as I tossed the bag on the ground and popped open another, letting a few stray puffs dance across the ground as his lip curled.

"Don't feel like it," I answered, throwing a pack of candy at him. "Screw off. What is it, like two bucks? I'm hungry."

"Damn kids," swore the man, hopping off a faded stool that creaked under his weight and ducking below the counter, a tuft of greasy hair stuck to the side of his reddening face. "Pay up, before I—"

I raised a hand, sweeping it in the direction of a display of beer that towered towards the ceiling, bringing it smashing down between me and the man just as I had pulled the cart earlier, the bottles shattering as liquid spilled out in a bubbling river on the floor. His eyes widened as I raised my other hand, the hot dog cart screeching as it fell atop the bottles, popping any that had survived the fall.

"I said," I repeated, my voice low and my eyes squinting towards him as he backed away to the counter, *"I was hungry."*

Chapter 14

"Shit, shit, eat what you want, kid!" shouted the owner as he jammed his finger repeatedly into a button behind the counter and taquitos flew at him like arrows with a swipe of my hand. And I took his advice - taking care to rustle the occasional shelf with a force point as he fled outside, sliding across the spilled beer in his haste, and slamming the door shut behind him. For all I knew, this could be my last food for days, and I made sure to stock up.

When the blue lights flashed outside, I launched a stream of soda cans out the window for good measure, aiming just short of the cars to shower them with cola as each exploded like a miniature bomb, acting as if I was tossing them nonchalantly over my shoulder as I raided the refrigerators.

"He came out of nowhere!" the owner was yelling outside to the several police officers who had arrived at the scene. "I ain't but only known one, but I know a Telekinetic when I see one! Nearly killed me, and my store is in ruins! Damn, do *something*!"

Just then, I looked up, my face portraying surprise as three officers cautiously approached the door, reaching my hands out in front of me to drag an ATM in front of them, purposely making it grind and screech more than necessary and forcing my arms to shake with effort.

"Son, just come on out— " started one of the officers as I toppled the machine, slamming it into the ground, and turned to run out the back exit. But before I reached it, the door exploded open, the officer reaching inside to toss the ATM back into the store as if it was made of cardboard. I shrieked, reaching upwards to make it rain ceiling tiles, releasing dust that had accumulated for longer than I had been alive and creating a smokescreen. Then I reached the back door, ramming through the *Emergency Exit* bar, and toppling into the parking lot. There, just twenty feet in front of me, was the owner's car - about twenty years ago, it would have been considered a luxury vehicle, but now sported rust to complement the racing stripes.

"Get back!" I shouted as the first of the officers emerged, the one who had bowling-balled the ATM. "I'm warning you, you don't know what I'm capable of!"

"Evade arrest, and we'll take you by force," he panted, his cardiovascular athleticism far less exercised than his strength. "Don't kid yourself into thinking you can escape. Already you're in deep trouble, and it's only going to get worse."

Beside him, the two other officers appeared, one a slim woman with close cut hair, the other a beanpole of a man, his uniform seeming to stretch impossibly to cover his entire frame. I lifted my arms once more, focusing on the car, creating a force point *just* powerful enough to start to pull weight off its tires and help the frame creak upwards.

"Don't you even think—" he warned, but I roared, the veins in my neck popping as I flexed my arm muscles, all while coaxing the vehicle upwards, bringing the back two tires off the ground as I shook.

And before I had a chance to raise the other two wheels, the short-haired woman next to him moved. Except *moved* wasn't the proper way to describe it - rather, she blurred.

The full force of her shoulder caught me across the chest so quickly my surprise was genuine, my breath lost before I hit the ground, spinning in midair as she maneuvered my arms behind my back. Cuffs latching around my wrists before I registered what was happening, cold metal tight against my skin. Then I was face down, my cheek biting into the gravel, her knee across my shoulder blades.

"Documentation," she commanded, grinding her knee into me more than was necessary as I choked. "Telekinetic, mid-grade, mandated by section A114 of city law."

"Screw you, and screw paperwork!" I retorted, trying to squirm away. "I'm not from here, I don't have to listen to your rules! Just like Dad said before you carted him off from the farm, and just you wait, he'll teach you!"

"Documentation, *now*."

"Didn't get none, don't need it!"

"Damn, this one's an idiot. Get the car, Jim; should be prime to keep rehab's hands full," she said as the other officers arrived, then started reciting my rights.

Chapter 15

"Don't you get any funny ideas," said the officer as he slammed the back door shut. "This car is lead lined and built with reinforced steel, but I'll crush it around you like a can if you get suspicious."

"You think you scare me?" I retorted, trying to spin in the seat but receiving a face full of window glass. "Just you wait!"

Ahead of me, he crammed himself into the driver's seat while the short-haired woman slipped into the passenger's side, shaking her head at my comment. We pulled out of the gas station lot, leaving the lanky officer to speak with the owner, the lights on his car still flashing in the mirror.

"Urlich, Larissa," crackled the radio from the front seat, and I recognized Officer Roland's voice from when he had spoken to Arial's father outside of the apartment, and I tensed. "Where are you? You're not in position. Why didn't you radio in?"

"Had a call north of the city," responded Larissa, reaching down into a cup holder and removing a handheld radio. I frowned, looking up at the separate police radio on the dashboard that had been buzzing with occasional traffic since I had been shoved into the back seat. "Mid-level telekinetic from farm country, nearly wrecked an entire gas station over a few candy bars and daddy issues. Figured he'd be a good way to get rehab off our backs what with the new vacancies. On our way back now."

"Hurry up and drop him off, then. We're doing sweeps in the next hour. Art wants the entire city combed. Sure he's nothing worthwhile?"

"Couldn't even lift a car, not worth our time," she answered. "We'll touch base in a few."

Then she leaned forward and played with the knob on the police radio, static flaring from the speakers.

"Siri, you there? This is car 48, Larissa. We've got a mid-level telekinetic prime for some reformation. Is your new facility outfitted with an appropriate holding cell? He's rowdy."

"Just finished this morning. This will make for a good first run. We'll have to keep him there over the weekend until we officially open," came the response, the light tone of a young woman floating atop the crackling. "We'll receive him out front. Documentation?"

"None apparent."

"All the better!" the voice exclaimed. "We'll be ready in five."

"Copy."

We drove into the city, hitting traffic that delayed Larissa's original promise of five minutes, Urlich's fingers gripping so hard around the steering wheel that it cracked when a car cut in front of him.

"Stop telling people I'm mid-level. I'm high-level!" I demanded from the back seat, kicking Larissa's chair while Urlich snorted and spoke.

"Son, you'd be best to keep your mouth shut. You can talk *all* you want when they load you into the cell. High-level, my ass."

"Let's see, closest region for Telekinetics is a hundred miles to the north, near the hot geyser springs," said Larissa. "With no documentation, your mother has no way to prove that you actually *were* born in a hospital, even if that is true. More likely she traveled out there on her own and had you in the dark, as I doubt you could afford it. And while that still may be practiced among the lesser civilized rural population, it still does bear the potential death penalty. So as Ulrich says, you'd best keep quiet. Or else your mother will be far more quiet than you'll ever be."

I shivered in the back seat as her steel eyes met mine in the rear view mirror, knowing that she had no idea the implications of what she had said. That for all I knew, that might be my mother's situation.

We pulled into the academy fifteen minutes later, two identical guards unbolting fresh locks on the front gate I had never seen closed, the fresh paint on the sign outside reading *Rehabilitation 1E*. Together they seized me from the car, their oversized hands gripping where my neck connected to my shoulder to guide me forward to the front door as the police car departed. Each of them wore white coats, their stature far larger than that of ordinary men, and their faces more blocky.

"Cut it out," I said and tried to twist away as their grips drew tighter. "No *way* am I going in there!"

With a carefully placed force point, I slammed the door shut five feet ahead of us, jerking my head as if to direct it. The guard on my right cuffed me across the temple, and for a moment, I stood dazed, my vision filled with stars.

"Try that again," he whispered into my ear, his voice low, "and you'll see we're capable of much more than a simple beating."

They ushered me inside, my sneakers squeaking on patterned tile floor as we passed a half dozen classrooms still in session. Dazed, I stared through the windows as we passed, only to be met with the shocked expression of a girl with brunette hair, her mouth open and brown eyes that widened as her gaze locked with mine.

Arial.

But in a half second, we passed her by, heading towards a door set in the back of the school, two thick metal bars placed across its frame. The guard hefted them upwards, grunting as they came free, and maneuvered the heavy door open to reveal a flight of stairs. I tumbled more than walked down them, the lighting poor, their hands practically shoving me forwards. And at the bottom, four doors jutted out from a central hallway, each made of varying materials with different locks.

With a creak, they pulled open the second on the left, throwing me inside so I fell upon the concrete floor.

"This room," announced one of the guards behind me, "has been engineered precisely for a range of classifications such as yours. Trying to escape will only bring punishment, and you will find the reward of freedom beyond you. Only through hard work and good citizenship can you find true freedom."

Then the locks in the door clicked into place, and I looked upwards to see two other forms in the dimly lit room. And one of the faces I recognized, clear as the first time I had ever seen it, the features unmistakable. The same golden hair that curled over his ears, the same sharp eyebrows, and same stocky torso. Except this time, all the parts of him were still connected.

"Lucio, how - how can this be?" I choked on the floor, the memories washing over me, my throat swelling to barely let words pass. "It's been five years since I saw you die."

Chapter 16

"Lucio," I choked again as I drowned in my thoughts, the memories flashing before my eyes.

How five years ago, we'd been on the eastern end of the city, at a crowded intersection clustered with cars ripping past far over the speed limit. We were playing marbles on a patch of dirt at the corner - hell, I hadn't played marbles in years now, and the rules were fuzzy in my mind. Lucio had been winning - Lucio, who had been my friend for my entire life, who I had met every day after school, who had been my top companion.

I still remember how he had claimed my prized marble just a few days before - we had nicknamed it The Black Galaxy for the spotted white stars that coated its glossy surface, and now he had it cocked behind his thumb and ready to shoot. Behind us, our parents were talking, since they had been good family friends since before I was born. And they hadn't been paying attention.

Instead of making the shot, The Black Galaxy ricocheted off of a rock when Lucio launched it, bouncing into the street where it made a kamikaze mission towards the storm drain. I'd jumped up to fetch it, but Lucio had beat me to it, leaping into the street to save our precious marble, his eyes never straying from the rolling sphere.

But Lucio hadn't seen the bus. None of us had.

The impact ripped the limbs from his body, his head soaring clean over the traffic light in the center of the intersection, his eyes meeting mine one last time. I screamed as my parents rushed forward, my father grabbing me by the shoulder, his hand wrenching my gaze away.

"Don't look!" he shouted, his dark eyes staring into mine. "Don't—"

Back in the holding cell, I blinked, pushing the memories away. And I spoke to the two faces in the darkness, keeping my voice level as it threatened to crack, shaking my head.

"I don't have a father."

The words hung in the air for a moment, then the second figure shoved Lucio, cursing at him as Lucio laughed.

"Damn it, Lucio, do you have to do this *every* time we meet someone?" Then he turned to me, extending a hand. "The name is Darian. And his power is the reason he's in here. He gets a kick out of meddling with other people's minds."

"Hey, he snapped out of it faster than most!" exclaimed Lucio from where he had fallen on the floor, his face still tugging at my memory. "What'd you think, was it *real*? A quality production? Too bad about your father. I could have kept it going much longer if you hadn't noticed that and I had known. But hey, I can't access memories - I can only plant them, and your mind fills in the rest."

"Was the part with the head really necessary?" I said, rubbing my temple and thinking back on the memory, realizing I had never played marbles in my life. That the intersection had been at the corner of 8th and Memorial Streets, which did not actually intersect anywhere in the city. And that besides this one memory with fuzzed edges, I could recollect nothing about Lucio, just attributes my mind had assigned to him. "And I don't actually know you, do I?"

"Now you do!" he exclaimed as Darian rolled his eyes. "Unless you want more of a back story? I can implant that as well! What do you think - maybe we met for the first time on a road trip or an adventure."

"No, I'd prefer you didn't," I answered, scowling. "Not that I would know, would I?"

"You get used to it," said Darian as he helped me to my feet. "Lucio has a very peculiar sense of style, a feeling to his memories. After a few times realizing that they are fake, they're easy to spot. The emotions come too easy. The colors too bright. The tone foreign."

"Hey," responded Lucio, standing back up and brushing dust off of his shirt from the floor. "If I wanted a critique, I would have asked for it! Besides, I'll get plenty of that when I make it back to Hollywood. It's where I was born, you see. The land of stories and motion pictures! And I'm going to be the best director you've ever seen. That's why I practice so much."

"And because you're a mischievous knucklehead," added Darian. "Anyways, we never caught your name. Looks like you're locked in here with us, so we might as well get introductions over with."

"SC. I'm a telekinetic," I answered and cast a look around the solid concrete room, a single light strip dangling from the ceiling, a series of bulbs rigged with low voltage, the walls polished to a fine finish. "How long have they kept you here?"

"Two days now after they pulled us off the streets," said Darian. "They caught Lucio here planting memories of having already paid for his lunch at a fancy restaurant we shouldn't have been at either."

"And neither should *they*!" Lucio exclaimed. "Two police officers, undercover, sitting one table over. We were being followed, Darian! They were trying to catch us doing something. And besides, I *told* you, that waitress was acting. I wasn't using my power."

"Sure you weren't," answered Darian and rolled his eyes again. "Either way, since I was there too, I was an accomplice. Anyways, SC, think you can get us out of here? Pull some telekinetic tricks?"

"I need something to throw or to move around," I answered, shrugging. "The walls here are bare, so I have no handholds. My best bet would be the lights, but they are too massless to cause any damage." Then I thought back to what the officer had said when I entered the back of his police car. "Besides, this room feels lead lined. I can't reach through it."

"Just like me," said Lucio. "Same here. All the minds on the other side are blurred. I can't focus on any of them."

"Then I suppose we wait," huffed Darian, sitting on the ground with his back against the wall, sighing as he threw back his head.

"Don't worry," said Lucio, his eyes glinting. "We have movies for entertainment."

Chapter 17

"Hey, what about lunch?" demanded Lucio as one of the guards opened the door to our cell and tossed in a stack of uniforms. "You forgot it today!"

"You would be best advised," answered the guard through his teeth, "not to attempt such an action again." He brandished a notebook, flipping open to a page showing a daily timetable. "I already fed you today. Your power can't change what is written on paper."

He checked his front pocket, then his back two, and finally his shirt pocket before finding the key as Lucio grinned, and locked the door behind him after slamming it.

"Damn, worked yesterday," Lucio said. "They're starting to get smarter."

I'd spent that night in the cell, shivering against the concrete and using my arm for a pillow. Lucio had snored for the majority of it while Darian had been silent, so quiet I couldn't tell if he slept at all. And I realized that for all I knew about him, he might actually be a Narcolept.

"What is your power, anyways?" I asked him when I awoke.

"Well, you and Lucio certainly share a disregard for manners," he answered, yawning.

"Oh, come on, Darian, why do you always have to be such a stickler?" needled Lucio. "It's not like you can use it effectively down here anyways."

"I'm a stickler because I like to avoid situations such as these, and I'd like to get out of them as soon as possible," said Darian in his deep voice, then turned his gaze back towards me, the whites of his eyes showing as he rolled them. "But to answer your question, I'm a Mimic. Born near a parrot sanctuary, because that's likely your next question. An illegal one, mind you, next to my hospital - the minor influx of Mimic children clued in the police. Typically, we're only from the tropics, but there were thousands of birds being smuggled in. Enough to bring a piece of their location with them, and influence children nearby."

"Interesting," I said, feigning curiosity, the hairs on my neck standing up as a chill rushed over me and I remembered the description of *Mimic* from the *Directory*. "What exactly can you do?"

"For a limited time, I can replay the powers of others as if they were my own. With far less strength, but still capably," said Darian. "But there are those that are more difficult to reproduce."

"Like mine!" spoke up Lucio. "Because mine requires a certain frame of mind and tons of practice. Because it's *art*. Not simply something that can be replicated."

"More because I don't have the obsession with it that you do," Darian retorted and kicked the door, the knock echoing in the room.

I stared at him as he sat back down against the wall, wondering about the true extent of his capability. Knowing that if he chose to replay my power, Darian would be far less skilled than I would be.

And that it would look nothing like telekinesis.

Over the next day, we heard the other doors outside opening and closing, sometimes accompanied by voices. Once, there had been a crash followed by a roar, and each of us pressed our ears against the door until the concrete started to heat up and we backed away, another roar quickly being stifled a few moments later as it was accompanied by shouts.

Another time, the entire room shook, dust falling from the ceiling as Darian paced and Lucio giggled.

We spent the next night in the holding cell, and the next, occupying the time with conversation and guessing games. For a few hours, Lucio broadcasted his movie ideas into our minds - one of which I found myself actively awaiting the sequel. And like Darian said, I started to pick up on the ticks and tendencies of each of his memories, finding myself able to sort through what was real and fake at a moment's notice. But as grateful as I was for the entertainment, his interference always made me uneasy.

It was Monday morning when the cell door opened wide, and the guard shouted inside, waking the three of us from slumber.

"Let's go, uniforms on! Five minutes until you're going upstairs. Cause trouble now, and you can be sure your name will be on a list for the rest of the year, and that it shall not be forgotten easily."

We dressed, ready when the guard arrived once more, the other doors in the hallway still shut tight. And he brought us upstairs to an auditorium, seating us at the far left side, an array of teachers watching us from below. Then more groups were brought up one by one from downstairs to join us - children all our age within a few years, each of their expressions varying - some with concern, others sleepiness, and several with anger.

Heat radiated from a small boy that stood next to me, holes already singed in several places in his uniform as he scowled, and three teachers from below kept their eyes warily directed at him. In front of me, a heavyset boy yawned, causing the entire section of students to waver as a wave of intense drowsiness passed over us and before departing in the span of a few seconds.

Then at the opposite end of the auditorium, students filed in a line to fill seats while staring down at us, their noses and chins high in the air. Students with freshly combed hair and ironed clothes, that looked like they had showered that morning, and that I recognized from my time watching recess in the rhododendron. Plus one that I particularly recognized, whose brown eyes never left me, and I avoided her gaze.

From below, a woman walked forward from the center of the line of teachers, dressed in a blue suit perfectly tailored to her shape. She tapped the microphone once, then smiled, as if oblivious to the glares directed at her from both sides.

"Welcome," she said, beaming, "to Rehabilitation Facility 1E, and congratulations on becoming members of its first class. I am Principal Siri, brought here from Facility 1A to help establish this institution. Before we begin, rules shall be established, starting with—"

"Why the Hell did you take me here!" shouted the small boy next to me, his shoes smoking, and I backed away as my arm started to heat up. "Who do you—"

But his voice was cut off as the woman leaned into the microphone, her eyes glinting, and the hard expressions faded from those around me when she started to speak in a sing song fashion:

"We gather here to bring out the best,
"That you should ever be!
"Forget your troubles, now you're blessed-
"Be calm, listen to me! "

Chapter 18

The heat died down next to me as Siri finished her singing, her eyes directly focused on the boy who had spoken up. His mouth ajar and his eyes glazed, he nodded slowly, blinking as if trying to push away sleep. It was quite rude of him to have spoken up, I thought. On our first day, interrupting the principal could only set a bad precedent.

"As I was saying," Siri continued, her voice returning to its normal quality and her smile wider than ever. "Now is the time to establish ground rules. Rule one - the usage of powers for any purpose outside of those dictated by your instructors is strictly prohibited and will be punished swiftly. We have been lenient on this matter as you have just arrived, but now you have been warned.

"Rule two, that classes will start at a prompt seven in the morning and end at five. Those who shall be boarding here," she inclined her head towards us on my side of the assembly, "shall continue with any other required activities and shall not be permitted to leave. The skipping of *any* required activities is forbidden.

"Rule three is that every one of you is now equal. Those who were brought in as part of the rehabilitation program, you are committers of crimes, and this is your second chance. And those of you went to the academy before - your parents owe the government for your education since you were on scholarship, and unless they can now pay it off, your participation in making the program a success will level the books. Unpaid debts are just as bad as stealing, so until you have completed this task, you are no better than your peers across the aisle."

There were several snorts from the other side of the auditorium as she finished rule three, and Siri raised her eyebrows, staring at each of the interrupters until the sound subsided. Again, I was struck by how rude they were - everyone knew we were supposed to be calm, and quiet, and to listen.

"Now," continued Siri as the other teachers stepped forwards from behind her, each standing in front of a section of students. "Today will be an evaluation of skills, meant to discern your potential path in education. Remember, we will instruct you on how to be your *best* for society. We will mold you and shape you, until you are *perfect*. Now, follow the instructors below, who will be conducting testing and determining where to send you for your first class. And remember," she said, turning her stare back towards the boy next to me, whose shoes had slowly started to smolder again but were quickly extinguished, "you don't want to set a bad impression."

From below, the instructors waved us into neat lines, keeping a ration of half and half from both sides of the auditorium. Ahead of me, Lucio and Darian were corralled together behind a woman with unnaturally bright teeth. Remembering Darian's power, and how we were about to be tested, I slipped out of that line and into another, falling into place between two previous members of the academy.

Blake and Peter, who had typically not engaged while the others played, but rather watched for the stragglers that they would throw stones at when the teacher's back was turned, or manipulate with their powers. When fights broke out, they were the first to arrive, jeering and spurring the parties on until the first punch was thrown, then laughing at the loser.

"Did you track some shit in?" came Blake's voice behind me, speaking over my head from behind. "Smells like a busted sewer pipe. *Just* under my nose too."

Blake swiped his foot forward, catching my back heel and making me stumble as my face turned red.

"Can't say I did," came the reply from in front of me from Peter. "Guess we'll just have to live among the filth until we clean them out, eh?"

He stopped suddenly, and I rammed into his back as Blake guffawed, reeling backwards, only to be shoved forwards again. I whipped around, my fists clenched just as an instructor walked by, casting a warning expression as Blake smiled.

"Go on," he whispered, just loud enough for me to hear. "First fight of the year, you won't do it."

I swallowed with the instructor's eyes still on me and turned back around, remembering why I had come to the facility. Starting fights with another student, however insolent, would only move me farther from my goal.

We marched from the auditorium and down the main hallway, splitting off from the other lines as they departed to other areas of the building. Then we turned left into a classroom and entered, the instructor walking up to the board and turning to face us.

"Take a seat. Each of you will be called up in turn have your powers measured, and each of you will perform to the best of your ability to be adequately separated into study groups. The highest performers will have the first pick of the meals, while the weakest performers will have the last pick at chores. This arrangement is temporary - there shall be ways to advance, if you can improve your worth to the facility. Now, let's see, who to pick first?"

I settled into a middle desk as he looked over us, and felt a sharp jab behind me. I ignored it, knowing Blake or Peter would only be trying to provoke me, but felt it again. Harder this time.

Angrily I turned, ready to snatch whatever they had been using to irritate me, but was met with Arial's face instead as she readied a fourth poke with her pencil. She must have slipped into the back of my line unnoticed, trailing me here.

"Why," she hissed. "Are you ignoring me?"

"You there, middle section, turn around. We'll start with you, since you're so eager to talk!" commanded the instructor, and I swallowed, standing up, realizing that Arial would be watching.

And that she still thought I was a Boreal.

Chapter 19

"Not only will this be a classification, but this too shall be a lesson," said the instructor as I walked up to the front. "During classes, much of what you learn will be about yourselves and your capabilities. But perhaps far more important is what you learn about *each other*. The ability to size up a Special and calculate your risks during a confrontation can provide an enormous advantage - by knowing their potential, you know how to stop it. The most dangerous foe, you will find, is the unknown enemy."

He reached into a bag on his desk, pulling out a copy of a book twice as large as the Directory and showing the title.

Painless Power Classifications.

"This is the textbook for my class, which many of you will be taking, depending upon your own classification. Right," he said and pointed to me. "You, what's your power? But don't tell me your power classification."

"Erm, ah—" I started, looking at Arial as the instructor drummed his fingers on the book, waiting. and watching. His dark eyes moved over my body as if he were measuring me, or as if I were a piece of fruit at the supermarket among a thousand others, and he was searching for defects.

"Let's go, boy, we have twenty other students. If each takes as long as you, we might as well send a runner to pick up dinner."

"I'm a Telekinetic," I answered with as much assertion as I could muster, breaking off my gaze with Arial to look back at the instructor, shivers running up my spine as I heard her speak up, her voice matter of fact.

"No he *isn't*. He's a *Boreal*, I've seen it!"

Damnit, I thought as the instructor cocked his head and spoke up. *Come on, think.*

"A Boreal *or* a Telekinetic? Two very different powers. Well, which is it?"

"Boreal" said Arial as I said "Telekinetic," and we each glared at the other.

"Boreal," she repeated again, insistent. "He *showed* me the dancing lights just a few days ago!"

"He did, did he?" said the instructor and made a note on a slip of paper on his desk. "How, exactly, considering you were at the academy, and he is here for rehabilitation?"

"I, erm," I said and forced my face to turn beet red, which took little effort as all the members of the class were staring at us. "I'm from the farmland a few miles out of the city. And, I, well, I'd never seen a city girl before." I shuffled my feet and looked down. "I just wanted to impress her. A Boreal is far more impressive than me."

From the back, I heard Blake snicker, and my face turned a further shade of red of its own accord.

"By showing her lights?" inquired the instructor, and he made another note. "Despite how much you wanted to impress her, that's outside the possibility for a telekinetic."

"We, well, we had climbed a tree, and it was dark inside, you know." The snickers in the back started to grow louder. "The leaves were blocking the sun, and I moved them around to let it shine through, like a light show. Only she couldn't see the leaves moving, since they were behind her."

"I bet that's not all he showed her!" shouted Blake, and Arial's face turned as red as mine as she whipped around.

"It wasn't like that!" she snapped at him as both Peter and he erupted into laughter. From the front of the class, the instructor slammed his fist against the desk, the sharp sound cutting off the conversation.

"Enough!" he shouted. "Enough! There is a simple way to solve this, and I won't have the first class dissolve into disorder. Go on, show us your power. I'm certain we will be able to tell the difference between the two."

Arial raised her chin as she stared, knowing she had me cornered, her expression triumphant. And I reached behind me, swiping my hand towards the board, scattering the erasers from a distance so they clattered across the floor. Her eyes widened, watering as she wiped them, and she whispered, "Liar."

"Morally ambiguous, but power certain. Telekinetic it is," dismissed the instructor slowly and flipped open his book, turning to a specific page. "Now, time for the power classification. Can anyone tell me how we could determine the strength of a telekinetic?"

"By how heavy of something he could lift!" spoke up a student on the far right.

"True," responded the instructor. "But there's nothing heavy enough in this classroom to be of use. In addition, during a confrontation situation, you wouldn't know the strength of his power until he showed his cards, which is an extremely dangerous position. Maybe he has the strength to drop a trailer truck on you, or maybe he can barely lift up a desk. Knowing can be the difference between life and death. So how else can we tell?"

The class remained silent as he waited, and he continued, thumping the book again.

"Good, this means that you'll have plenty to learn from my class. Powers do not just exhibit their classification when they are at full capacity - no, you can judge them far easier, assuming you know what to look for. In the case of a telekinetic, not only is it difficult for them to lift heavy objects, but also to lift tiny ones. Similar to how a grain of sand might slip between your fingers, those objects are difficult for them to grasp and can be a quick tell in a fight. For instance, back when I was on active duty, there was one who could control the very dust in the air, formed pictures with it as he approached, and to this day, I have never seen someone with such control or strength."

He tossed a paperclip on the ground in front of me, the metal *tinging* as it bounced on the tile and coming to rest at my feet.

"We'll start small. Go on, try to lift that without damaging it."

I frowned and reached out with my power, creating the force point above the paperclip just as I had done with the grocery cart, concentrating it into a narrow cone. But similar to a true telekinetic, the field I produced was too strong for something so delicate, and the metal shriveled into a ball.

"Right there is about the borderline between high and mid power class, as documented in this book. If you ever come into a fight against a telekinetic, and you find paperclip-sized objects coming at you with some accuracy, know that you are in for trouble. Now, try this."

He tossed a pen cap on the ground, and this time, it started to float upwards before slipping into the force point and cracking. With frustration, I dropped the two halves on the floor, letting them bounce away. Here, I needed to show that my powers were capable enough to get me into the better classes. Not so strong as to arouse suspicion, but enough to make my time at the facility effective.

"Now this," he said and tossed a rubber eraser the size of my thumb down.

This time, the object floated obediently at my command, and I lifted it gently, spinning it in a loop and placing it back upon his desk.

"Mid-level, near dead center," announced the instructor, making a final note on his paper, "And that, class, is the advantage. I now know how dangerous he is, because I know exactly what he can do. He can't surprise me! And because of that, I can win. Now, who's next?"

Chapter 20

One by one, the other students of the class were called forward, and the instructor demonstrated simple tests to determine their powers. Behind him he had, written *Mr. Linns* on the board to match the nameplate on his desk, underscoring several times with a marker. And for each of them, he had a separate page in his book, which I could now see was classified by power groupings so that several powers had the same tests to determine their strength.

For instance, the same test he had used on me for telepathy was used for Anthony, the student with powers over controlling the wind, by seeing how small of an object he could steadily levitate under an air current from several feet away. Similar to me, the eraser was the point where he lost control of his power, but for his power, that correlated with a higher than average strength, though not quite high powered.

Blake went next, flashing skin that turned to crystal under his command, making him a member of the Diamond Exterior power type. He flashed a smile as he walked to the front of the room, light sparkling off of a temporary diamond grille that replaced his front teeth, and flexed his arm, the muscles ripping into sections of glittering stone.

"Interesting, see here, class!" said Mr. Linns, leaning forward, his finger tracing along Blake's arm. "Power levels for Diamond Exteriors are determined through flexibility after the skin to stone conversion! See how he can still bend his arm, even though it is crystalline? As well as his knees! Truly marvelous. The rationale between this classification is that, in their hardened state, Diamond Exteriors are near indestructible and can produce razor sharp edges. And an indestructible foe with swords for limbs running at you is far more dangerous than one who can simply stay put and take a beating! Yes, this is high power here, due to the sheer defense."

"Of course I'm high powered," scoffed Blake, taking the chance to flex again and make rainbows cascade out of the prisms on his bicep, "with the papers to prove it."

"Yes, I'm sure," responded Mr. Linns, then waved him away. "Next!"

Arial walked to the front of the room, still cross but with regained composure, and refusing to look at me.

"Ah yes, Fliers," observed Mr. Linns when he saw her feet were actually a few inches above the ground as she waited. "A more difficult power to determine in the confines of such a small room. Typically, Fliers are classified through acceleration values, which directly correlate to the amount of lift force they can produce. Later, I will describe how to evaluate these in a more open environment. However, there is another method, one we will employ here. For Fliers, power generation occurs vertically - it's extremely difficult for them to hold a stationary angle. See how she is vertical now and at ease? But if she were to tilt backwards, even a few degrees, maintaining steady posture is far more difficult without forward motion. Observe."

He walked behind Arial, whose eyebrows were scrunched together with curiosity, and held his arm vertical.

"Now, Miss, tilt at the same slope as my arm. I'm going to move it slowly backwards. Ready?"

"Sure," answered Arial, rising a foot off the floor and watching his hand. He started to pivot at the elbow and she followed, careful to keep the motion slow and moving from perpendicular to more parallel to the floor.

At fifteen degrees, her teeth clenched.

At thirty, I could see her neck muscles straining.

Forty-five degrees and she started shaking, her breath held as she kept pace with Mr. Linns.

And at sixty, she collapsed to the floor, Mr. Linn's arm shooting out to catch her before she met tile, bringing her back up to vertical where she started floating without effort again.

"Another medium high, quite impressive," he said, and made a note on his paper. "Personally, I've never seen a Flier make it past seventy degrees, and seventy-five is absolutely unheard of. Well done, well done. Now, next!"

The heavyset boy whose yawn had spread like wildfire in the auditorium made his way to the front, his chubby face disinterested as Mr. Linns looked him over.

"Groupthink," he said before Mr. Linns had the chance to ask.

"Look, boy, you will speak when you are spoken to in my class!" reprimanded Mr. Linns, slamming a ruler against his desk with a *snap*, "Who do you think you are?"

"Connie," he answered, still disinterested and voice slow. "But my friends call me Connor."

"*If* I wanted to know who your friends were, *I* would have asked!" Mr. Linns practically shouted, and Connor flinched as the rest of the class pulled back in their seats.

"Hey, I don't know what I did here— " he started but was cut off by another shout.

"Maybe you should think about it, then! Walking up here like the class belongs to you, disrupting it, not paying attention in the back. I've half a mind to send you away right now!"

At his side, Connie's hand formed a fist, and he retorted to Mr. Linns, "I don't know what burr lodged its way up your ass, but go ahead, then! See if I care!"

"Yeah!" shouted Blake at the back of the classroom. "What the Hell is your problem, teacher?"

"Leave him alone!" two more voices called out as a few students stood, shaking their heads in disgust as their chairs screeched backwards.

"Seriously, he did nothing wrong!" I joined in, my right arm tightening as I considered putting a force point behind Mr. Linns' desk to scatter his belongings to the floor.

But Mr. Linns raised his hands and flashed a smile, speaking quickly to the aroused class.

"Well done, Connor! Class, Groupthink is the ability to transmit your own emotions to others, often marked by a suppression of emotions in the individual that holds the power, unless provoked. And Connie here has shown he is particularly adept - ten seconds ago, the back row was practically asleep in their seats. Now they're about to challenge me to a fight. I apologize, Connor, for yelling at you - but evoking emotions is the best way to test Groupthink."

"So I did well?" Asked Connor, his face confused as the rest of the class tilted their heads to the side, their own expressions perplexed.

"Marvelously!" commended Mr. Linns as Connor's face broke into a proud smile, beaming.

And the class rose to their feet, erupting into applause as he walked back to his seat.

Chapter 21

Mr. Linns folded his notepaper as he cast a glance over us.

"That's everyone, then? We'll be heading back to the auditorium then; let's go."

He led us from the room, the mood slowly fading as Connor's expression returned to disinterest, passing groups of other students that were performing their own tests in side classrooms. One was focused on a steel marble in his palm, his expression locked in concentration as veins of gold spread outwards like spider webs of the metal. The door to another room was open, and as we passed, I felt a frigid breeze accompanied by the chattering of teeth, with several blue faces staring out from the inside.

"No, don't go up in the seats!" he said as we arrived in the auditorium and started to climb the bleachers. "Down here, in the center, stand and wait! The rest should be here in a moment."

One by one, the other classes arrived, gathering around us in a growing crowd, the teachers collecting at the front of the auditorium and passing around slips of folded paper to Principal Siri, who transcribed them into a small bound book.

"Welcome back!" she said, holding the book in the air. "Each of you have been measured, your initial dignity determined. Next, you shall be separated accordingly into three groups - Upper, Average, and Bottom. Uppers will congregate in the seats to my left, while Average and Bottoms will share the bleachers on my right. Bottoms, you shall not sit.

"Uppers - you are free to go after you are sorted, you only have to return tomorrow for classes. Consider today a half day for you in reward for a job well done! Averages and Bottoms, you will remain here for further instruction."

She cleared her throat, scanning the open notebook in front of her.

"The following ten students shall be Uppers," she said, reading from the list, though there we only two names I recognized, the last two to be spoken.

"Blake and Connor!"

The called upon students sifted through the crowd, nudging past us to the left seats where small packs of snacks and bottled drinks waited for them. Academy and street criminal alike, all of them stood a little straighter than they had only a few minutes before. And the rest of us remained waiting as Principal Siri licked a finger to turn the page and started speaking again.

"Averages are next, starting with Kimmy," she said, as a girl to my left sighed with relief and started to walk away, soon joined by three more students in my nearby vicinity. A slew of other names followed, each of the students grateful to depart. Arial was in the middle of them, and she left without looking back.

"And finally," Principal Siri said, with only a fraction of students left, "SC."

I departed, making my way into the seats as Principal Siri smiled to the remainder of the students.

"Bottoms," she continued, staring down at them, the one boy who had made heat pour away from him and had shouted earlier glaring back up from their center, "you are the remainders. Go on, claim your area. Own it."

Then she turned to address us all. "Everyone, these are your current classifications. Know that while these were judged off of power rankings, you have the opportunity to make them change. You may move upwards, or you may fall downwards - at the end of each week, evaluations will occur to determine where you belong. But remember, your position relies entirely upon your demonstration of worth. And high worth shall be justly rewarded.

"Uppers, you are now free to go. The rest of you will assist in cleaning this facility. Averages, move down to collect your chores now from the instructors, and Bottoms, the remainder of chores belong to you. Until all are finished, no one eats except for the Uppers. And Bottoms, I suggest you employ a sense of urgency, for when they are done, you will be scrubbing the dishes."

My chore list was simple - to sweep the main hallways, then mop afterward before returning for a new assignment. And since I was mobile, I saw what tasks preoccupied the others.

The Averages were dotted around the classrooms and corridors, given chores like sorting books, dusting, or cleaning the windows. And the Bottoms congregated with cleaning chemicals in the bathrooms, their noses wrinkled as they worked, an instructor overseeing each group. Only once did I see one of the Bottoms start to pitch a fit, but in moments, Principal Siri was beside her and whispering in her ear, until the girl picked the sponge back up from where she had thrown it and returned to the bathroom.

The Averages arrived to dinner on time, a meal that most complained about, but I found better than the school food I had endured in the past. The Uppers were there early, laughing at a table by themselves, the Bottoms arriving just in time to start clearing plates away. Then they ate what remained of dinner, the portions smaller since most of it was already consumed, sitting at a table at the far end of the room with uneven legs. The Bottom table, it was known on the first day.

By the second day, it had already been christened the Ass Table.

Chapter 22

"Listen up!" commanded Instructor Cane, a mountain of a man with the foothills of a stomach to match, his gut warbling alongside his voice. "And quit your yawning! This is important!"

From the back, a few heads snapped upwards, and I flexed the muscles in my back, trying to roll out a knot that had formed the night before. We were standing in the center of the recess field, the fence containing us, and in a circle around Instructor Cane.

Of those who now lived in the rehabilitation facility, the Uppers were the most rested, with private rooms outfitted with brand new mattresses that the Averages had helped carry inside. And as an Average, I had received a narrow and lumpy padded bunk bed for the night, the room's temperature just slightly too warm, and two out of my eight roommates carefully ensuring that not a moment passed without the sound of snoring. Still, I had it better than the Bottoms, whose room was a single one of the basement holding cells for all of them. Each sported bloodshot eyes and wavering attention as they tried to focus.

"As I was saying, it is in your best interest to listen carefully," he continued, tapping an ear, "because this pertains directly to your current status! Your performance from here forward determines who shall eat dessert, and who shall clean the plates upon which it is served! Your first chance for change comes this Saturday, and in all my years of teaching, I have yet to see a more ill prepared lot. Soft, but I can change that!" He laughed, rubbing his own stomach as he watched our blank expressions, then continued.

"Much of your success depends on your own power. But first, we focus on your physical stamina! What use is it to have the strength of ten men if you tire out after only fighting two? This is why each morning before breakfast, you will report here, to me, so I can scrub the fat off of your bones!"

A few students groaned, which only broadened Instructor Cane's smile.

"I see you are eager to begin! Well, who am I to delay you any longer? Remember, no powers today, only muscles and willpower. We'll start with a three-mile run around the perimeter. That's thirty laps. The first ten to finish mile one do not have to run the next two, and the first ten to finish mile two do not have to run the third! The rest of you will continue until mile three. Ready? No? Good. Let's go!"

He blew a whistle and the class started off at a sprint, maintaining that pace for the first half mile until the wheezing of out of shape students far outweighed the easy breathing of the top athletes. I fell to the back of the middle pack as the days of malnourishment and nights of little sleep slowed my steps, my chest heaving as the first group finished, Blake among them.

"Let's go!" he shouted as a group of us jogged by. "You're holding back the class!" A few muttered swears were returned his way, and Connor rounded the corner behind us, coming alongside Blake as sweat poured from every inch of exposed skin on his body.

"Come on, Fatass!" Blake jeered, kicking a mound of dirt towards him. "Hurry up before I come catch you!" Head down, Connor increased his speed to escape, the next lap only bringing him back to Blake and the other finished students.

"Taking your damn sweet time!" Blake shouted as Connor stopped, one hand against the fence and the other on his stomach, his chest heaving. Then he retched, the night before's dinner coming up to splatter on the dirt.

"Like I said!" Blake gloated. "What a—"

But then he stopped, his face suddenly green along with anyone else in Connor's vicinity. And he doubled over, instantly nauseous, the sound of dry heaving populating their end of the field. Each lap afterwards, I sprinted by them to avoid Connor's effects, until I finished with the majority of the class on the third mile.

"Push ups and sit ups, let's go!" snapped Cane, allowing only a minute's rest. "On my mark. Now!"

Together, the class dropped as he counted, each student struggling to keep up with his cadence as arms and legs quivered.

"Jump squats!" he commanded next, pulling aside a still shaky Blake to demonstrate. Then came a slew of other exercises engineered to use our body weight against us, from lunges to pull ups and abdominals.

Sprints came last, several of the students collapsing at the end, their breaths coming in gasps.

"You're welcome for going easy on your first day," said Instructor Cane, "Now, ten minutes until breakfast, be changed beforehand. Then fifteen until your next class. I look forward to seeing each of you tomorrow! Don't worry if you miss me throughout your day; it will be here soon enough."

Chapter 23

Class one was with Instructor Linns. Not for everyone, of course – that was simply for the Averages. The uppers had their own teacher next door with a far smaller class size, while the Bottoms had been escorted somewhere else in the building by Instructor Cane.

"I see you enjoyed your morning session; some of you certainly smell like it," he remarked as we filed in. "From now on, showers prior to class are mandatory. I would have thought that would be common sense, but it appears many of you are not well versed on the subject. Take your seats. Let's begin."

He brought out copies of textbooks from the back of the class, letting them drop with a *thud* in groups of ten on the first student's desk, and instructing them to distribute them down the row.

Even lifting the books was a strain for students that now could barely move, their muscles protesting against the hard seats after the morning workout. Several groaned as they picked them up, while others attempted to move them with as little effort as possible.

"Now, you are aware that the first session of the day is physical. Second session shall be mental. And third will focus on individual power development. Here, we will study how to outsmart your opponent, rather than how to outlast or overpower them. Now, before we begin, who here knows the strongest power ever to exist?"

His eyes sparkled as he asked the question, and he walked to the board, waiting with the marker poised against blank white space. He waved his hands, encouraging answers from the silent class.

"Hurricaners!" shouted a student in the back. "When I was five, one leveled an entire block when he got too drunk and had the spins!"

"Hurricaners," repeated Linns as he wrote the word on the board. "Interesting, but not quite. Like the actual storms, their powers wane, so they are easy to defeat on a downswing. Next!"

"Electro sparks!" said Arial from several seats to my right. We still had not spoken, and she had been in the group that had finished the second mile early, though I noticed her feet didn't always touch the ground. "Hard to fight back against a bolt of lightning!"

"Another good suggestion, but again not quite. With proper grounding, it's actually quite easy to defeat one of them. More, anyone?"

A few students scratched their heads, and then gave up answers summoned from watching incidents on the news. And Instructor Linns added Dashers, Quakers, Magmas, and a dozen more to the list on the board. Then he took his marker and drew an "X" through them all, and turned back to face the class.

"All of these are wrong, but they are also right. There is no *one* power that is most dangerous - rather, for each of you, there are ones that will cause far more damage than others. Weaknesses that can only be exploited of certain types, regardless of power level. In fact, some of you may be far more at risk with a low powered Special than a high powered one, simply due to the nature of their power and their susceptibility."

"But surely one type is most dangerous!" said Lucio from the middle of the class. "Or at least, more a threat to most types of Specials! There is a reason why some Specials are classified as high powered and need more documentation!"

"Indeed, yes, there is. Which was the point of our last lesson. The most dangerous power is the unknown power, the one that you cannot defend because you cannot identify it."

"Come on," responded Lucio, rolling his eyes. "There's no way an unknown of low power is more dangerous than someone with high power."

"Oh, really?" asked Instructor Linns, stroking his chin. "I don't suppose you've heard of the Faceless Battle, have you? Many consider it legend, but I assure you it is real - I've read many firsthand accounts myself. Let me tell you a story, and see if it will sway your opinion then, of the unknown power."

Chapter 24

Long ago, before airplanes and cars, before transportation was available to the masses, the power diversity was far less than it is today. Many of you have likely visited towns known for their power, perhaps a mining town where nearly all the inhabitants can shape rock with their hands, or a oceanside town where breathing underwater is second nature. But before massive cities, that was how the majority of the world used to be. It would be extremely rare, for instance, to find opposing powers in close proximity, as that would mean that their owners likely traveled countless miles from their birth location.

Knowledge of powers, therefore, was limited. A nation knew all the powers within its own borders, and likely those next to it, but that was typically the extent of their expertise. Perhaps an anomaly would be born among them every few years to help expand their knowledge marginally, but these were few enough they may as well have been myth to the common people. We know from ancient texts that there are even societies that denounced the very existence of powers that are ubiquitous today, simply because in their region they had never interacted with them.

Now, two peoples were at war during this time, the Aeta and the Remis, both native to the Asian plains. The Remis were an expanding empire, their number far outstripping the Aetas, who had been a thorn in the side of their borders for years. The Remis decided to end the Aetas, to corner them and force them into single final battle. Realize that the Remis not only had the Aeta outmatched in number, but also in technology and in power types - this should have been a battle that would end in minutes.

To the surprise of the Remis, the Aetas met the Remis on an open plane, with some records saying their numbers were as few as a five to one ratio. To any general, this was an easy opportunity to eliminate the enemy. In a single swoop, and the Remis leapt at the chance. Here, now they could finally end the nuisance that had plagued them for years.

However, the Aetas held a secret. A deadly, yet low power, secret.

Deep in their jungles, there was a spring so clear it is said you couldn't see the water. And the Aetas discovered that anyone born near this spring developed the power of invisibility - a power regarded as low today due to easy detection and precaution, though it is still rare. And what the Remis did not know, was that one thousand Aeta citizens waited hidden by their own power on top of a small hill in the center of the battlefield.

When the Remis charged, they split around the hill, leaving the Aeta forces untouched. And the Aeta main force met them in defense, not attempting to attack but rather to survive, blocking the Remis with enormous shields as they waited for their brothers and sisters on the hill to creep behind the Remis forces.

The five Remis generals were slain within thirty seconds of each other by invisible swords, and the ranks below them eradicated moments after that. Death befell the Remis force from behind, silently cutting the throats of wave after wave of unsuspecting soldiers, and leaving only bodies in their wake, targeting high power individuals first, wiping out any with high power levels before they had a chance to use their power.

When the Remis finally discovered what had happened, they panicked with no high level officers in command. And the Aeta force crushed them despite all disadvantages, in a move that is said to have brought about the end of the Remis empire when it collapsed a few years later.

All this occurred due to one unknown power. Today, the ways to spot Invisibles are well known - to use mirrors that reveal them, to look for footprints, or for the telltale shimmer when they move. No general in their right mind would have conducted the attack. But to the Remis, this was knowledge that came too late.

So that is why even a lesser power is most dangerous when it is unknown. The effects are too hard to predict, the battle uneven. Class, this is why knowing your opponent is more important than anything else. And why your first move should be to find out all the information you can about them.

Countless times in history, this trend has repeated itself - that the first party to discover a new, secret power has a weapon of almost unimaginable strength while that power remains a mystery. And even today, the discovery of new and seeking of rare powers is predicated upon this superiority, of an ability to decimate an enemy before they can react.

It's what spurred exploration of the new world. It's the reason that empires remained empires, due to their access to varieties of powers. And it's why today, every power must be classified and documented, even if their power is so weak that they're practically a Regular.

Chapter 25

"Our first unit of this class will be on the capabilities of each special Variety, so you stand a chance defending against them," said Linns as he paced the area in front of the board. "You'll learn the telltale signs of when Josh, the Flamethrower here, is preparing to launch an incendiary in your direction. We'll go over why Arial, our Flier, would have a hard time following you if you run a complicated zig-zag pattern. And we'll explain the rationale behind SC being unable to simply rip you limb from limb with telekinesis, rather than hurling objects at you. One day, I promise you, this education will save your life."

He returned to the book at his desk and opened it, holding it up for all to see.

"To start, turn to chapter three. Each power can be placed in a group depending upon its abilities, which makes these facts far easier to remember. The same wall that will stop a Flamethrower will also stop a Tempfluxer and a Blizzarder. For this reason, they are clumped together in your studies, under the grouping Temperature Modulators. They share many of the same strengths, and many of the same weaknesses, with footnotes of exceptions at the end of each chapter. For now, I want you to memorize every group and their components, then later, we will dive into the details. Study up!"

He walked back behind his desk, taking a seat and watching us pore over the pages, dozens of charts that marked power families and their members. For instance, Telekinetics and Lucio's power, Memwriters, were under the same grouping, which explained why we had been taken to the same holding cell.

Class was dismissed for lunch at eleven, then we were directed to the academy's old gym. One room over, in the auxiliary gym, I could hear Blake's voice, which meant the Uppers would be in there. But since breakfast, I had yet to see a single Bottom.

The gym itself had been transformed from what I assumed had been a regular open multi-sports space to a training arena. Body bags hung from the ceiling on chains at varying intervals, specific ones marked with red flames or other symbols to indicate the power types they were designed to withstand. On the floor were a variety of obstacles, from nets and dirt mounds to an actual flowing creek that cut through the center of the room. The walls were padded, the windows replaced with boards, and the lights far above surrounded with protective cages.

"Welcome," rang out a voice from behind us after we had entered and were milling about, our eyes on tape markings that crisscrossed the ground, "to general power training! Here we will cover tactics that are common across many powers, from projectiles to strategic positioning to close combat. And here, you will learn to defeat your enemy."

We turned around to find the source of the voice, but there was only air, the space between us and the door empty. My eyebrows came together as I searched for the instructor, and the voice rang out from behind again.

"To defeat your enemy, you must know how to predict his every move!"

We whipped around as a class back to the gym, but still there was no one, only the equipment swaying from the rafters and the dim shafts of light that made their way through the cracks in the boarded windows.

"You must be one step ahead every time! Always with the surprise, and always with the advantage!"

This time, the voice cascaded from directly above us, raining down from the ceiling. But yet again, as we searched, we found nothing, except for a thin trail of dust that trickled down from one beam.

"Ready to strike with the perfectly timed punch for absolute decimation!" came the shout, as directly in front of Arial a figure materialized, his knuckles held an inch from her nose as he held a fist in the last stages of a strike, his body in a fighter's stance. She squeaked, throwing herself backwards and ten feet into the air, bowling over the students behind her.

"And that, that is how you defeat your enemy," continued the man, holding his pose as Arial stayed aloft. "Only when your instinct knows their actions before your mind, when you feel their movements instead of seeing them, when you react to actions that have not yet come into existence. Only through discipline and repetition can you learn this. And I, Instructor Peregrine, shall teach you."

He disappeared before us, then materialized behind once more, his voice like a bark.

"Now line up! Your lesson starts today, today we train your instinct, your reflexes. Your animalistic nature! That's it, behind the line of tape. We start with basic exercises, those beneficial no matter your strengths and weaknesses. The first, a sense of urgency. Move! Let's go!"

Chapter 26

"No, Josh, concentrate! Thinner, more accurate!"

Instructor Peregrine flashed beside Josh the Flamethrower, putting a hand under the bottom of the boy's elbow, redirecting a stream of fire slightly upwards. The target at the other end of the gym was a piece of white paper, six inches by six inches, with a red frame around it.

"Remember, you must only hit the inner target!" he commanded as fire splashed across both red and white paper. "Fire is dangerous, destructive. You must learn to contain that danger, to control it, or it will claim many lives, including your own."

Then Peregrine stepped away from Josh and into nothingness, only to appear in front of Arial, who floated twenty yards in front of a pitching machine stocked with tennis balls.

"First precision, then power!" he said as she dodged the first projectile by launching herself several feet to her right. "Too much, too much. I want the tennis ball to just whiff the hairs on your arm, for you to just barely avoid it. You must be agile, nimble, not clumsily leaping from place to place!"

It had been three days since Instructor Peregrine had given us our first lesson - three days filled with soreness courtesy of Instructor Cane, mental exertion from Instructor Linns, and power usage from Instructor Peregrine. Day one had been easy - simple stretches he advised us to perform in the morning, bed, and before workouts.

"It's for alignment," he said as we reached upwards, our backs arched. "You cannot be separate from your power. You must feel it within and around you, a crucial piece of you, not merely an ability. Stretch and feel where it begins and ends. Where *you* begin and end."

"Sounds pretty hokie," muttered Lucio as he held his hands upwards, then jumping when Peregrine appeared just behind his ear and whispered, "Far less hokie than your memory games, Lucio. But here, I teach you how to make them far more than games."

Lucio swallowed and kept his arms stretched towards the sky as Instructor Peregrine disappeared once more, flitting away to correct another student's form.

Day two had been an analysis of each of our powers, then matching us to our assigned tasks. And day three had been practicing those tasks over and over again, repeating the same motion for hours until exhausted. Soon the actions felt like chores, or boring, the repetition growing tedious.

"We are ingraining the motions past your thoughts, past your memories, into your instincts and reflexes," he said as my breath came heavily and I prepared to repeat my assigned task once more, and he appeared on my right.

Nausea washed over me when he appeared, a feeling that occurred whenever he used his power close to me and I felt the space around me shift, a hole opening and closing in a split second where he passed through. It was similar to when I created the black spheres, the feeling alien when not generated by myself, and different than I used it. Where I pushed the space, he tore it open, a sensation similar to scratching nails on a chalkboard.

"SC, concentrate," he shouted as I focused on four tennis balls that rested on the floor. "Aim! You must have the control to strike multiple targets, you must have the precision! Practice. Ready, go!"

Flicking both my wrists upward, I raised the four balls, then hurled them at the far wall. Four painted targets showed where I should have directed them, but with my ability to create only two force points, the balls clustered together, striking two of the targets off center.

"SC, you are dragging the projectiles forwards. Instead, you must grip each individually, guiding their path. Do not hold back!"

"I'm trying," I hissed as the balls rolled back.

"Try harder and practice!" he commanded and disappeared again, this time nearly making me retch. And after a few hours, I found I could accurately direct the ball clusters, but never striking more than two targets.

After his class were dinner and chores, then another shower and bed. And bed was something I welcomed after the tiring days, humming a song as I prepared. Always the same song, though I could never quite remember where I learned it, nor the words.

Until the night I was awakened by my window blowing open, and I heard the voice singing it. And I realized there was nothing more I wanted to be than the perfect student, the strongest in all three classes. The example for all.

Chapter 27

SC, are you listening to me?

The voice trickled down through my consciousness, echoing among my thoughts. I blinked, my eyes drooping from the night before, stifling a yawn. For three hours, I had crept away in the dead of night back to the auditorium where Instructor Peregrine trained us, repeating the drills over and over deep into the night. Working on my form and my technique. Trying to become the perfect Telekinetic.

To be the perfect Telekinetic, the perfect student. And that, of course, was something I wanted above all else - to move to the rank of Upper, and join those in high favor to Siri.

I frowned as I practiced, whipping the balls past me to hit the targets, my aim improving each time but still failing to hit all four of them perfectly. A *good* Telekinetic would be able to do that, I thought. Since I was a mid-range, I should be able to as well. What was wrong with me and my power?

Then I shook my head, laughing in the auditorium, a hand over my mouth as the sound reverberated off the walls. Of *course* I couldn't hit all the targets; Telekinesis was my fake power. My secret one, not my real one. Though now, after five days at the facility, I rolled the word off my tongue. *Telekinetic.* It sure sounded much better than *unknown,* so much more welcoming. And they needed Telekinetics on the police and military forces - I would fit in well there to help them as a Telekinetic, to help the state.

My frown turned to a smile as I kept practicing, the sound of tennis balls hitting the painted targets with soft *thumps* akin to the ticking of a clock as the night grew deeper, and I lost more sleep. But this was more important than sleep - I knew I must become better.

SC, are you listening to me?

The voice sounded again, and I jolted out of my memory, my hands flat on my desk and my eyes on Arial, who sat next to me one desk over, her sentence a hushed whisper.

"What?" I asked, stirring, seeing that Linns had momentarily left the classroom. Behind us, several of the other students were socializing, particularly those who returned home each day after school, those who had been members of the academy before it was converted. The others stared off into space, some of them holding light conversation, and many with bags under their eyes as deep as mine.

"I was *saying*," she said, her voice a hiss, "I'm switching schools next week. My admission papers to my new school were held up due to the sudden change of the academy, and they don't want to take me in until the end of the quarter. But they'll be going through by next Friday at the latest. Father was going to pull me out entirely, but I wanted to keep coming because I saw you arrive here. He only agreed because he wants to hear what goes on in the rehabilitation facility. I'm still angry with you, by the way."

"Oh, I'm, I'm fine," I answered, tracing the outline of a wood knot on my desk with my index finger. "Just haven't been sleeping well. I'm sorry for tricking you, Arial. I didn't mean to make you mad."

"So that's it, then?" she asked with narrowed eyes. "You know I don't buy what you told Linns, and I don't buy what you're saying now. What goes on here at night when I go home?"

"Oh, just sleeping," I answered and offered a grin to dissipate the inquiry.

"Riiiight," she scoffed. "I'm going to find out, you know, before I leave. You make about as good a liar as a Telekinetic - mediocre. Besides, I have a bad feeling about this." She lowered her voice and continued to speak, her eyes darting towards the door where Linns had left. "Like I said, my father let me stay because he wants to know what's going on inside here. I think something is going to happen, SC. He said he wants me to keep an eye out for anything unusual. And he said he wants someone else to do it for me, when I'm gone. To help the police."

"The police?" I asked, suddenly more alert and sitting up in my char. This could be an incredible way to start contributing to society, just as we were being trained to do. To accelerate my path to Upper.

"Yes, the police, dummy. You know they contract him out for his power. Anyways, I mentioned that you were here with me, and he said he's sorry for the way he treated you at dinner. But he wants to know if you would help report back to him. To keep him informed! He says that while the rehabilitation facilities feed into the police system, since they're owned by another branch of government, they have no insight."

"Of course, I would be happy to!" I nearly exclaimed as Arial tilted her head. "Just let me know when I can start!"

"You sure?" she asked. "I thought you would be reluctant, after that dinner."

"No, no," I answered. "He was only doing his job, Arial. And I'd like to help with that. I was lying, after all."

"If you say so," she sighed and tapped her fingers on my arm. "Are you sure you're okay, SC? You're different. Even your voice sounds off."

"Never been better," I answered as Instructor Linns entered the room and I opened my textbook, the motion filled with purpose as he started writing on the board.

"I'm going to find out, you know," Arial repeated in a low voice. "Just you wait. Is this really how you want me to remember you, SC, when I'm gone? The boy who never told the truth?"

I rolled my eyes and focused on the lesson. Halfway through, I dropped my pen, locking eyes with Lucio across the room as I bent to pick it up. Both his and Darian's gaze focused on me, and Darian nudged Lucio just as a sudden memory flashed across my mind of Lucio speaking to me before class started.

"After class, we need to talk. Meet us as soon as you can, SC," he had said.

To my annoyance, I remember having accepted. I was hoping to study in those moments, to make use of them, but if I already said yes to Lucio, I owed him a few minutes.

Chapter 28

"Today, we learn of the strengths of powers and how they are directed," said Linns, tapping the board. "This lesson comes courtesy of the research of Claudius Eriste, the primary contributor and collector of *The Directory*, whose edge experiments on the subject have been highly informative to understanding the nature of powers themselves. Now, class, we separate power into two dimensions - type and strength. First is type - who can explain the origins of power type?"

"That's easy!" exclaimed Lucio. "Where you are born determines the type! Everyone knows that."

"True, but there is more to it than that," said Linns.

"Conditions affect it as well," said Darian, his voice deep. "Location only affects it due to the conditions present in the location, what that location provides."

"Yes, that is closer to the mark," agreed Linns. "Think of it this way - an area is not considered volcanic because of where it is on the map. Rather, it is the volcano that makes it volcanic. A region is defined by its attributes, not the attributes defined by the region. Similarly, powers are defined by attributes. Can anyone tell me why that occurs?"

The class was silent, except for a voice in the back.

"Well, they just *are*, aren't they?"

"Not quite," said Linns, and he drew a blob on the board, one the size of a person. "Here, this represents power itself. The larger the area is, the more strength a power has. Now, before birth, the general size of this blob is determined - there may be slight fluctuations, but we know from Claudius' research that these are minor. Does anyone here know how we know this?"

"The twins disparity!" said Arial, speaking up next to me. "That's how they found it out!"

"Correct!" answered Linns, jabbing a finger towards her. "Correct! Claudius studied identical pairs of twins around the world in what we call bimodal sites - these are regions where two power types tend to develop in equal proportions. Location only plays so strong a role in power type - for instance, ninety percent of children born in one region may be one power type, but there will *always* be outliers. Anyways, at these bimodal sites, there was an equal chance for two separate powers. And Claudius found pairs of twins where one twin developed one power, and the other developed another, though all factors were nearly identical such as time of birth, extraneous circumstances, and of course, location.

"And what he found was extraordinary - that despite their differences in power type, twins always had nearly the *same* power level in respect to their type. An Electrospark born in the center of a storm was just as strong as a Weathermancer twin, a Tempfluxer in the desert just as skilled as the twin Sandblaster. So Claudius determined that location plays near no role in power strength. Rather," he said and drew a square over the shape of the blob on the board, "it simply shapes it! Into power type A, or for example," he took the marker and drew an oval over the square, "power type B. Does that make sense?"

"Kinda," said Lucio. "But there are some powers that are just weaker than others. How does that work?"

"This only determines strength within a type," answered Linns. "Each power has a general known upper bound and lower bound - initial power before formation simply determines where individual lies between them. *This* is why location matters so much, because individuals can jump entire power bands, in addition to some locations being potent enough to apply a minor power boost. A mid-level Telekinetic, mid-level Flier, mid-level Flamethrower, mid-level Duster, mid-level *anything* tends to start with the same initial power, even though some are considered far more dangerous than others. That danger level is simply the way we perceive them after their shaping. Now, does anyone know the name Claudius gave to this effect of power formation?"

"Egg in the nest syndrome," spoke up Arial again, her voice bored. "We went over this last semester."

"You did, but not everyone," chastised Linns. "But that is correct. Claudius postulated that unformed powers seek to conform to their environment as soon as they enter this world. In zoos, we see examples of dogs raising lions when their natural mother is not present, and the lions pick up many attributes of common dogs. Powers are similar - upon 'hatching,' they cling to the first identity they can find, and are thus shaped."

On the board, he went over the edges of the square again with the marker and erased the other shapes so that was the only outline left.

"Remember, power is the size," he said, shading it in. "And type is the shape. Important, yet again, because what is perceived a low power type can actually hold high amounts of strength. And I fear we've run over on time now - go on, next class! But remember this idea, the idea of intrinsic power. That everyone starts the same, and it is only the circumstances that change us."

We started to file out, and I felt a nudge as Lucio prodded me in the ribs and Darian took my elbow. And as the rest of the class turned left towards lunch, they dragged me right into a small side closet.

Chapter 29

"Quiet," ordered Darian as my eyes widened, and put his arm on my shoulder. "We only need a moment."

"What's going on?" I demanded as Lucio looked left and right outside before shutting the door behind us, the only light coming from underneath the crack in the door.

"We have a secret for you, SC," whispered Darian. "But we have to know we can trust you."

"A secret?" I repeated, feeling a broom handle jam into my shoulder blade as I stepped backwards. "What sort of secret?"

"One about what happens at night," hissed Lucio. "The singing, have you noticed it?"

"At first," continued Darian, "I thought it was Lucio here planting memories in my mind, trying to mess with me like usual. We were fortunate enough that I know how mischievous he is and immediately accused him of trying to meddle with my thoughts. I wish I had been right."

"What about it?" I asked. "I like it. It sounds beautiful."

"Damn it," cursed Darian, looking at Lucio, who spoke up next.

"Look, SC, that music is poison. They're doing something to your thoughts, to all of our thoughts. They're changing who we are, every night, without us knowing."

"Well, maybe that's a good thing," I protested. "They should be molding us to become better contributors."

"SC, that's not what they're doing at all!" urged Lucio. "They're trying to use us, like tools! Siri is trying to—"

"Hold on now," I said, anger flashing across my face in the darkness. "They're giving us an education, and lodging, and food, and you're accusing them of not looking after us?"

"It's not like that," said Darian, shaking his head. "They're not giving us anything. They're taking from us."

"I've half a mind to report you!" I retorted, my voice raising. "For your sheer ingratitude! That's what they say to do!"

"*Who* says to do? *Who*?" Darian asked, and I bit the inside of my lip as a lyric flashed across my mind.

The protesters, the fouled mouthed roommates,
Report them away as ingrates!

Send them to Siri to show them the way,
So they can be molded today!

"I-I—" I stuttered, blinking, before my common sense came rushing back. "Siri did, you know that as well as I do. Let me out of here. This is ridiculous. You ingrates."

Lucio and Darian looked at each other, then turned back to me.

"Look, here is our secret," said Lucio, changing his tone, his eyes softening. "We've been recruited as part of a secret team to help Siri. That was all just a test, SC. You should change your sleeping arrangements to be with us for a night. We'll show you what we mean!"

"Exactly," confirmed Darian, trying to place a hand on my shoulder. "She promised us it is the quickest way to become an Upper. Just for a night, you should join us."

"After what you said," I answered, "I'm not falling for your tricks. Let me out!" I pushed past them into the hallway, nearly tripping over their feet and stumbling over tile before turning back. "I'm not going to report you because I'd still like to be your friend. And I hope you see the truth. But if you try this again, I will! And maybe I still might!"

I stalked away, heading to the lunch room, irritated that I would likely be eating after the Bottoms and have less food than normal. From behind me, I heard the hushed whispers of the two of them as they followed, just barely audible.

"Should we nab him?" said Lucio, and the muscles in my back tensed as I prepared to use my Telekinesis.

"No, he's a goner. Useless," answered Darian, and they fell away as I entered the cafeteria, taking the scraps of food on my tray before finding an empty space to sit. In moments, Arial stood up from the other end of the table and joined me, her expression concerned.

"Where have you been?" she asked. "You're late, you don't want to get in trouble with them." She nudged her head towards the two guards that had escorted me into the facility on the first day, that now guarded the lunch door to keep anyone from leaving early. I paused, thinking back to what had happened, the memory coming to me a bit slower than normal. But once it arrived, it was fresh.

"Rolled my ankle leaving the classroom," I said, looking down to my foot. "Had to go to the nurse to have it looked at. Feels fine now, almost as if nothing happened."

Then, at the table two across from me, Lucio and Darian sat down as I scowled. Hopefully, they had reformed their thoughts after cornering me in the closet yesterday. And now that I could think about it, I did remember Lucio apologizing later that afternoon. Good, I wouldn't have to worry about them then.

"What's your plan for the weekend tomorrow?" I asked Arial, starting to take a bite.

"Tomorrow? It's only Thursday," she answered, laughing, "Don't get ahead of yourself! School isn't *that* boring."

"Thursday?" I said and looked up towards the menu. Today, I ate lasagna, and that *was* marked for Thursday. "Hmmm. I guess you're right. Strange."

Then I finished my meal and prepared to meet Instructor Peregrine once more, hoping the last night's secret session would show some improvement in my power.

Chapter 30

"Josh, inside the target! No splashing, we've been over this!" shouted Instructor Peregrine as the arc of flame leaving Josh's fingertips singed the entire target, and not the white square that had been shrinking every day since we had started training. Now it was a mere two by two inches instead of the original six by six.

"What's the point of this?" Josh said in exasperation. "Why should I even aim at a target? Why not just make fire explode out from the target itself?"

He pointed his finger, and flame erupted from the white parchment, originating in the center instead of his hand.

"Class, stop your activities and come here!" demanded Peregrine. "Josh has asked a question every one of you needs to hear about your powers. Let's go, now!"

He disappeared to materialize on top of a ten-foot obstacle in the center of the floor, bits of ice and frost falling from him as he appeared, and we circled around him.

"Every class, without fail, someone inquires why we do not use our powers directly upon someone else. For my own power, that would raise the question of why I don't simply reach inside an enemy's chest and pull out his heart still beating!" He flashed a smile, while Arial shivered. "Not that I haven't tried. For Josh, why not start a fire inside their cranium, so that steam flies out their ears? Or SC perform a dissection from a distance, removing body parts until the target is incapacitated? The answer is quite simple."

He disappeared, and I felt nausea again as he appeared at the base of the obstacle, a heat wave following his entrance, and his voice lowered.

"On Regulars, such tactics may work. But for Specials, it is different. Surely Linns has told you the origins of power types? A fascinating subject, with one important implication - all of us, though separate flavors, are the same. To cast your power directly upon someone else, you fight their own power that resides within their body. You infringe upon territory that is not your own, something so difficult to do it is nearly impossible. Josh, now, will illustrate. Go on, Josh. Start a fire in my chest, a real bonfire!"

"Wha-what?" stuttered Josh, stepping backwards.

"You heard me," commanded Peregrine, following Josh. "Give it your best shot. Burn me to a crisp."

"I don't want to hurt you," started Josh. "In case—"

"Do it, boy, and do it now!" shouted Peregrine, appearing inches from his face, and Josh threw a hand up against Peregrine's shirt, sweat trickling down his temple. And he gasped, his cheeks turning white as nothing happened.

"A slight pressure, and a slight increase in pressure, but look how exhausted he is," said Peregrine. "Useless in actual combat. But for those in control of their power, such tactics do work on distant extremities. Such as you, with your forearm, Josh."

The last few words came out low from Peregrine as he put his own hand in front of him, and his fingers disappeared into nothingness, though I felt space rip open before them. And Josh shrieked, looking down to his arm where several wiggling bulges appeared under the skin. Peregrine's fingers, with the nails just visible, nearly breaking through the barrier.

"Stop!" Josh shouted, trying to lurch his arm away but finding it locked in place, the fingers gripping bone from the inside. "Agh, it hurts! Stop, let me go!"

Eyes flashing, Peregrine pulled his fingers back through ripped space, whipping the bloody tips in streaks against a practice dummy. Josh shrieked again as depressions formed where the fingers had been, shaking his arm as it was released.

"Relax, boy, compose yourself. You'll see worse than that in the field. After class, report in to the nurse."

The class was silent as Peregrine walked back up to the front, his steady footsteps contrasting with the uneven wheezing of Josh's still panicked breath, and looked back towards us.

"What are you waiting for?" he demanded. "I answered the question, return to your drills. Anthony, it's your turn to be Lucio's partner. It's time we switched one out."

The students rushed to break apart, hurrying back to their stations. And Anthony took a seat next to Lucio, where I heard Peregrine instructing them with the only interruptions the thumping of practice dummies and targets.

"Now, Lucio," Peregrine started. "You are progressing well, but you are still adding too much of your influence into memories. The subject should not be able to discern between your additions and their own past. Consider their minds a wild jungle - you must plant the seed of a weed, one not indigenous, and let it grow on its own. Let it draw nutrients from their soil, from their air, from their sunlight. The more you nurture it, the more foreign and well gardened it will be. That is unacceptable, the memory must be indistinguishable, because you have only created the spark. Let them fill in the blanks, let them create the rest. Begin."

Chapter 31

On Friday, we were informed that school would continue on Saturday.

"You will report in at ten in the morning, this Saturday and every Saturday," said Siri at lunch, standing at the head table, her sapphire blue eyes moving across each of us. "We have graciously permitted you the hours of extra sleep. Ensure you are not late, and ensure that you are prepared. Saturdays will be the culmination of every week and you will be given Sundays for recovery and chores. Though some of you will receive more of one than the other."

Speculation grew that night as we readied for bed, with several of my bunkmates speaking up.

"They said that weekends were when we would be given a chance to strive for Upper!" said Josh the Flamethrower, rolling a small ball across his knuckles absentmindedly, the flame jumping an inch every time it crossed a ridge. "Makes you wonder what we have to do."

"Hopefully not hit a small target!" smirked Lucio, a toothbrush hanging out of his mouth as he passed by the door.

"Nobody asked you!" retorted Josh, the flame skipping an entire knuckle as it doubled in size. "Or invited you in here!"

"You're just jealous because I got the good room first!" said Lucio. "A lot nicer when you only have two! So roomy. You wouldn't know. SC, though - the invitation still stands."

"No thanks," I answered. If Josh was right, I'd be moving to the far nicer Upper dorms soon when I could prove I was worthy in the morning. There would be no point to changing bunks now.

"Suit yourself, SC," said Lucio, and I rubbed my back, remembering how bad the last few nights had been from the lumps in my mattress. "Are you sure, though?"

"I'm sure," I answered. One more night wouldn't be that bad. And when I did climb into bed, the lumps I had remembered must have been smoothed out.

That next morning, we met in the auditorium, the typical yawning reduced from the extra few hours of sleep, and the instructors leading us into the smaller practice gym, the one next to the daily Average practice with Instructor Peregrine. We lined up, the Averages along the long wall, and the Bottoms and Uppers facing each other from opposite ends of the rectangle.

The center of the gym was raised on a flat mound of dirt two feet high piled atop the floor, chalk lines creating a segmented oval with two circles on both ends. Obstacles were erected between the two circles – a car door was embedded into the dirt, a large wooden wiring spool was tilted in the middle, a low ridge of granite stones ran diagonal, and a long knee-deep puddle ran in an arc just inside the chalk line.

Perpendicular to the edge of the mound stood a table with two flip boards on it, one green and the other red, with numbers between zero and three. The two guards who had dragged me inside the first day sat behind each of the boards, their eyes on us as we entered, and their palms flat on the table.

"Welcome!" exclaimed Siri, climbing to the center of the mound and standing atop the wiring spool. "Welcome to Saturday activities! As promised, this is where you will have the ability to control your future positions in Upper, Average, and Bottom. Each week, Bottoms will be given the opportunity to challenge Averages and Averages the opportunity to challenge Uppers. Uppers, it is upon you to defend your position! Should more than one person challenge the same contestant a rank above them, they must fight each other for the opportunity to advance."

Siri spread her arms wide, pointing to the two edges of the oval where the circles waited.

"Contestants will start on both sides, with the more senior choosing their preferred circle. The winner will be determined when the first contestant scores three points - each point signifying a death stroke, or an action that either incapacitates or has the potential to kill an opponent. Applications will come one week in advance and may be submitted at any point prior to the end of today. Simply fill out a form with your own name as well as the name of the person you wish to challenge and drop it inside the box located at the entrance of this gym. By the next morning, brackets will be on display in the auditorium of the coming week's matches.

"This means each of you will have one week to prepare, one week to gauge the other's weaknesses, to determine how to best defeat the other power. Obviously, this does not reflect an accurate fight, so as we progress through the year, this time will shorten and brackets will be displayed later and later into the week. Seven days will be reduced to six, then five, then all the way down to the minute before the competition. Accordingly, the points to win will also be diminished from three to one. Bear in mind that this places the advantage upon the challenger, as they will still have a full week to prepare."

She smiled, turning from Upper to Average to Bottom.

"So, students, take a close look at your peers. Who among you will be changing their position next week? Who among you will become an Upper? It's up to you! That's all for today, but prepare for next week. And don't forget your submissions!"

The submission box was closest to the Bottoms, and every single one of them rushed into the front of the line, their eyes flickering from Average to Average as they considered their options. After a few moments, they shoved their slips into the box and the first of the Averages arrived, their own hungry gazes already shifting across the Uppers. Several Averages had already left the gym, particularly those who did not stay overnight at the school, Arial among them. But of those in the dorms, nearly all remained.

I considered my options among the Uppers. Should I choose someone too easy, there would be too much competition to reach them, and I'd be exhausted before the fight that actually mattered. And should I choose someone too difficult, I'd waste my opportunity to jump a rank and have to wait another full week.

But after a few moments of thought, I wrote a name upon my slip and jammed it into the box.

Then I waited for the next day, when the brackets would be displayed.

Chapter 32

"Oh ho ho, SC, I hope you're ready for a fun week!" shouted Josh as the door to our room slammed shut and I sat up in my bed, still groggy from sleep.

"What-what's going on?" I asked, blinking, and seeing that outside the sun had just started to rise.

"Woke up and I had to pee like nobody's business, so I figured I'd check if the brackets were posted. And they are! A few Bottoms beat me to it!"

Blankets flew into the air as the rest of the students jumped up, scurrying down the hall in bare feet, rushing forward to see the brackets. Of those in my room, every one of us had challenged an Upper. And every one of us was excited to win.

Three brackets were painted onto a banner the size of a van and hung from the auditorium wall, high enough that even the shorter students in the back of the growing crowd could see them clearly. First, there was the largest banner, the Average versus Average. Here, those that had put the same name down to challenge an Upper were dueling each other first in order to move to the Upper vs Average bracket. The largest sub-bracket was filled with ten names, all fighting for the opportunity to duel Roger, the Upper who was largely believed to have his position due to his father's large donation to the school the prior year. Though his power was strong as an Electrospark, Roger rarely looked others in the eye, and during initial testing, there were whispers that the instructor spent twenty minutes trying to coax his power out of him.

Relief flooded over me as I saw that I had bypassed the Averages bracket entirely and moved to the Uppers vs Averages, no one else stepping forward to challenge my opponent - Blake, the Diamond Exterior, whose power relied upon direct contact with me. And since the contest was scored by striking your opponent, as long as I could keep my distance and use my power at a distance, I would have a chance. Better than simply becoming an Upper, it would be my opportunity to retaliate against his earlier comments. And when I did become an Upper, it meant I wouldn't have to share a classroom with him.

But then I saw an footnote next to my name, and the smile froze on my face. There, on the Bottoms vs Averages bracket, I had a challenger. Someone who I would have to defeat before facing Blake.

Fino.

The student who had stood next to me during the assembly on the first day, whose shoes and clothes had smoldered before Siri turned her attention on him. Who now watched me from the other side of the gym, his hand on the wall, his eyes meeting mine. Then he turned to go, an ash handprint left behind, and a poster on the wall curling away from heat as he passed.

I swallowed and turned back to the bracket, making sure no one else had challenged me. A few were bracketed against Arial, another had chosen Lucio, and a third against Darian. The other names were not so familiar to me, though I knew in the majority of cases the Bottoms would have trouble - with powers like theirs, they stood little chance of making their way into the Average ranks.

Except for my opponent, who should have been placed among the most powerful had he not misbehaved.

Which meant this coming Sunday, I had to fight not just one Upper, but two.

Chapter 33

Late Sunday night, I made my way to the training gym, the steps along the dark hallways now familiar as part of my routine. The singing had just finished, and I felt the usual rush of motivation flood through me, spurring me forward, pushing me to train. To become an Upper and defeat both Blake and Fino.

But halfway down the main hallway of the school, I stopped cold, seeing a door creak open a dozen yards in front of me. With a single side step, I darted into a dark classroom, holding my breath as I strained my ears, my heart seizing as a tree branch scraped against the side of the building and the wind whistled. I craned my neck, my eyes trying to discern shapes but finding nothing that moved, wondering if it had only been my imagination.

Slowly, I crept out from the classroom, my eyes on the door that had opened, my feet making no sound on the cold floor. Still there was no movement, but I frowned, knowing that if I crossed the door's threshold, anyone inside could see me. And *pretty sure* that the door had moved, but not *one hundred percent* sure.

So I backed away down the main corridor, keeping my eyes pinned ahead until I turned the corner. There, along a slightly longer route, was a side corridor that I could take instead. One that looped along the sleeping quarters, then passed behind the cafeteria, but would still bring me to the gym.

I darted like a shadow, ducking under each of the incremental windows set into the wall, resisting the temptation to break into a run. The confines of this smaller hallway made the hairs on my neck stand up, the tight turns concealing each new length, the moonlight shining through the windows keeping my pupils just small enough to hide the darker shadows.

Which was why I never *saw* the small meeting, I only *heard* it.

"Every minute she spends here is increased risk!" hissed a voice from ahead on my right, and I froze, dropping to a crouch inside a broom-filled maintenance closet. Just ahead I could see the dim light around the edges of an ajar door, the teachers' lounge, and I swallowed as I recognized the speaker.

Peregrine.

"He picks her up each day while the rest of the students are cleaning. I've watched them - every time he drives by, it's slow as he peers through the gates, searching for something. He's suspicious. And I'm sure she provides him with a highlight reel each night."

"If you're acting accordingly, you should have nothing to worry about," came the second voice, and my eyes widened as I recognized it too as Siri. "I've been running rehabilitation centers for ten years, Peregrine, with hardly a hiccup after the first center. We're far cleaner now than back then, and we've closed the records on those students - the ones that entered the mental wards are there for PTSD from the front lines of the wars, and the ones who haven't are so loyal to the state that they died for it. Besides, the police know we are the hand that feeds them - if they were going to bite us, they would have done so long ago, and if they want trained Specials to populate their ranks, then they have no choice but to comply."

"Yes, the *police* might not try anything, but he's an independent contractor with a knack for looking in places he shouldn't," Peregrine protested. "Technically, he's not bound by their rules - he can act rogue, or at least claim that, whether or not he is colluding. They can deny any sort of interference on their part."

"But your project is well hidden, is it not? Just three weeks ago, you assured me that no one would ever find it, even with a map," responded Siri, then her voice turned low and hard. "Or do I have reason to be concerned, Peregrine?"

"I didn't expect a damn Hunter to be on my tracks."

"You've dealt with them before, deal with them again," she said, her voice drawling. "You're being paranoid, Peregrine."

"It's not strategic. Let's remove her before she causes trouble, expel her or cause an accident, or facilitate her entry into a new school," he demanded. "I might be paranoid, but you're reckless."

"It is strategic, Peregrine. If her father suspects something, he'll find a way to keep investigating. However, there's only one way to hold him at bay," she answered. "Do you know why my singing power works? It creates a desire so strong that everything else is eroded away. Once you have a person controlled by their desire, you can steer them any way you wish. And desire comes from something you can't have, something that is taken from you. Do you follow me, Peregrine? Why give him back his daughter?"

"It's risky," he answered slowly. "But I agree that it does make sense. While we have her during the day, he can't make an advance. He has to be cautious, so we only have to watch for him in the hours she isn't here."

"Of course, but you misunderstand me. If she is *always* here," hissed Siri, "then you shouldn't have to worry about him *ever*. I think it's time Arial realized that the rehabilitation facility is where she belongs."

Chapter 34

I smiled as I awakened the morning after overhearing Siri and Peregrine, jumping out of bed to prepare for physical exercise. Even in the short time that I had been in the facility, my muscles had already started to firm from the morning sessions - I could feel it in my back when I climbed up to my bunk, or my legs when taking three stairs at a time was easier than just one. And in the mornings, my joints and limbs no longer groaned from the previous day - rather, there was a permanent soreness in them that was almost satisfying, a deep sensation deep under the skin that thirsted to be stretched.

After becoming accommodated to regular meals and a having a mattress under me each night, my physical scores reflected my growing muscles as well - now I started placing in the upper fifth of the class, completing the exercises quicker to afford longer breaks, and watching as the other students improved as well. Even Connor could now keep up with the remainder of the class - though his times were poor, he actually completed the routine instead of stopping midway.

When I arrived to Instructor Linns' class later that day, I couldn't help but feel happy for Arial as she sat next to me - she would be receiving special attention from Siri, and soon she would not have to be around her father as often. I laughed, remembering how I had wanted to help him before Siri's comments about him the night before - obviously, he was someone to be avoided. Plus, this meant Arial wouldn't be leaving me for a new school. Besides Darian and Lucio, she was one of the only students I spoke to on a regular basis.

And even though the sides of my mouth raised when I waved at her, my heart twinged just for an instant, my face struggling to hide jealousy. Hopefully, it wouldn't be long before I, too, had some individual time with Siri.

"What are you so happy about?" Arial asked after class as I walked with her towards lunch.

"Oh, nothing in particular," I lied, not wanting to spoil the surprise. "Just ready for the brackets this Saturday!"

"You realize it's ridiculous, right?" she huffed, shaking her head. "Them turning us against each other to try to become Uppers. Life is perfectly fine as an Average without everyone staring at you like they want to stab you in the back."

"It's an excellent opportunity to advance, Arial," I lectured, and she rolled her eyes. "I have a feeling you'll change your mind eventually."

Then it was onto Peregrine's class, where we continued to hone our abilities. I frowned, realizing halfway through that Arial had not come with us - hopefully, she hadn't already left for home. Since seeing the brackets, everyone was practicing with increased ferocity, particularly in areas that they thought would expose a weakness in their enemy.

No one wanted to volunteer to help Lucio and take time from their own routine, so Peregrine selected a student at random every few minutes. And next to me, Darian practiced with Miles since no one else could muster the strength to hold the dummies that Miles slammed with punches that would dent the side of bank vaults, or spot him as he lifted several thousand pounds in lead weights. But for Darian, once he mimicked Miles' power, the task was easy.

I rushed through chores after dinner, hoping for a chance at a nap to recover from the night before and revive me for the chance to go to the gym while the others slept. Today, I had been assigned yard maintenance, one of the quicker tasks, in particular to rake leaves scattered around the physical training ground.

"Create piles, bag them, and dispose of them behind the dumpster at the back of the school," one of the instructors directed me, his voice a drawl. "Once you're finished with that, you're free for the night."

But the dumpster was at the far end of the school, and each of the trips would take just as long as the raking itself. Holding a hand over my eyes to shield them from the sun, I scanned the yard as I finished my first pile, looking for where else I could dispose of them. Then I turned around and nodded as I saw the fence behind me.

There was the rhododendron tree I used to climb, which had a perpetual mound of leaves at its base, one that no one would notice if they were to become slightly larger. All I had to do was throw the bags over the wall, empty them after I scaled the fence, and return back to the yard. Overall, it would be far quicker than the dumpster.

I looked left and right as I turned the first bag into a pendulum, swinging it from my right shoulder until I was sure no one was watching. Then I heaved it upwards, releasing it in a long arc, and watching as the bag started to sail over the wall in a trajectory aimed for the tree.

And just as it cleared the lip of the wall, it exploded.

Leaves showered down in trailing arcs as my mouth opened, watching as the bag ruptured against the air, splitting open and toppling down half full on top of my head. Shaking it off, I squinted, trying to see if anything had collided with it. Then I picked up a rock from the ground and lobbed it upwards, watching as bounced away off of *nothing* and back into the school yard. Curious, I climbed, my hands finding little nooks in the bricks, and placed my palm against where only air should be.

And instead, I felt a cold, smooth continuation of the wall. An invisible object that extended as far as I could reach, and that shimmered just slightly on contact with my palm, barely enough that I could see a disruption.

Strange, I thought, my eyebrows coming together. This part of the city wasn't that dangerous and certainly did not warrant extra security to protect us from outside. And everyone loved the facility, so surely it was not meant to keep us in – who would ever try to leave?

Collecting the rest of the leaves, I hauled them to the dumpster, biting my lip as I walked. Just thinking about the invisible wall made my stomach feel unsettled, though I wasn't sure why. Surely it meant me no harm.

And after I finished, I rushed back to the dorm, eager to take a quick nap. Most students were still completing their chores, so I would have plenty of quiet, a luxury that was near nonexistent at the facility. Settling into bed, I closed my eyes, then cursed as I realized I had left my shoes in the bathroom next door. With I sigh, I sat back up, rising to fetch them, and walking barefoot onto the cold bathroom floor.

But my shoes weren't by the door like I thought they had been. Actually, now I couldn't remember using the bathroom at all. And my forehead wrinkled as I tried to remember why I even would have left my shoes here, just as I heard someone step forward from behind me.

Before I could move, I was shoved against the wall, my hands pinned behind me with fingers clenched around my wrists like vise grips, my shoulders nearly ripped out of the sockets, and a pressure applied to the small of my back that expelled my breath in a gasp.

"This has gone on long enough, SC, it's time we set you straight," whispered Lucio's voice as I struggled to turn. "Let's go, move him. We don't have much time, and I'll need all I can get."

Chapter 35

"Cut that out, or I'll snap your neck!" growled Darian as I squirmed, my arms still pinned behind my back as he lifted me into the air, one of my kicks catching Lucio in the chest as I struggled. "I've borrowed the strength to do it!"

"Hel—" I managed to shout before Lucio's hand clamped over my mouth and they started to move, rushing me towards their dormitory room, the rest of the beds along the way deserted as the other students completed their chores. My face flushed red as I reached out with two force points, ripping a shower curtain away from the rod and flinging it over Darian, who swore as he struggled to remove it while the metal hooks clawed over his skin. Next came the collection of shampoo and body wash bottles, spraying over Lucio and the floor as Darian struggled forward, now slipping over the layer of colored soap coating the tiles.

Stumbling, he dropped me as he fell forward, and I slid on my back over the gel until I struck the far wall with the back of my head, my vision flashing as I raised a dazed hand. A stack of toilet paper rolls pelted Darian like machine gun fire as he recovered, and with my other hand, I prepared to rip the toilet stall doors straight from their hinges. But then Lucio threw the ripped away shower curtain over me like a net, cutting off my vision as Darian whipped me around like a rag doll inside the folds of the plastic, bundling me tighter than a burrito as he hoisted me over his shoulder.

Without my vision, I could no longer see objects to launch at them, and I groped out at random as they dashed away. I heard the sound of bunks screeching as I pulled them towards us, then books being ripped off of the provided study desks, and chairs toppling onto the floor. Then my ankles smacked against the door frame of their room, Darian unrolled the shower curtain like a carpet, and I tumbled on the bed.

"Don't you even!" hissed Lucio as I reached a hand upwards, immediately taking hold of a lamp with a force point and flinging it towards him while struggling to sit up, but he ducked out of the way.

"We're trying to help you, you idiot!"

"I should have never trusted you in the first place," I shouted back and launched myself from the bed just as Darian raised a hand, and I slammed into an invisible wall that domed over the top of me. Tiny ripples spread away from my point of contact as I fell back onto the mattress, the springs rebounding me upwards to smack against the invisible wall again as Darian grimaced.

"Hold still!" he commanded, but I punched upwards, my fist striking the wall in an explosion of pain, the sensation of the material the exact same as the bubble that encapsulated the facility. Then I reached outwards, pulling a broom that had been leaning against the doorway over the barrier so hard that the handle snapped, splinters scattering around the room.

"SC, it's no use, cut it out. Like Lucio said, we're here to help," continued Darian, his voice slightly muted. "Keep quiet, or we'll have more trouble on our hands."

"*You'll* have more trouble on *your* hands!" I answered. "Let me out of here! Stay away!"

For an instant, the wall disappeared, only to be replaced by one that was smaller, giving me only a half foot of space to move. The barrier was now so close I could feel my exhalations striking the inner top of it, and the hairs on my neck pricked as Lucio moved in closer. My breath came quicker, my chest heaving up and down as I pushed against the invisible material, my thoughts giving way to panic.

And I felt myself doing something familiar, something I hadn't done in quite some time, something that happened more out of instinct than intention.

My index finger found its normal resting place between my thumb and palm, and with a *flick,* I snapped space downwards, a black orb forming directly above me. Light spiraled into the sphere and I fed my own shirt into it as it gained stability, the fabric splitting apart at the thread level as the sphere gained weight and size, the sheets underneath me rushing to jump into the orb as well.

"What the Hell is that?" exclaimed Darian, his deep voice still managing to portray calm as his eyes widened and the dark sphere moved upwards to meet the invisible barrier. At the edges, the wall glowed purple as the sphere approached, neon sparks flying away as the two entities met. And then the sphere broke the barrier, the wall swirling inwards to join it like water down a drain. I laughed as the outer edges of the dome receded into the orb and Darian created a second barrier, only to have it disappear into the orb as well.

"Lucio, a little help!" cried Darian, sweat pouring down his forehead.

"Right!" shouted Lucio and leapt forward, his hand coming down over my forehead, "but this isn't going to be easy! I would apologize, SC, if you weren't being such a prick - but this is going to hurt."

Then I smiled, the world before me dimming as I entered a daydream, a memory more fresh than reality. There, just in front of me, Arial floated, smiling as the wind caught hold of her hair and streamed it out like a cape, the setting sun behind her illuminating each of the individual strands with a golden halo. A creek bubbled just off to my right, and green meadow stretched into the distance on the left, meeting snowcapped mountains a few miles away.

"I've always wanted to show you this place," she said as I relaxed, taking in the scenery. It was beautiful, just as beautiful as she was as she stared at me, her pupils dilated, her face lit by a glow that drew me in. "Remarkable, isn't it?"

I nodded, my mouth slightly open, my brow furrowed as I tried to remember where we were. Nowhere near the city could I find somewhere like this, not even when I took the bus into the outskirts. Maybe she had flown us here.

And as I fought to remember, I felt something at the back of my head. Not *outside* my head, but *inside* it, like a worm burrowing through soil. And Arial disappeared in a burst of color as singing filled my mind, singing so loud that my hands covered my ears and I could practically see the dancing notes. They moved in front of me, becoming more distant as they pulled away, the feeling similar to floss being pulled through my teeth and out from the back of my throat.

Paralyzed, my body rigid and my muscles tensed, I watched the music depart, the sounds leaving a burning sensation wherever they touched, reaching backwards as they fled and trying to catch my thoughts, to hook themselves back into my mind. But they were cleared away by a sweeping motion, like a squeegee over a window, letting no remnants remain.

I opened my eyes as Darian and Lucio stood over me, both of them tense and staring as I spoke, my body shaking as the memories of the last few days came flooding back. But it was as if I were rereading a book several years after the first time, the meanings of sentences altered on the second rendition, my more matured mind picking up parts that had been previously been hidden between the lines.

"My God." I whispered, looking up at them. "Arial."

Chapter 36

"SC, when you're finished, I'm going to need some help here," said Darian from above me.

I retched again over the side of the bed into a box that had been full of books just a few moments before, graciously provided by Lucio as soon as my face turned green. With each beat of my heart, my head pounded, the sensation rushing from the outer edges of my skull inward, and I winced with each pulse.

"What?" I managed to ask and looked upwards to where Darian stood, his hands two feet apart. Caught between them was the black orb, hovering in place, and as I watched, a pen from the other side of the room zipped towards the center like an arrow, only to be consumed into the mass.

"Oh, that," I said, feeling out for the orb where I had left it during the memory daydream, and feeling Darian's mirrored presence holding it in place. "Let go, I've got it now."

With a sigh, he released the orb, pulling his hands backward, and I took hold of the sharp depression in space. Slowly I opened it, releasing a stream of light that danced around the room, illuminating Lucio's and Darian's faces. Then, with a small pop and flash of light, the orb ceased to exist, dust floating to the ground from where it had been, while the two spectators jumped back in shock.

"Telekinetic, my ass!" said Lucio, pointing a finger at me. "That girl Arial wasn't lying on that first day of class with Linns! What are you?"

"Well, before we get to that," I said, staring into the mess accumulating at the bottom of the box, feeling my stomach lurch again. "What did you do to my head? I thought you said you couldn't alter memories. And what's going on? I feel all muddled."

"Until you can speak properly, we'll go first to fill you in. But then you owe us or else I'll broadcast this power over the entire facility. Something tells me they would be eager to find out about it," answered Darian. "Lucio, want to explain?"

"You're right, I can't modify memories," responded Lucio. "Provided that they are *actual* memories. Your problem is that Siri implanted her songs into your head - they're near memories, so I can't alter them either, but I can find them and remove them. It's like cutting away brambles stuck to jeans - I couldn't help it, some of them will make you bleed. But they needed to be removed."

"Thanks," I said, the word all I could muster as I remembered the sensation.

"Since day one," continued Darian, "Lucio has been removing the singing from my head each morning. And while I'm nowhere near as skilled as he is, I can emulate his power enough to remove a day's worth of singing from his head. Much more than that, though, and I would be useless. Siri's song has to build upon itself - multiple days are needed for it to really take root. They have to be layered."

"Not entirely true," said Lucio, raising a finger. "From what I can tell, she *could* enchant someone in a single session, but it would be dangerous. Basically, she would have to rip open their subconscious, and at that point, she would have far less control of the outcome. It's much safer to gradually take root."

"But even if it is safer," interjected Darian, "you can still tell who has been altered by their mannerisms. She has to be careful - after some of the stronger nightly sessions, the recipients act out of their minds. SC, we watched you try to write on one of Linn's quizzes with an eraser for ten minutes once before you realized it made no marks. Another time, getting changed after physical practice, you took the same pair of pants on and off five times. It's as if you're concussed - the brain needs time to recover."

"It sure does," I said, closing my eyes, the world swimming. "God, we need to find Arial. They're talking about giving her a full-on session."

"She's gone for the day," said Darian. "I saw her leave. But how, exactly, would you know that?"

"I'll need to start from the top," I answered. "But if I tell you this, you have to keep it a secret."

"Hey now, *you* were the one that was about to run blabbing to Siri!" insisted Lucio. "I think Darian and I are more trustworthy in the secrets department."

"Fine," I sighed. "But first, tell me - am I really scheduled to fight Blake *and* Fino at the end of this week? Lucio, tell me that's one of your memories."

"Nope," he answered, shaking his head. "Like I said, the singing makes you crazy. And in your case, plain stupid. At least more than normal."

"Damn," I responded. "That's going to hurt. And why did you use the daydream of Arial to calm me down?"

Lucio chuckled, a sly grin forming on his face. "I didn't. I just planted the seeds for happy thoughts, fantastical ones. But for the future, that's good ammunition."

"Damn again," I groaned. "As if you need that."

"Not like it wasn't obvious already," Darian stated. "Now focus, SC. You owe us a story. The others will get back any minute. Wait, hold on - Lucio, let's clean the best we can before they see anything! Hurry!"

And when they returned, I started, my voice low so others couldn't overhear.

"There's a reason why you didn't recognize my power," I said, pushing the box of vomit away. "It's because, to my knowledge, I am the first of my kind. And the only."

Chapter 37

"I still can't believe you're from space," whispered Lucio from across the table, his face alight. "I mean, I *believe* you, but it's still crazy! I'd almost believe that you are a Memwriter, not me!"

We were at lunch, Lucio leaning across the table with his palms flat on the surface. The night before, I'd switched rooms, moving in with Darian and Lucio while leaving the others behind, using the excuse that their snores had driven me off. And in the morning, we'd awakened ten minutes early - even after one night of the singing, I felt groggy, as if I had barely slept the night before, and thoughts seemed to stop halfway through my mind. This time, when Lucio reached out to my mind, the process only left me slightly disoriented.

"It's like the dentist," he said. "Last time, I had to remove teeth. This time, I only have to polish them. It'll be much less painful."

And now, at lunch, Darian put a hand against Lucio's chest to push him back into his chair.

"Keep your voice down or the whole cafeteria is going to hear," he chastised. "Don't be an idiot. This secret is the greatest weapon we have right now - it means we can exit the force field. It means we can escape."

"Sure, sure," said Lucio, hesitant. "But you forgot something - SC said he came here on purpose. We can only escape with him, unless you use his power."

"Which is something you should avoid doing at all costs," I hissed back to Darian. "Look, I'm here because I'm hiding. I told you about the Hunter - if you use this power on the outside, you'll draw him in like a magnet. Anyways, how long can you hold on to my power?"

"That's all the more incentive for you to help us then," countered Darian. "We saved you, now you save us. Anyways, I can only store a few powers at a time. The stronger they are, the less I can keep - it's as if I put them inside a box, and the box size is only big enough to contain a few. And they're always weaker than the original source. But I'll hold on to this one as long as I need to."

"I promise I'll find a way to get you out of here," I answered, looking directly into his eyes. "But you have to promise me you won't use my power to do it first. Look – I know you hate Siri as much as I do. She's planning something, something big – how great would it be to really stick it to her and the rest of the instructors when we leave? And if we do it right, we might shut down the facility by the sounds of their relationship with the police. Besides, if you're caught escaping now, all that will happen is that the police will bring you back – let's make sure there is nowhere they can bring you back to."

"I'd be in for sure," Lucio said, cutting off Darian. "Let's start trouble."

"Fine," Darian ceded, crossing his hands over his chest. "I promise. But you better hold up your end of the bargain, SC. I'm in this to escape."

"Like you said, I owe you, so I will," I answered. "But we'll need a plan, and right now I don't have one."

We fell silent, and I considered potential ideas. Unlike Darian, I was not ready to leave the facility – I still had to learn to fight. Additionally, I still had no solid leads on my mother, but spying on Siri as they became further pitted against the police might help. Perhaps they might have clues on why my mother had been taken, or perhaps I could lead them into investigating why.

I racked my brain for ideas, letting my gaze wander over the lunchroom. There, the Ass Table was still empty, the inhabitants having just reached the front of the line for food. To the right sat the Uppers, laughing as Blake threw an orange into the middle of the Bottoms still in line and they fought each other for who could claim it. I narrowed my eyes as they pushed over each other – in only moments, they would also have food, but something as rare as fresh fruit rarely remained long enough for a Bottom to find it.

I was so busy staring at the Bottoms, I didn't realize that Blake had met my gaze, his own eyes turning hard as the outer edges frosted into crystal. Within that instant, I knew both our minds were focused on the same topic – the bracket and this coming Saturday.

Casually, and still locked in a glare, he reached for an apple in the center of the table. And he raised an index finger, the edge glinting as it caught the lighting above us, and sliced clean through the apple to the core with a single swipe. The top of the apple slid away and fell to the floor as juice trickled down his palm, and he held the apple towards me before crushing it in a diamond-encrusted fist.

Swallowing, I looked away before he tossed the mass to the Bottoms, just as Lucio nudged me.

"Hey, SC, look who's coming! It's the girl of your dreams - well, *our* dreams, since I gave them to you! I'm sure you'd love some more, eh?"

"Shut it, Luc—" I started just as Arial sat next to me and placed a bowl of tomato soup on the table. I started, remembering that we needed a plan to expose Siri. And I realized that she might hold the answer.

"Arial, does your father still want information on the rehabilitation facility? If we could find out some secrets, could he share them with the police? Secrets bad enough that we could then leave this place?"

Arial frowned, staring at her soup, a fork in her hand. She dipped the utensil in the thin liquid, the soup drizzling away before it had a chance to reach her mouth, spilling over the table. With a sigh, she tried again with the same result, her brow furrowed when only a fraction of a morsel was actually consumed.

"Arial?" I repeated, and she looked up at me, tilting her head.

"Leave, SC?" she asked, dipping the fork into the soup once more. "Why would I ever want to leave?"

Chapter 38

Arial turned to face me, her eyes meeting mine as chills ran down my spine. For an instant, I could have sworn they were a bright sapphire blue - but when they came into focus, they resumed their normal brown color, the pupils sliding over me in search for a handhold but finding none, as if they looked past my features and I was just a piece of the background.

"I already leave too often," she mumbled, biting her lip. "To perform as a student, I need to focus more. To immerse myself in learning."

"Arial!" I said, snapping by her ear and letting my hand fall on her shoulder. "Arial, stop it, no you don't. Lucio, can't you help her?"

"Help me what?" she asked as Lucio scanned the room.

"Not here," he answered. "Too many distractions, and it would be too obvious!"

"If you would help me be Upper, I would be happy," Arial contributed, smiling, and twirling a finger around a lock of her hair. "We can be Uppers together! Wouldn't that be sweet, SC? Should we start now? The more we train, the better our chances."

"No, Arial," I responded, shaking my head. "Later, later, we can do it. We'll, ah, help you become an Upper, then."

"Good!" she said, standing. "Until then, I'm going to head to the practice gym. I've been falling behind; it's time to get ahead. Since I'm only a Flier, I'll have to work harder than the others to make it ahead."

The table was quiet as Arial departed, until Lucio broke the silence.

"See how we felt?" he stated. "That was you, not too long ago, until we shook you loose."

"And so much for the idea of using her father, SC," Darian snorted, rising to follow Arial. "*That's* not going to happen. But one thing is certain, whether or not you listen to Siri. If we become Bottoms, we'll have no time to develop a plan. And if we are separated, the singing will drive us mad. So I suggest we train. And SC, don't think for a second that if we become Bottoms I'll stick around - at that point, you can consider your promise broken, because I'll know you won't be able to make a plan."

The lunch room was half empty and Darian out of sight when Lucio spoke up, shaking me from thoughts that had turned to brooding.

"You know, it's not really that bad here," he said, his voice a flat monotone, unlike the typical prying dance that it normally performed. "At least not for the three of us, since we're now immune to the singing. I don't see why Darian hates it so much - but you, you still want to stay. How do you feel about it?"

"I feel like there's something going on that I don't know," I returned, forcing myself to finish the food on my plate though I was no longer hungry. "Something that could be a clue to find my mother. But even if it isn't, I came here to learn to fight. And I still have a long ways to go."

"So you're saying that you'd just leave otherwise?" he asked, leaning in. "If there was no fighting and no clues about your mother? You'd just up and go? As if nothing happened, as if we never met?"

"I wouldn't really have a reason to stay, would I?" I answered, picking at a few crumbs on my plate before deciding they weren't worth the effort and setting my fork down.

"I suppose you wouldn't, but after this, what then? Darian, he's always trying to find something new. Even without this facility, he'd be trying to escape something. We've only known each other a few weeks and already I can tell that. But what are you going to do?"

"Find my mother. That's my only goal."

"But *then* what?" Lucio practically yelled, then crossed his arms and sat backwards. "You're just going to off and leave once you do that, aren't you? Did I ever tell you where I was born, SC? Why I have this power?"

"Yes, Hollywood. You said it when we met. I'm sorry, Lucio, I don't know what you're getting at."

"Right, Hollywood. The land of movies, but also the land of forgotten faces, forgotten actors and actresses and stories that never made it to the screen. Of dreams buried under Sunset Boulevard. I was born to a mother who didn't want me, SC. In an alleyway behind a bar, a forgotten baby, left behind while she drank enough tequila to forget everything else in her life. *That's* why I'm a Memwriter – like Linns said, when we are born, our power clings to whatever it can in the outside world. And I think in that moment, even newborn me knew that I too would be forgotten unless I did something about it. Unless I created memories."

Lucio's chair stuttered backwards as he stood, and with a start, I saw his eyes glistening with moisture.

"And for once in my life, I'd like to create some real ones. To not be the forgettable orphan. Because at least inside here, I have friends. And when we leave, that's something I don't want to lose."

Then he stalked away, turning so I couldn't see his face and leaving me at the table. Alone. And without a plan.

Chapter 39

"Since the challenges have been issued and the brackets are up, it's only normal to experience anticipation," stated Instructor Linns from the front of the classroom that Wednesday. "But that does *not* mean you have a free ride to doze off or act up in class. Pay attention! Those of you who do will be grateful this coming Saturday, and those who do not will likely regret it. Consider this some free coaching."

Instructor Linns whipped a ruler against his teaching desk, the *crack* making several students in the back start.

"Now, many of you aspire to become Uppers, an admirable position. But there is a reason that the current Uppers are Uppers - to be frank, their powers are more advanced than your own. Without training, I would classify you as crazy to fight them - but with training, you stand a chance. Now, class, who remembers why an unknown power is so difficult to defeat?"

"The element of surprise!" shouted Lucio, directly into Darian's ear and making the larger student jump.

"Well demonstrated," commended Instructor Linns with a nod, "and correct. Remember, the advantage comes from the enemy being unable to find an angle of attack - with no knowledge of a power, there is no way to know their weakness. And far worse, there is no way to know if you are exposing your own weaknesses against an unknown power! But this Saturday, that rule has been turned on its head. Now, several days in advance, you not only know the powers you will face, but you have the opportunity to choose them as well. You know their weaknesses as well as your own. And you should understand how to exploit them."

"But they'll know what's coming!" whined a student in the back, and Linns shook his head. "There's no way we can sneak up on them."

"*Some* will, those more prepared. But remember, they are proud to be Uppers. Many think they are intrinsically better and this fallacy of pride will be their downfall - from my experience, more warriors fall from pride than any other weapon on the battlefield. Here, let us work through a few examples - however, I won't be going through any from this coming week, as that would be an unfair advantage. Let this a lesson to you on the importance of choosing not the weakest Upper, but the best match for your own power."

Instructor Linns turned to the board and wrote two powers in large, looping letters.

Electrospark and *Vibrant.*

"Now, which of these are more powerful? Which would *you,* if faced off in a fight, prefer to avoid?"

"Electrospark, obviously," yawned Lucio. "Vibrants can only make plants grow - lower levels can probably even be defeated by skilled Regulars. But an Electrospark would turn me into a Barbeque, and complement the meal with a few of the Vibrant's vegetables."

"Again, correct! Electrosparks are feared and feared for good reason," said Linns and turned back to the board to circle *Vibrant* twice. "But in the field, Vibrants are one of the top powers used to diffuse Electrosparks. In fact, with proper training, a Vibrant will defeat an Electrospark consistently, which is why Electrospark and Flamethrowers are often paired together. Can anyone here tell me how?"

"Plants aren't very conductive," said a reluctant Darian when no one else spoke up, his voice drawling. "A shielding could be created from leaves, such that the Vibrant sacrifices plants against the lightning."

"Close, but not quite. *Most* plants do not conduct electricity, but what's interesting is that some varieties are *excellent* at being conductors. Take aloe vera, with heavy electrolyte fluids, or any plant that is comprised primarily of water. Instead of creating a shield, Vibrants use a technique called the Walking Vine against Electrosparks - that is, they grow conductive vines like veins around them, and these vines sink into the ground to take root with each step. Should an Electrospark attack, the lightning is absorbed by the vines and dissipated into the ground before any damage can be done to a Vibrant, rendering any electrical power useless. And at this point, the battle is no longer a Vibrant against an Electrospark. Rather, it has become a Vibrant against a Regular. Does that make sense?"

"Sure," I said, waving a hand. "But that example seems pretty extreme. For most of us, our powers will not completely neutralize an Upper, no matter how much planning or preparation we use."

"True, but it will provide an advantage, such that it is no longer Upper versus Average, but more similar to an Average versus Average," said Instructor Linns, illustrating his point by leveling two of his palms from an uneven formation. "Now, any more questions?"

The class was silent, most students scribbling on their notepads as they thought ahead to the fight in just four days, and others showing visible regret. Had this lesson occurred a week before, many would likely have made different choices in who they would challenge.

"Any suggestions for difficult powers to combat? Remember, *everyone* has a weakness."

"A Teleporter!" I spoke up after a moment of silence, deciding to take a chance. "How could any of us defeat Instructor Peregrine? Any of us."

"Your aspirations have jumped far above Upper!" Instructor Linns laughed, his eyes sparkling. "Peregrine himself would be more difficult to defeat due to his experience in the field - fighting him is something I would not recommend. But for a normal Teleporter, let's take Arial as an example. Or any Flier, for that matter."

"Me?" asked Arial, suddenly stirring. "How would I do what?"

"Defeat a Teleporter, Arial. Please, pay attention - this lesson is designed to help you," Instructor Linns chided. "Now, Teleporters are an interesting breed. On flat terrain and armed with a blade, they can cut down vast numbers of troops before there is time to react. But Teleporters have an interesting property that Fliers can exploit - have any of you have felt slight breezes of warmth or cold coming from Peregrine as he uses his power?"

"Yeah!" exclaimed Lucio. "Near burned me once when coming down from the rafters!"

"Precisely, precisely," continued Linns. "When working with different heights, Teleporters have to account for energy deficits and expenditures typically associated with climbing and falling. When traveling downwards, they release heat - when moving upwards, they absorb heat. Due to this restriction, jumping too high or low is *extremely* dangerous, and Fliers can take advantage of this to drain Teleporters or dodge beyond their reach. The rest, I'll leave to your imagination, as class is ending and I have one final piece of advice."

Students started packing their bags, and Linns continued speaking, drawing a rough depiction of the fighting arena on the board.

"If you have learned anything from this class, let it be to use knowledge to your advantage. Study the arena and terrain, reduce the number of unknowns that can affect the fight. And use those unknowns against your enemy. Now, for the next two days, I will be answering questions to help you on Saturday. Come to the next class prepared."

Chapter 40

I was so worried about Saturday that I nearly missed its arrival.

"Get up, SC!" shouted Lucio, shaking me. "We're going to be late!"

"What - How did we oversleep?"

"*We* didn't oversleep, *you* overslept," lectured Darian, leaning against the door with his arms folded across his chest. "Come on, let's go. Wouldn't want to miss our chance to be an Upper, would we?"

"Figured you could use the extra sleep," continued Lucio as I dressed, hopping into my gym clothes as we had been instructed the prior morning. "With all the extra training over the last two days, it will only help. Besides, there was no singing last night - I think they want us to be extra alert. Makes for a better show, right?"

"Right," I muttered. "Might as well give them one, then."

At breakfast, the plates were notoriously empty - even the students who stayed overnight could only muster half a bagel, and those known for piling their portions high every morning now stared at their food in silence instead of eating it. Only a few conversations broke out across the room, and those were snuffed out quickly, like match heads that flared up before dying only moments later. The silverware clinked like the ticking of a clock, each chime a reminder that soon the tables would have new inhabitants. Some for the better, and some for the worse.

Then the last fork was dropped onto a tray, and the inhabitants of the cafeteria stood in a wave - the decision unanimous to depart, and together we trickled into the hallway. Opponents skittered away from each other, some refusing to make eye contact, while others attempted to use stares for intimidation.

We arrived in the secondary gym to find bleachers erected - a large section in the middle for Average with two smaller ones on either side for Bottoms and Uppers. Beyond, the brackets had been moved to cover the far wall, a number placed next to each fight to indicate when it would occur. And behind the table where the point scoreboards rested, the two guards that had dragged me through the front doors on the first day sat, their expressions stone as they watched us trickle into our seats, their hands drumming on the table in a mirrored cadence.

Here, even the breathing of students seemed subdued as we waited, staring at the clock above the entrance door as the second hand seemed to resist the palpable force of anticipation. With five minutes left, Siri walked to the center of the combat field; Instructor Linns on her left and Instructor Peregrine on her right. With two minutes left, she cleared her throat. And with thirty seconds left, she produced a microphone from within the pocket of her blue suit, tapped it to make sure it was working, and spoke to the waiting crowd.

"Welcome, welcome. Today is the day you've been waiting for - the day to prove yourselves to *me*, the day to become an Upper. The day where your training will pay off, and we will see who among you is worthy, and who among you is fit for only lower duties. Come, show us. Show us not who you are, but who you *can* be."

She walked back to the judges' table, and gestured at the brackets.

"First, the Bottom versus Bottom matches will occur. Next, the Average versus Bottom, then the Average versus Average. And finally, the Average versus Upper will be the culmination of the brackets. Ties, should they occur, shall be awarded to the higher rank. Any interference from the audience will be punished, so do *not* interact with those inside the arena. Now, Peregrine, clarify the rules."

Peregrine stepped forward to take the microphone, then appeared directly in front of us, an eager smile playing across his face.

"Leaving the confines of the arena counts as a point for the opposition - this applies to all circumstances, so should you find yourself cornered against a painted line, I would encourage you to fight your way back in with every ounce of energy you have. Fighters will start at opposite ends of the arena, and after each point is scored, they will restart at their original ends. Remember, the only way to score a point aside from forcing your opponent outside the arena is to deal a death or debilitating stroke, and remember, the final point *cannot* be scored by forcing your opponent outside the arena if the other points have been scored in this manner. May the fiercest among you prosper. Linns?"

Instructor Linns walked across the arena to take the microphone from Peregrine and paused before speaking, his words coming low and steady.

"The fiercest, or the brightest," he countered, looking back to Peregrine. "Though both are necessary traits. Remember what you have learned, remember what we have taught you. And show us how you have improved over the last two weeks. I wish none of you luck - rather, I wish you the sense to use your ability in its most devastating capacity."

"And with that," finished Siri, plucking the microphone from his hands, "let us begin. Bout one, to the judges' table! Show me you deserve to be more than Bottoms, even if I don't believe you."

Chapter 41

Match one was between Brianna and Mason.

"This is going to take forever," complained Darian next to me in the stands. "Neither of their powers is of much use, so waiting for kill strokes is going to be boring."

"Speaking of kill strokes, last I checked, you can only die once," added Lucio. "So unless there's a healer in here somewhere, this won't work out well. Unless these two are cats and hiding eight other lives. You can never be sure, and I wouldn't want to assume."

He squinted, looking down as the two competitors reached opposite sides of the arena and Darian rolled his eyes. The two guards watched from behind the table, each with one hand palm down, the other one clutching the side of the score cards. And below us, Brianna and Mason turned rigid as Siri's hand hovered above the buzzer.

"May the winner advance to the opportunity to fight for Average," she said, addressing the entire crowd. "And the loser remain a Bottom. Prepare to begin."

Brianna reached a hand upwards, checking that her blonde shoulder-length hair was still tightly tucked away, her sharp nose tracing paths through the arena. There was the stream to be avoided, the granite stepping stones that might aid in a speed boost, the obstacles for shelter in case of an unexpected attack. And there was the target, Mason, with his stare fixed on her, his face expressionless. Already he had dropped in a sprinter's crouch, his fingers twitching against the side of his leg. Then, without notice, Siri pressed the buzzer, the sound screeching through the gym as the two rocketed forward.

Mason rotated his arm along his cuff mid-stride, slinging a wave of water from the stream towards Brianna, his aquatic power barely managing to push a few scattered drops across her path. Without blinking, she darted through the wave, the water just enough to darken the fabric of her shirt, and danced around the car door. Mason reached back for another strike just as she leapt, her Jumper power propelling her a dozen feet into the air and clean over the spool in the center of the arena. Mason tried to stop, sliding on mud that he had created, his eyes widening as she arced through the air before him and rolled into a landing at his feet.

With two fists, she bundled his shirt at the collar and forearm, ripping him sideways and attempting a trip. Sidestepping, Mason avoided her swinging foot, breaking the grip on his collar by rolling his arm around hers and popping it away. Brianna fought for the grip back, leaping forward with her power into him, and he deflected to let her momentum carry her past him.

"Look, their powers are so weak, they're fighting like Regulars!" jeered Blake from the Upper stands. The students clustered around him laughed. But below, Brianna and Mason continued to struggle, their actions seeming to flow from memory rather than from panic. From the outer edge of the arena, Instructor Cane watched, nodding in approval once Brianna secured a hold on Mason's collar again.

And this time, he had no chance to break it.

Brianna sidestepped once, then turned, swinging her hip into him as she dragged his leg over her own outstretched thigh, forcing his front heel to leave the ground for an instant. Dropping, she twisted, pulling his body over hers in a throw that arced his ankles high above until they smacked against the dirt, following his back, which struck just a fraction of a second earlier. He gasped as the breath left his lungs and Brianna oriented herself on top on him, her hand forming a fist and descending in a punch that carried her entire weight.

Without hesitation, she struck the center of his throat, her aim to cut off his windpipe in the kill stroke.

But the fist never made it to the target - instead, it glanced away against a shimmer of light as the guard keeping her score outstretched a hand. There, just above Mason's throat, a tiny force field had formed, existing just at the edge of our vision from where we sat in the bleachers. Then her guard reached a hand to the score, flipping the number from zero to one.

The force field dissipated just as Siri's finger pressed the buzzer once more, causing Brianna to roll away. Then they both made their way back to their sides of the arena, their chests rising and falling with exertion, and prepared to start again.

Chapter 42

The score was three to one when Brianna dealt her last blow, a strike to the back of Mason's spine as he stumbled over in a mixture of exhaustion and defeat, wincing away from the assault instead of raising an arm to block. When she stepped away, he gasped on the dirt, mud sliding down the right side of his face, his shirt torn from Brianna's whirling throws. His hair was plastered down not from sweat, but from where Brianna had held him underwater, her fingers clasped directly behind his head as bubbles surged up around him in the stream in the center of the arena.

That had been more powerful than any physical blow - for an Aquatic, water was home, a sanctuary. In higher powers, some even had working gills. But for Mason, his power was so weak that, even in his element, he faced defeat - and in the final round, it was more embarrassment than lack of skill that finished him off.

When they returned to their section, the next bout started, populated with two more Bottoms with equally as weak powers and resorting to the same Regular-based tactics as Brianna. I frowned as one reenacted the same motion as when she earned her first point, performing a perfect mirror of her twisting throw and following up with a similar strike to the throat.

In the Upper section, Blake's jeers grew louder until one in particular caught on in a chant that erupted every time a Bottom started to form an advantage, the sound surprisingly loud for the few students occupying the stands around him.

"Who needs a Regular when you have a good Ass!" they shouted as the nearest Averages smiled, though the expression appeared on none who had an upcoming bout with a Bottom. Then the second Bottom match finished with a score of three to two, the final point more luck than skill, and both left equally as ragged from the encounter. The third Bottom match began, lasting only half as long as the previous, the two attacking each other in a flurry with such ferocity that all powers were forgotten and animalistic instincts took over. And when that fight finished, bite marks and scratches were as visible from the stands as the light behind Siri's eyes.

"Bout four!" announced Siri. Quiet rushed over the stands as dozens of eyes turned to the Average waiting below and several hands clapped against the Bottom's back who rose to meet him. They were both the same: same tall body type and size, both male and lanky, and both walked stiffly to their positions at the opposite ends of the arena.

But only one of the faces showed fear. Anthony, the Average, with the power of wind.

Against Slugger, the Momentive.

"I'm pretty surprised they made him a Bottom initially," whispered Lucio, careful not to shatter the silence as Anthony and Slugger looked to Siri, who was conversing with the guards. "Used to play pick up baseball with him in the old lot behind the train station - with a swing like his, we used to joke that he could hit the ball farther than the next stop. I was never any good, but people seemed to forget that when picking teams."

"It's because for a Momentive, he's pretty low-powered," answered Darian, his whisper doing little to conceal his own voice. "From what I've seen, he has to have direct contact with objects to affect them. Takes away a lot of possibilities."

"You haven't seen enough of him yet, then," countered Lucio, barely containing the excitement in his voice. "His nickname applies to more than baseball. My bet is he probably gave some lip to Siri and she sandbagged him."

Siri turned from the judges, and Slugger spoke up from his end of the arena, shaking out curls of red hair as he leaned against a foot-thick concrete pole obstacle, one similar to those found in parking garages to prevent cars from entering certain sections.

"Oi!" he shouted, straightening and bouncing back and forth inside his circle, holding up his fists in a mock fighting stance. "We about to get started here? I'm through with cleaning the jacks, and this is going to be good craic! Anthony, don't look so nervous, lad! Yer lookin' like you've never traded fists! Only hurts bad for a second."

Anthony turned bright red, rolling his neck as he avoided eye contact, and Siri pursed her lips at Slugger. The crowd leaned forward as her hand hovered above the buzzer, particularly Wendy, who had moved to the front of the Average section, her knees bouncing in anticipation and sending rhythmic waves throughout the stands. From across the aisle in the Upper section, Connor looked from her to Anthony, and a chorus of *boos* sounded as Anthony managed to wave to the bystanders.

Then the buzzer sounded, and the fight began.

In all fights up until this point, powers had acted as accents to physical techniques. Brianna, with her jumping ability, had been able to enhance her throwing skills, but the finishing strikes had always been the result of a more Regular-style fighting. In other Bottom fights, the same pattern had occurred where powers helped the combatants but never seemed to play a major role.

But for this fight, the dynamics shifted, made apparent in the first ten seconds as Slugger pushed against the pole obstacle he had been leaning against, likely testing its rigidity, and yanked it from the earth as if it was a twig. He swung the metal and concrete pylon above his head, laughing with each revolution, the *whooshing* sound reaching us in the stands as it carved a path through the air.

"Slugger O'Sullivan steps up to the plate!" he shouted, dancing forward with short stuttering steps. "The fans have been waiting for this stink all off-season, for the prodigy of the playoffs to return! And the pitcher winds up, it's gonna a fast one, a real fireball, and Slugger swings!"

He whipped the concrete pole forward, stepping forward and throwing his weight into the motion.

"And it's a hit outta the park!" he bellowed, launching the pole forwards as he released it, the rotating mass whirling directly towards a wide-eyed and frozen Anthony, who had yet to move at the arena's opposite end.

Chapter 43

Anthony reacted when the pole was halfway across the arena, as the collective audience was holding their breath. Raising both his hands, he screamed, the sound more fitting for someone several years younger, and a blast of wind coursed past him to pummel the flying object.

It was a desperate move, one of instinct rather than thought. For no matter how powerful his wind was, the pole was concrete, and its course would only be altered a few inches. The action *should* have been ineffective, like trying to stop a semi truck with a ping pong ball.

But instead, the wind caught the pole like a leaf, throwing it off course and slamming it into a far wall, where it fell to the ground without even chipping the paint.

"What the Hell?" said Lucio as the crowd gasped, and Anthony's face showed the same level of disbelief.

"Don't you ever study?" huffed Darian.

"I consider the ripest fruits of knowledge to be delivered by life, not books."

"Or you can't read," countered Darian. "Did you plant the idea you can tell vowels from consonants in my head too?"

"If you *had* studied," I said, cutting them off, "you would know that Momentives can change the mass of objects. Slugger made the pole lighter to throw it – if he had been a higher power, he would be able to change the mass back *after* the throw. But since he can't, it looks like it just reverts back over time."

"So what was the point of throwing it, then?" persisted Lucio, his eyebrows scrunching together. "Wouldn't it just feel like getting hit with a twig, or—"

"*That,*" interrupted Darian, pointing below.

Anthony had stumbled back with the force of his torrent and had nearly recovered by squaring his feet. But racing down the left of the field at full speed was Slugger, tossing obstacles from his path as if they were made of paper, dirt spraying up from behind him with each step, and streaking like a bullet towards Anthony.

Anthony shrieked when he looked upwards, seeing Slugger's fists raised, and ducked under an initial blow before sprinting down the left side. Slugger was faster, but Anthony's head start carried him halfway to the other side before he could turn to pursue.

"Get back here, ya gimp!" Slugger shouted when Anthony zig-zagged around him again and took off back towards his original starting point. "I'll make it quick!"

"Don't you come closer!" yelled Anthony, stopping, the two facing each other with twenty feet between them, and the crowd booed again.

"Oh, that's grand, just grand," laughed Slugger, and launched himself forward. "We're not here to chat, lad."

Anthony raised his hands, directing a torrent of wind to blast against Slugger and pushing himself backwards. But Slugger plowed forward, his feet creating trenches in the soil, lowering his head as strands of red hair whipped around his ears. He gritted his teeth, his progress slow but controlled as Anthony retreated toward the back of the arena, and Slugger was careful to box him in this time from the center to prevent an escape.

Then Anthony's back foot reached the painted line that was at the edge of the arena and he balked, pinwheeling his arms to maintain balance, while Slugger launched himself into an attack to take advantage of the momentary weakness.

But as soon as Slugger's feet left the ground, Anthony panicked, changing the direction of the torrent in a sideswipe that caught Slugger in midair, buffeting his body left before he could recover traction. The wind howled and Slugger cartwheeled over the row of granite stones, trying to catch one as a handhold, but his fingernails only left smudges against the rock, and he toppled out of the arena, onto the gym floor.

The buzzer sounded as Slugger stood and shook the dirt off of him, and Anthony released a smile mixed with relief and disbelief.

"Point one for fleeing the arena!" announced Siri as one of the guards adjusted the score.

"Come on, you're going to let that pass?" Slugger retorted to Siri, and her eyes flashed as the crowd booed.

"Competitors will return to the starting position," she said, the ice in her voice cutting off the crowd's reaction. "Or forfeit the next point."

"Grand, just grand," he exclaimed, his voice exasperated as he threw his hands in the air but walked around the outside of the arena to his original end, and twisted his torso in a stretch as he waited for the buzzer. And this time, when Anthony took up his position, the fear had left his expression.

Then round two began, and Slugger started to walk towards the center while Anthony maintained his ground, waiting, rolling his wrists as Slugger advanced. And once Slugger reached halfway, Anthony struck.

First the wind howled from the right, but Slugger dug in, refusing to let it drag him outside the arena again, bracing his muscles against the force as his shirt flapped around him like a sail. Then the direction of the wind changed, crashing in from the left and nearly toppling Slugger, halting his advance but failing to knock him off balance and outside the arena once more.

For a full minute, Anthony pummeled him with currents and Slugger absorbed them, his muscles bulging while sweat poured down Anthony's forehead, both of them wearing down but neither letting up ground. Then Slugger shouted, his voice carrying above the wind, frustration biting into his words.

"Oi, so that's how you'll play?" he yelled, the spittle from his mouth flying back into his face. "Fleeing instead of fighting? Might as well get this over with, then. Last I remembered, only two of the three points can be scored from leaving the arena."

He darted left and jumped, sailing past the out-of-the-bounds line and landing in a crouch.

"And now that that's done," he continued, his voice calm now that the wind had died away, and Anthony's mouth hung slightly open. "Let's begin."

Then he turned to the guard at the table and tilted an imaginary hat.

"Two to zero, lad; you'll be wanting to fix that."

Chapter 44

When the buzzer sounded, Slugger reached down and gathered two fistfuls of dirt, holding each at waist height. The muscles in his arms strained when he moved forwards, the steps short and deliberate instead of the running leaps from earlier, his feet sinking deeper into the earth.

And when Anthony started building up currents of wind once more, Slugger gripped the dirt tighter before continuing to walk through the storm.

"Clever," said Lucio, his two feet resting on the bleacher in front of him, the student ahead of him casting back an annoyed look. "Weighing himself down with the dirt. Why doesn't he just make his body heavier or something? That's easy enough for me at lunch!"

"When you can't pass Linns' class, don't try to cheat off me," remarked Darian, speaking over the howl. "That was literally the first thing we learned about Momentives, that they can't change the mass of their own body. It's how you can tell one is approaching you - they'll often have on knuckle wraps or gloves to make their punches land, or be holding a non-traditional weapon."

"See? That's interesting. You should try that more often, Darian! We need to find a good Comic for you to mimic. I could use some laughs. In the meantime, you and SC need to pick up the slack on the joke telling."

"SC is already busy plan making," Darian said, turning his eyes back to the fight. "Or he should be. There will be *plenty* of time for jokes when we get out."

"That's right," I mumbled as the fight below progressed. "But one step at a time. Let's get to Upper first."

I swallowed, watching as Slugger cornered Anthony, packed the dirt in his hand into a ball of mud, and wound up like a pitcher on the mound. Then he threw the makeshift baseball directly at Anthony, stumbling over with the force of the fastball, but managing to create a trajectory that ended with Anthony's solar plexus. And thrown just hard enough to sting, had it been a regular mud ball.

"*Ooooomph,*" gasped Anthony when the projectile connected, driving the wind from his lungs as he flew backwards, his gangly arms and legs struggling to keep up with his torso that appeared to be hit with a wrecking ball. Ten feet he flew backwards, easily clearing the edge of the arena, and toppling onto the ground as a heaving and crumpled mass, a hand clutched over his heart as he stared upwards.

The buzzer sounded and Slugger walked forward, extending a hand to Anthony from above.

"Lad, get up. This has gone on long enough, dontcha think? Come on, t'was just a bit of dirt."

"Contestants will return to their starting positions," commanded Siri, pursing her lips, but Slugger ignored her.

Anthony shook his head, and Slugger reached down to take his wrist, pulling him to his feet and clapping him on the back once.

"Lighten up; let's either make this quick or fun, shall we?"

"Contestants will return to their starting positions," repeated Siri, this time in a singsong voice that made the crowd above stir, but Slugger rolled his eyes.

"Cut that out, Miss!" he retorted, shaking out his hair and cracking his neck. "Going as fast as my wee legs will take me, and they're longer than most!"

Shock flashed over Siri's face, then was gone in an instant, her expression turning as conservative as the blue suit she wore, and the muscles in her neck tightening. Then the next round started and was over in under a minute, Slugger aiming a punch at Anthony's face that was so strong that the protective force field lit up with a flash sparks when it connected to his fist. And when he prepared for the final round, the final strike to end the match, Siri turned to whisper in one of the guard's ears.

"And now, for the grand finale, the bottom of the ninth!" shouted Slugger when the buzzer sounded, and he picked up one of the car door obstacles, holding it above his head. "Truly a one-sided game, but Slugger will not let his fans down! No, he'll leave with a grand slam, a nail in the coffin! And a warning to future challengers!"

He trudged forward with the car door, his legs straining as it gained weight, while Anthony appeared ready to wet himself. But two-thirds of the way across the arena, Slugger tripped on something, though there was nothing but bare earth beneath him. And there, so faint I could barely see it and appearing only for a split second, was a spark just under one of his feet as he careened forward.

The car door slammed down on top of him, the mass enhanced, and his guard raised a hand to generate a force field only after his body bore most of the blow. The door rolled off, revealing Slugger's face to be splattered with blood that rushed from his nose and was lapped up by the earth, staring back at the spot where he had tripped with disbelief as the buzzer sounded.

"Congratulations to Anthony, the winner!" announced Siri as she smiled. "Remember, students, humility is a virtue! And as we watch you grow, we will be sure to nurture the virtues necessary for you to thrive. For what is a vine without a trellis, or a bush without pruning? Let the next match begin, and may the winner be deserving of the prize!"

Chapter 45

Of Lucio, Darian, and myself, my match came first. And after watching all the physical techniques of the Bottoms, I felt ready – I knew their top moves, their throws, how they set up a punch. While at first it had seemed near mystical, now I realized there were less than five combinations, which made perfect sense considering the short amount of time they had to train. And each of the combinations had an equally as simple counter – a side step, a twist of the hips, a dodge. So long as the move was recognized before full implementation, it would be trivial to evade it.

But for those who had no foresight, it was deadly.

"Match seven!" called Siri, and I stood, walking down the bleachers to the arena below. Each of my steps seemed to echo off the far wall as I descended, and from the corner of my eye, I saw a figure keeping pace. Both he and I reached the judge's table at the same time, waiting to be assigned to a corner. Next to me, I felt the heat radiating from his body in pulses that could only be a heartbeat, and straightened my shoulders while raising my chin, making a point to make my body as large as possible to combat the space occupied by his power.

Then we walked to opposite ends as I felt the earth crunching under my feet in the still dry regions, and passed several new obstacles that had been added after Slugger's fight – a fresh car door, a new pole in the place of the one he had ripped out, and the scattered granite stepping stones realigned in their place.

I looked up when I arrived at my position, meeting Fino's eyes, the ever present fury flaring up just behind them. I steadied my breath, taking account of the terrain, preparing my muscles to leap into action. And I remembered Linns' lesson on Fino's power type, Furnaces.

Often emotionally driven, untrained Furnaces face problems with containment – too easily do they let their power boil over, their embers turn to wildfires. At that point, they lose control, and are as much of a danger to themselves as they are to you. So remember, the more power they use, the less ability they have to direct it with precision.

Siri's finger rested on the buzzer, and the crowd took a collective breath, knowing that this was no Bottom against Average fight. And aside from the Bottoms, none of us had seen the extent of Fino's power since the first day. But with strategy, quick reactions, and Linns' advice, I should be able to counter it.

Then the buzzer sounded, and I saw Fino's power before I felt it. Hands raised, he screamed with rage, his face as red as the flames that licked up from his feet, smoke billowing away from the pillar on his left as the paint crinkled and bubbled. The air warped, shimmering like the layer just above pavement on a triple-digit day, and blossoming towards me in a visible shock wave that expanded outwards to cover my entire side of the arena.

Reaching ahead with two force points, I took hold of both the car doors at opposite ends of the arena, dragging them backwards and together just in front of me, the glass shattering as metal twisted together at the center seam. Crouching, I ducked under the metal, driving the edge of the doors into the dirt to form a small mound in front as the heat wave struck, the structure becoming a shield.

The faded leather on the interior of the doors cracked instantly just as the remaining glass in the side mirrors exploded, sending not shards but powder raining down in a cloud. Above, I felt the heat reaching down to attack my eyebrows, threatening to burn them clean off, while the tips of the metal on the outside of the door already glowed a faint orange. Any moisture left in the dirt fizzled away behind me, the mud splitting open as steam billowed upwards, any organic matter immediately turning to ash.

Then the blast was over, like opening and shutting a grill for only a second, the remaining heat dissipating into the rest of the gym. Hearing nothing, I stood, chancing a look over the lip of the doors and meeting Fino's eyes once more.

Ahead, in the direct line of the blast, there was only char and destruction - nothing remained intact, even the granite stones were chipped at the edges. And Fino had not moved, his hands still outstretched, his eyes widening as I entered his view, and launching a second blast that rolled towards me like an ocean wave.

Diving back down, I weathered the second blast, hearing his shout of anger as the car doors held. I thought of my next move, remembering Linns' advice to spur a Furnace on until they lost control.

And I realized Fino was long past that point without my intervention.

Chapter 46

"Coward!" I heard Blake shouting from above as the third blast came, closer this time, and I huddled under the door again to escape. "Get up and fight!"

Only twenty seconds had passed since the buzzer, but I knew I had to move. I readied myself, gritting my teeth as I realized my black spheres would cut directly through Fino's heat, likely absorbing it on their path, and would constitute at a kill strike before he had a chance to move. But using the spheres would expose my power, and therefore expose me. This fight would have to be won as a Telekinetic.

I waited, listening, holding my breath for the fourth wave. Then, just as it passed overhead, I slammed two force points past the car doors, flinging them open and hurling them at Fino. They spun through the air like cards, the outside glowing red from the heat, the interior an ashy black, churning through the heat while gaining speed. And Fino, his chest rising and falling with exertion, had no time to move.

They smashed into the force field generated by one of the guards, the energy on impact enough to split them into several pieces, the metal brittle from cycling heat and an exterior oxidizing layer. But without the protection, they would have hit Fino directly.

"Point one!" shouted a voice in the stands, and I turned to see Lucio with a finger raised even before the buzzer sounded. "Not too average for an Average!"

Darian nodded beside him as Fino turned his back to walk towards his starting position and wait for the next round, the shimmering air around him turning into a frenzy as he held in the heat. With each step, it surged, seeming to be corralled in just barely by force of will, and eager to be released.

"Not bad!" shouted Blake from the stands, a smile forming over his face that made warning bells go off in my mind. "But let's see how you perform without a shield!"

Chills ran down my spine as I turned, looking to the remains of the two car doors on the ground in front of Fino, now nearly entirely disintegrated. And as Fino followed my gaze, a smile raced across his lips, matching Blake's while his laugh shrieked across the gap between us.

Seconds later, Siri pressed the buzzer, and I dove to the earth as the first heat wave struck with no time to develop a better plan. Immediately, the guard generated a field above me as the heat came crashing down, and the buzzer sounded again a mere five seconds after the round began.

One point Fino, one point me.

The next round, I flung the granite stones at Fino, hurling them like comets towards him - but while he could dodge the stones, the wave he propelled was as wide as the arena, and there was no dodging its breadth. Instead, it caught me head on with no defense, and the blast of hot air burned my arms before the guard generated a shield.

Two points Fino.

For the final round, I tried lifting the earth in a shield, my powers pulling upwards at flecks of dirt in two tornadoes to form an insulating wall, heaving the mass upwards with the strongest force points I could muster and bringing the stream water with it. But the earth broke apart in clumps as the gravity took hold, and the stream water turned to steam by Fino's third wave. With both points focused on maintaining the wall, I had nothing left to utilize in an attack - and when the fourth heat wave came, it flew through my cloud like water through a strainer, completely unaffected as thoughts raced through my mind, last-second possibilities that came too late. And I realized that today, I would only be fighting once.

That as the buzzer sounded, I'd be making my way back to the bleachers.

And I'd be watching the rest of the fights from the Bottom seats.

Chapter 47

"Sorry SC," whispered Darian as he brushed past me, walking the aisle between the Average and Bottom bleachers. "But I'm not going to spend the rest of my time here scrubbing toilets, as short as it may be."

"Darian," I hissed back. "No matter what happens, don't use my power, or we'll *actually* be stuck here. It's our only way out, understood?"

He paused, looking back towards me from where he had continued walking down the steps, and nodded.

"Understood," he answered. "Besides, I wouldn't need it until the next round anyways. Not like I'm about to lose to a Bottom."

Eleven minutes later, I rubbed the blisters forming on my forearms while Darian sulked next to me, his scowl deep enough for both of us, maintaining silence for the next four matches.

"It's absolute bullshit," he outburst eventually, slamming a fist down on the seat next to him. "She should have clarified the rules before the match. I sat in the front row for your battle to absorb Fino's power, I spent twenty minutes this morning picking up Flamethrowing from Josh. It should have been over in an instant."

"Looks like we're sticking together, then," I said, "depending upon the outcome of Lucio's match."

Beside me, Darian huffed, and I suppressed a smile recalling the details of his match - or rather, the *detail* that mattered.

"Remember," said Siri, shortly before the match began and staring directly at him, "all interference is strictly forbidden." She smiled, and her tone took on a light quality as realization dawned across his face. "*Of course*, that includes the powers of others outside the arena. Ready? Begin!"

She slammed her hand down on the buzzer as Darian stood, stunned, and his opponent tore across the arena towards him. And in the entirety of the match, no powers were used, the Bottom relying solely on physical combat techniques. Techniques that Darian had utterly no training in using.

Darian managed to score a single point with a rogue punch, catching his opponent off guard, but the remaining three were scored against him - with no power to absorb, he too was powerless, and even worse, unprepared. And though he walked away from the arena with no injuries, his face was still bright red when he sat next to me, and he avoided eye contact with the rest of the students, including Lucio as he was called to the arena and his own fight began.

"You better be watching!" Lucio had said the night before, scribbling on a piece of paper before bed. "It's going to be a real show!"

"Just make sure you win," Darian had lectured.

"Eh, I'm not too concerned about that. Besides, Darian, I want to be a movie director, not a warrior! How about you judge this off of the entertainment value?"

"Just know I'm not waiting for your ass if you lose," Darian had answered and jumped into his bed. "All that matters in the end is the score."

And now, in the arena, Lucio looked our way as Brianna prepared on the other side. Then both dropped into a sprinter's crouch, their eyes turned towards Siri, and their muscles tensed. As soon as the wall of sound broke the silence, they launched themselves forwards in a dead sprint, their arms pumping and thighs straining for extra speed. But Brianna had the advantage - with her jumping power, a leaping start placed her slightly ahead of Lucio, tilting their collision course towards his side of the arena as they raced closer, neither slowing but rather speeding up with each step, their faces staring directly ahead.

And just as the crowd winced, preparing for them to slam together with a sickening crunch, the opposite happened - they ran right past each other, barely brushing shoulders, until they arrived at opposite ends of the arena. Nearing the edge, Brianna jumped the last ten feet, sailing out of bounds past the painted line as she raised a triumphant hand.

"Point one to me!" she shouted, beaming. "Never lost a race in my life. I *knew* I would win the racing round!"

"Sneaky bastard," whispered Darian as confused whispers broke out in the crowd.

"Maybe you won the race, Brianna, but not the point!" answered Lucio, tapping his forehead as a blush formed across her face. "I'll be taking this one!"

"That's cheating!" she protested. "That's not fighting; that was a trick!"

"I don't recall saying anything. Maybe you should be a little less trusting of your memories. It's quite easy for them to turn even the best of us into fools."

"Well, this time, it's not happening again," she countered, raising a clenched fist. "I'll hit you before you have the chance."

"Be my guest," he said, sweeping an arm in front of him and bowing. "Just don't miss."

With the start of the next round, he dove behind one of the car door obstacles and waited for Brianna to approach, staring into the mirror on the side to watch her movements. She crept forwards, then suddenly changed her path halfway across the arena, moving toward the second car door with nothing behind it, passing Lucio without a second glance and failing to see him where he hid.

Tiptoeing, he maneuvered behind her and followed, exaggerating her steps as she prepared to pounce, his arms raised like a puppet master. In the crowd, giggles started to erupt as he pulled a face, and Brianna froze, sensing something was amiss.

"Briaaaana!" he called, dragging out her name from right behind her as she jumped like a surprised cat, spinning in midair. But before she hit the ground, she recovered, lashing out with a punch that caught a force field just before Lucio's face and scored her the point.

"Rats," he said, snapping his fingers from his fallen position on the ground. "Don't know how I didn't see that one coming. Guess I'm just too clumsy, aren't I?"

The next two points were scored in a similar fashion - each time, Lucio led Brianna around the arena as if she were blind, planting memories of false move combinations in her head that made her trip over her own feet or convincing her that she had already won the match to drop her guard. Each time, he came within striking distance, but not once did he move to attack, Siri's eyes narrowing as she noted each missed opportunity.

"Now *that* was fun," he said a few minutes later when he took a seat next to Darian and me in the Bottom section, the crowd laughing and applauding as he bowed after the match, though the scoreboard showed a clear loss. "Sorry to keep you waiting, and hope you enjoyed the show. I'll be expecting critiques later! Anyways, I suppose I'm just not good enough to stay an Average, according to the score board. Worked out well, then, with the outcomes of your two matches, didn't it?"

Chapter 48

The rest of the matches progressed over the next two hours, some devolving into little more than scrap fights while others showcased powers in a fashion that appeared more similar to dancing than pugnacious. Arial defeated her opponent to remain an average with little difficulty, simply lifting them into the air and dropping them, and several Uppers started to relax as their competition eliminated itself in the lower brackets.

When it was Connor's turn, even Darian couldn't resist lightening up as waves of comfort and warmth washed over the assembly, the floating feeling displacing negative thoughts and brooding. Students slumped in the bleachers, relaxing and yawning, their thoughts turning to places and people far away. Together, Connor and his opponent skipped outside the arena twice to score him two points, and his opponent smiled from his position on the ground as Connor raised a granite block high into the air and dropped it directly on his face to win the third round.

Then the day was over, as Siri stood in the center of the arena and the bleachers looked on with a mix of emotion. Some faces were crestfallen, others triumphant, and a minority neutral. Few were without cuts, scrapes, and sweat, though the shields from the guards had borne the brunt of the strikes. Still, a small line had formed to the onsite nurse at the right of the bleachers below, who had already sent two students to the on-campus infirmary consisting of three beds erected inside the old theater room, along with a smattering of medical equipment to immediately treat most varieties of mid-grade injuries.

"New placements shall take place immediately," announced Siri, her voice filling the gym. "Some of you should be proud of your actions. Others, quite the opposite." She scanned the crowd, until her gaze found Mason, and spoke the next word in a somber, low note. "Ashamed."

He flinched backwards, the blood running from his face, and even from my position, I felt the impact of the word, my ears burning and my gaze avoiding contact with the other students. And the truth hit home - we had lost, while the others had won. We were exactly as our name implied - the Bottoms, those who couldn't keep up and were dragging down the rest. We would have to try harder, we would have to become Uppers, to become perfect students.

Then I blinked, feeling Lucio's touch inside my mind that pulled away the thoughts, and looked to the other Bottoms as they cringed before Siri, some even balled up, their feet folded under their seats and hands in their armpits. As if they had been caught by a parent in a truly heinous act, like torturing a pet, or standing before a judge after committing a murder. And I realized that was what I had felt just a moment before.

When Siri finished speaking, it was the responsibility of the Bottoms to clean and restore the arena, the work taking several hours and lasting long past dinner. I went to bed hungry and exhausted, taking my belongings to the holding cells downstairs, and was packed together inside one with several other bottoms. We shivered through the night, our only blankets the clothes on our backs and our laundry, which still allowed the concrete floor to wick away the heat and grind against pointed bones.

And at one in the morning, I gave up on sleep. Even keeping my eyes shut had proved difficult as I realized I had no inkling of a plan. As I wondered if perhaps it was better to escape the facility and try to teach myself to fight, to take Lucio and Darian with me and work together, to start something new. But I knew that even together, we would be unable to imitate the lessons given by Instructors Linns and Peregrine, and that somewhere out there, The Hunter was waiting for me to reappear, and that he was ready to attack.

I turned to look at Darian in the darkness, knowing that in the morning, I would have to convince him to stay or risk exposing my power. That he would take nothing less than a concrete objective, and that might not even be enough prevent him from leaving.

Sitting up, I left the others in the holding cell, the lack of their snoring meaning that I was likely not the only one who would be exhausted in the morning. And I started walking towards the place I had heard Siri and Peregrine a few nights before, my spirits leaping as I saw the familiar light and the voices ahead, and I stood stock still listening for their conversation.

"I need space," Peregrine was saying, his voice rushed. "And he's making that next to impossible. You said you would take care of him."

"I did, and I will," Siri responded, her voice annoyed. "She starts full time tomorrow, just like several of our other previous commuters, and he won't dare come near again without a reason from the police. And the police know better than to come snooping. Relax, Peregrine, the situation is under control. We've talked about this every night for months. Your paranoia is starting to be more of a problem than the police."

From my position, I shifted, moving closer to hear the voices more clearly and hide behind the broom closet door, holding my breath, praying for details that would help my situation.

"Siri, I'm mere weeks away from completion, and when this project is finished, it will be far more dangerous than it is now. Without secrecy, we lose all advantage. But when it's finished, the advantage will be incredible. I trust you've secured the building for the new facility?"

"Of course I have, Peregrine. All the steps have been taken, and your secrecy is top priority in exchange for your loyalty. *Nothing* is going to happen, even if they knew about our project, they wouldn't be able to find it. And The Hunter's daughter starts full time tomorrow, so he's under our thumb."

And as Siri spoke the next few words, the muscles in my shoulders tensed, and I felt a chill run from my neck to my ankles, and I bit the inside of my lip to keep from gasping.

"*Every* precaution has been taken. The location, The Hunter, the distractions, the maid we captured for you to keep your precious project out of their prying eyes. Now focus on finishing it. You're driving me over the edge."

And she changed the quality of her voice, song entering it. "And leave the rest to me and retire for the night."

"Of course, Siri," he answered, his voice slightly more dull than normal. "Of course."

He left the room, turning away from me and walking down the hall, not seeing me from my hiding place behind the closet door. And from within the room, Siri started to sing once more, softly and to herself.

Focus on the end and naught more,
Forget what brought it there,
Of those dashed upon the shore,

Dust under the rug not shared.

Forget father, who met his end,
After his last command,
I decided my will shan't bend,
When I took my final stand.

Remember the power to move,
To inspire, shake, to drive,
Of loyalty they're possessed to prove,
When it means their very lives.

"Of course, of course," she muttered from within, her own voice now dull. Then she shut off the light and followed Peregrine's steps into the darkness. "Focus."

Chapter 49

Thoughts raced in my mind as I hurried back to the holding cell and I repeated Siri's discussion in my head.

Even if they knew about our project, they wouldn't be able to find it.

The maid we captured for you to keep your precious project out of their eyes

The maid, my mother, with her power to hide even the most obvious of details. That *had* to be who they were speaking about.

Without secrecy, we lose all advantage.

Now that Arial was at the facility full time, that secrecy would be a guarantee. For the first time in my life, I wished that the police would be *more* involved. That I actually wanted their help.

And in my mind, a plan started to form, one that solidified with the slap of each of my footsteps against the cold tile floor. A risky plan, one that might even get me caught. But even if I *was* caught, it might be worth it. It might expose Siri and, in doing so, free my mother.

I was so absorbed in my thoughts that I failed to see the shape growing larger in the darkness in front of me, the slightly darker blotch blending into the shadowy surroundings. Only once I walked into it did I jump backwards, feeling the cold hand that cupped the back of my neck, barely catching the scream in the back of my throat.

There, hanging and just barely visible, was a body with a rope tied around its neck, swinging from the rafters from the force of my collision. The ankles dangled several feet off the floor, one of the shoes kicked off, and two swollen eyes staring forward like miniature full moons. And I recognized the face as I rushed forward to help him down, to see if I could still save him.

Mason, who had lost the match earlier that day to Brianna.

There was no warmth to him as I reached up to find the knot, stumbling over a chair in the darkness that he had used to climb upwards and fit his head through the noose. No breath passed through his lips, and as I felt his wrist, no blood pumped through his veins. Swallowing and shivering, I knew that there was no Mason left inside to save. And I pulled my hand away from the knot where I had started to untie it from my position now standing on the chair, and I hesitated.

Then I climbed down and walked past Mason, leaving him alone in the darkness.

Knowing that if I had been caught wandering the halls at this time of night, it would only raise questions. That Siri might suspect I had been listening in to her conversations. That I might find myself in a special session with her.

And that helping Mason now would do nothing to bring him back, no matter how guilty I felt as he stared into my back.

We were awakened the next morning with a scream down the hallway, and I worked to keep my face as confused as the others as we surged out of the holding cell, searching for the source, infusing my voice with panic as we caught sight of the body.

It took little effort, and the fear came quick as I beckoned it - the details of Mason's body in the daylight introduced fresh shock into my emotions. A shaft of sunlight caught him across his face as he twisted, the rope biting into his neck, and blood trickled down from where he had bit clean through one of his lips to stain his shirt to puddle on the floor.

As Siri arrived, one of the guards cut the remains down, carting what was once Mason away, and she spoke to the gathered crowd, her voice slow but not quite melancholy.

"A terrible, terrible outcome," she said, shaking her head. "Truly unfortunate, particularly considering we saved him from the streets. No family or relatives to speak of, and this is how he shows his gratitude. No, he shan't be remembered, not after this."

She shook her head again and placed two fingers over her lips before continuing to speak, turning from where Anthony had been to stare directly at the Bottoms.

"Perhaps if he had been an Upper, this never would have happened."

Then she walked away, her heels clicking against the floor, her tightly wound hair bobbing with each step.

"Oi," said Slugger, gripping me by the shoulder. "Did you see this when you got up last night, SC? Be hard to miss, wouldn't it?"

Ahead, the sound of Siri's steps stopped, and she half turned around, one pupil moving to look at me out of the corner of her eye.

"Of course not," I answered quickly. "Without dinner last night, my stomach was killing me. Just had to use the restroom is all. This sight made it no better. I'm going to be sick again."

Click, click, I heard as Siri's steps resumed, and I quieted my sigh of relief as she turned the corner ahead. Around us, the other students made their way to the breakfast hall. One of them cracked a joke from ahead, and there was a chorus of laughter in response that changed from nervous to raucous. Then, just twenty minutes after finding Mason, we departed to our first class.

After all, Siri had commanded that he would not be remembered.

And the students obeyed.

Chapter 50

"Don't even try, SC," panted Darian after the morning run. Without sleep, we'd fallen into the back half and had to run extra laps as a result. As usual, Blake sneered from each passing lap, and even Connor was hot on our heels. Next to him jogged Wendy, who typically finished in the top third but had taken it upon herself to improve Connor's times. And it was working.

"Like I said, don't even try," he repeated, sweat trickling down from his forehead. "I'm leaving. After last night's misery, it's not worth it. I'm out, and we both know I have the means to do it."

I caught him by the elbow, my grip tight on where muscle met bone, my voice level but menacing.

"You want to escape? Fine. But give me one more night," I said. "One more, then you're free. I'll even give you a fresh dose of my power in case it has started to wear off. But we do this my way, understood?"

"Understood." The words came through gritted teeth, but they still came in agreement. "But don't think you can keep putting this off."

"I don't. This is for real, Darian, and part of the plan." I stated, finally gaining control of my breathing. "Details tonight. And I can promise you more than just your freedom. How about a hot five-star meal and some special treatment? A soft bed in a top hotel?"

"For that, I'll wait, SC," he continued and strode towards the body weight-training portion of the class. "What's the plan?"

"Tonight, we'll talk tonight. There's something I have to confirm first."

"I'll be waiting."

After workouts, instead of reporting to Linns, we started a separate class, one tailored to the Bottoms alone. One vastly different than the Averages' and led by Instructor Cane.

"Welcome, welcome," he said, tapping the board. "Fortunately, we are all acquainted! And I have the pleasure of seeing several faces that otherwise would have departed to be with my softer friend Linns. Fear not - I'll be sure to make up for all the time you've missed."

He chuckled and turned on an old overhead projector, a flurry of dust rushing out of the vent as the fan kicked to life. And he pulled out a stack of transparent laminations, shuffling through them until he found a specific sheet and placed it on the flickering light. A few crumbs sprinkled over the image as he smacked a small chocolate chip cookie from a foot-tall tower on his left, and he pointed to Slugger before beginning.

"Ay, milk maid, you're still in my class, aren't you? Don't make me think you're slacking this Monday morning - not if you ever want a figure as pristine as mine!"

He laughed again and slapped his stomach, the reverberations rolling down to bulge resting on his knees, and gestured back to a small fridge in the back of the room.

"Oi, wasn't planning on making this prompt of a return," groaned Slugger, sighing as he stood and made his way to the fridge. "Can't you tell how excited I am to see you? It's grand, just grand."

"Maybe you should have won your match then, princess," retorted Cane. "Besides, I think you'll find yourself far better suited here than above. And the rest of you would do well to think likewise. Ah, that's it, just one glass for now. Froth it up!"

Cane leaned to his right, where Lucio was sitting, and commented out of the side of his mouth like he was sharing a dirty secret.

"Mind my words, Momentives make *the top* baristas. No one can froth a glass of milk the same way, and don't even get me started on Momentive bakeries. Had a scone so light once, it floated out of my fingertips and into the sky. If I had my way with that one, he'd be in a different type of school right now."

"I'll make ya a mean shepherd's pie," Slugger commented, shaking the glass, the milk scattering on the inside as if it had forgotten gravity. "The meanest."

"I'm sure you'd love that, wouldn't you? So mean it would probably off me, wouldn't it? That'd be a real stretch with my power, you'd have to make something so atrocious to earn a place in the history books. But we both know how much you'd miss me, that's the real reason you're back, isn't it?"

"Course it is," Slugger answered and dropped the milk on the projector, letting a few drops splash over the edge. "Ya read me like a book. How much longer do I have to wait until the adoption papers are signed?"

"Peh, I have standards. Why would I ever want to take in someone who wanted to be an Upper? Pure snobbery. Now, enough of this nonsense, back to the subject matter. And before moving forward, let's clarify something. No matter what you hear, or what anyone else thinks, Bottom is where you want to be. It's where you learn. And it's where change occurs."

He cleared his throat, coughed, and turned a knob on the projector so the shadowed image came into focus. Squinting, I could see a pair of bodies moving around the screen, with arrows and shading highlighting certain muscle groups or regions, and step patterns etched underneath.

"For those who are new, let me clarify my purpose. Here, I teach you not how to use your powers. Here, I teach you not technique that may fail you during inopportune circumstances or upon the nullification of your ability. No - here, I teach you to *actually* fight. And as many of you who used to be Averages have noticed, it works *damn* well across all the power ranges."

Chapter 51

It wasn't until lunch that I was able to talk to Arial.

It'd been nearly a week since we had spoken more than a passing word – between training for the matches, Arial's unavailability after school hours, and the events of the weekend, finding a spare moment was nearly impossible. Furthermore, since her personal interaction with Siri, any conversation was difficult to move past even the most basic of small talk – though she had been improving.

"Congratulations on the match," I said, placing my tray down on the table and sitting next to her. "Happy to see you won! How have you been?"

"Of *course* I won," she sniffed and rolled her eyes. "I was against a *Bottom*."

She moved her food tray away from me and shifted a foot on the bench, staring straight ahead, then swept her hair to the side to form a curtain between us. For a moment, she was silent, the muscles in her jaw working as she chewed, her lunch already three-quarters of the way finished since I had arrived late.

"This *isn't* the Bottom table," she said to the air. "That would be over there."

I swallowed, then bit my lip, pausing. From anyone else, from a time before Siri, that statement would have warranted a harsh response. Growing up poor, I had received my fair share of dismissive comments from those more fortunate, from people who could not see past class, or thought that their powers from birth made them inherently better than me. But hearing it from Arial as she held her nose high in the air, and her words still bearing the slight slur of a person mildly intoxicated, I felt only concern. And I remembered when Siri had held a grasp on my mind, knowing first-hand the complete lack of self-awareness Arial now possessed.

"Fine," I countered, standing up and placing a palm on the table. "But if you want me to leave, you'll need to answer a question first."

"I don't have to do anything a Bottom tells me to do," she huffed.

From across the lunch room, there was a shout, and Arial turned bright red as Blake's voice cut through the buzz of conversations.

"Look at the two lovebirds! If I had standards that low, I'd be scouring the soup kitchen for dates! I suppose even devastating failure can't stop true love!"

The Upper table erupted into laughter, and several chairs away, Wendy whipped around to stare at Blake, then us.

"I'm not—" Arial started, but then stopped and snapped at me, her brown eyes hard and no longer the inquisitive ones that had found me in the rhododendron when we met. "Make it quick, and don't come back."

"Your father," I started, crossing my arms in front in me as if they could block the words. "Does he still come by the school? What did he think when you told him you were starting full time?"

"Of course he isn't happy, but he never was. At least here, people care," she answered. "He hasn't agreed, of course - but he won't have much of a choice, since I said I would give Siri a report of him abusing me."

"You did *what*?" I stuttered, my eyes widening.

"It was the only way to make sure he would let me start full time," she said. "Besides, it's for the best and should never come to light. Is that all?"

"One more question. Remember that night I came over for dinner, and he had to leave in a rush? Is he still on that work assignment?"

"He won't shut up about it; he's obsessed," she answered. "Mother's even concerned for his health. Either way, I don't have to care about that anymore now that I'm not going back. Is that it?"

"Sure, that's it. Just know that you've changed, Arial. This isn't you."

"Stop being a Bottom, then we can talk," she retorted. "And if you're an Upper, we can be friends. Then you can talk to me about change."

Shaking my head, I left the table and sat with the other Bottoms in a cluster between Lucio, Darian, and Slugger, but still several feet away from the others.

"Nothin' to be sad about, lad," comforted Slugger, putting a hand around my shoulder. "She's cold-hearted to be treating you like that. Not worth your time. Seems like everyone in this place is like this - practically obsessed."

"Yeah, you could say that. It's not her fault, though. She's different," I said.

"That's some bullshit; she snubbed you!" Slugger continued, and Lucio raised an eyebrow. "Don't be giving any excuses for that. We have a word for that in the home tongue, wouldn't welcome one like that in all of Ireland."

"All right, I'm just going to broach this subject now," said Darian, cutting through the conversation and pointing to Slugger. "What's your deal?"

"My deal?" asked Slugger.

"Oh, come on," pestered Darian, rolling his eyes. "Do we have to spell it out?"

"What he's *trying* to say," interjected Lucio, "is how come you aren't affected by the singing like everyone else is?"

"The what?" asked Slugger, raising an eyebrow. "Are you drunk? Because if you are, you better be sharing."

"The singing," pressed Darian. "I have a feeling you damn well know about it, so let's hear it. Either that or move to the other side of the table."

"Hold it, hold it, what's with the aggression? You're as bad as the Flier friend, lads."

"Hate to say it, Slugger, but I'm with Darian," said Lucio. "I've known you for some time now, but it's suspicious. Why aren't you affected by the singing every night, by Siri's words?"

"Those are *words*?" exclaimed Slugger, hitting himself in the forehead. "God, it's like awful screeching, keeps me up sometimes, but everyone else seems to sleep right through it. Worst music I have ever heard in my life, if you can even call it music. Makes sense that it comes from Siri. I thought she just screeched at you all during the day when she wasn't happy. Anyways, when I get tired, it's hard to understand the American accents, especially if they're in a song. Guess I just never knew there was a message."

Chapter 52

That afternoon was spent with Instructor Cane again, along with several of his assistants who aided in demonstrating techniques. During the morning session, we had learned the theory of moves I had seen Bottoms performing the week before – the steps required to perform a trip or a throw, or the proper variations of stances. But studying a combination of moves was far different from actually performing them, and everyone who was new to Cane's class found themselves stumbling every few steps, twisting and turning in ways more robotic than fluid, and catching the occasional accidental impact.

"God, Lucio, one more time and I'll strangle you," vented Darian, his voice nasally and his eyes watering as he clutched a hand to his nose. "You are supposed turn left, not right, and I swear your elbow might have broken cartilage this time."

"Sorry!" exclaimed Lucio, winking at me as Darian wiped his eyes. "I just can't seem to remember which way. I promise I'll get it right next time."

"You better," came the response as Darian returned to a stance and grabbed Lucio, acting out the motions as he spoke them. "Now it's my turn. Okay, so left hand on the elbow, right hand under the armpit and up the back, twist and *crouch*!"

He ducked, spinning as his right arm lifted the much smaller Lucio high into the air, his feet following as they leapt off the ground. Darian caught him just before he landed on the practice mat, then lowered Lucio to the ground, still letting him fall the remaining six inches with a thud.

"Not bad," I said from where Slugger was critiquing my stance, showing me the differences between staggered, square, and upright. "You're picking up on it quick."

"Copying is my specialty," he answered and threw Lucio again, harder this time, a flash of pain crossing Lucio's face as one of his ankles landed off the mat and his breath whooshed out of his lungs. "And don't even complain, Lucio. That was payback. You should have paid attention this morning on how to fall."

"It would help," I interjected, glaring at the two of them as Slugger trotted away for a quick water break, "if neither of you injure yourselves before we go over the plan tonight. I'll need you both in top shape - if things go south, we'll need it."

"Yeah, yeah," said Lucio, tapping his forehead. "Top secret plan, I get it. Hate to break it to you, SC, but if you need me for anything on the more physical side of things, you'll be out of luck. My strengths are up here."

"I just don't need you in a wheelchair, understood? You have to be mobile."

"Truly happy that our interests align on that front. Hear that, Darian? SC says you need to be more dainty. You should have dropped the macho man persona after you lost your match, eh?"

"On the contrary," I countered. "We'll be needing that even more. Tonight, at dinner, we'll talk. Get a table far away from the others. And keep your voices down."

"Done deal," said Darian as Slugger returned. "Until then, we'll wait."

"Wait for what?" asked Slugger as he walked me through the steps again, pushing and pulling me through the motions.

"For our chance to not be Bottoms anymore," concluded Lucio, which I suppose held some truth.

When dinner arrived, Lucio and Darian found a table on the far right, waiting until Slugger sat down elsewhere and removing all the chairs until only three were remaining. Lucio played with his food as he waited, while Darian's plate was untouched, a fork standing straight up in the inferior food provided to Bottoms.

"Since you've promised a five-star dinner," he commented as I arrived, "I elected to wait to eat."

"That I have, but not just yet." I said, pulling out a chair and taking a seat, the food on my own plate jiggling as I set down my tray. "Tomorrow, actually, if we pull this off correctly. And right after dinner, so you have twenty-five hours. Now, are we ready?"

They both nodded, and both leaned inwards as I started to explain - Lucio's face growing more excited with each passing moment and Darian's darkening.

"It's all just a big trick!" exclaimed Lucio. "Some well-played mischief."

"That's the plan," I said. "And if we do it right, no one will ever know."

"But if this does come crashing down, and the illusion is caught, what then?" asked Darian.

"Shouldn't matter to you, should it? By then, you'll be long gone."

"True," Darian answered as Lucio's expression fell. "I suppose I will."

"There's one condition I have," demanded Lucio and held up a hand, while both Darian and I waited.

"Yes?" Darian asked after a few seconds, and Lucio continued.

"If we pull this off, I own the film rights!"

Chapter 53

Chores arrived after dinner, in a far longer list than before, and interlaced with far nastier tasks. There were the bathrooms, which we had known were coming. But there were also items like taking out the dinner trash, which leaked through the bag in spurts with every other step, scrubbing down the cooking equipment until the coating of grease atop it now lived under our fingernails, and performing laundry for the entire rest of the facility.

Then there was also the opossum that had died over the weekend in the crawlspace, and whose removal had been appointed to Darian, though Lucio and I came to watch.

"Oh, that's foul!" exclaimed Lucio as Darian dropped to all fours, shining a flashlight underneath the building and poking a dark object several feet away with a stick. "SC, watching this is the exact type of break we needed. You're going to have to touch it eventually, Darian, and I bet that thing is like a bug piñata."

"Screw that," said Darian and threw down the stick, backing out from the hole with a green face, holding the end of the stick that had touched the carcass far away. "SC, what do you say we move this plan forwards?"

"Not sure about that," I answered. "I'd rather be more prepared, have another day to make sure we've thought it through."

"Why not? Shouldn't matter if it is today or tomorrow, and it's pretty simple."

"C'mon, Darian," interjected Lucio. "Don't end our entertainment. SC, make him give it a few more pokes first!"

I gagged as a particularly foul wisp of wind escaped the crawl space, accompanied by several dozen flies that swarmed away like scrambled jets, and held a hand over my nose.

"Fine," I said. "Let's move. Front of the school by the main street. From there, we'll make moves. But at the first sign of trouble, we bail, understood?"

"Understood," answered Darian. "Let's go."

The sun had started to set in the distance, casting long shadows over the academy, and allowing only the tips of brightness to stretch over the low wall. As we walked, we carried tools for the chores - rakes, shovels, and wads of garbage bags - to appear like we were busy, keeping our faces down and our shoulders slumped. We moved counterclockwise from the back of the school to the front, hugging the building and ducking under the windows.

But once the gate was in sight, we stopped, seeing that someone had already beat us to the entrance.

He stood just outside the force field, with two squad cars filled with officers behind him, his finger jabbed towards the front steps of the school where another small party stood consisting of Peregrine, Siri, the two guards, and Arial.

"My daughter is coming home!" shouted Arial's father, his voice slightly muffled by the shield but still managing to maintain a hard edge. "Or the police will be forced to intervene!"

Taking Darian's and Lucio's arms, I dragged them back behind the corner of the school staircase before we could be seen, holding a finger to my lips.

"I'm sorry," said Siri, a hand on Arial's shoulder as she spoke. "But that would be Arial's decision, would it not? And she has elected to stay with me."

"Considering she's a minor, the decision does not lie with her," retorted The Hunter. "I don't have time for games, Siri. The police have overlooked your... *operation*, here, but if you force my hand, we *will* act."

"We, Art? You're no member of the force, so don't start putting on airs. Besides, this is not a police issue as much as it is a child protection issue."

"Absolutely ridiculous," he sputtered. "An investigation would find nothing."

"Oh? But it's by her own word, Arial's own admission. A sad story, really. She's happy here, Art. Do you really want to disturb that? She'll be home for the holidays, and I assure you she'll be having the best of education and a *competent* family to look after her."

"You bitch!" shouted The Hunter, starting forward with several police officers, but behind Siri, there was a flurry of movement as she raised her right hand. The bodies of Uppers streamed out from where they had been hidden inside the door, clustering in front of her to form a small wall, and standing shoulder to shoulder with faces of stone.

"There's no reason to be violent, Art," continued Siri. "We'll take great care of your daughter. And when she returns home, she'll be reformed into the perfect citizen."

"Arial!" shouted The Hunter as Siri turned. "Arial, come over here. We're going home. Stop listening to her."

Arial froze halfway through a turn, blinking, a confused expression flowing over her face.

"Arial!" commanded her father. "*Now.*"

"Don't you dare, darling," sang Siri, so softly I could hardly hear it, as the muscles in Arial's jaw tightened. From where we stood, I could see her legs shaking, and her breath coming in quick rising and falling motions. "Today, you belong here, with us."

"Arial!" shouted her father one last time. "I won't repeat myself again! To me!"

Arial looked between her father and Siri, her eyes wide and afraid, her lips trembling, feeling the pressure on both sides mounting. Her father's command versus Siri's power. And caught like a marble between two hard walls, she escaped by flying away, leaping upwards with her hair streaming behind her, streaking towards the sky in a route that took her far away from both her father and Siri.

But Arial had never performed chores in the yard. When students like her from the outside arrived and departed, the force field bubble had been temporarily disabled. Now, flying at full speed at an angle to just clear the gate and the brick wall, she knew nothing of the invisible barrier between herself and the outside world.

Until she collided with it fifty feet above the ground.

And even from where we stood, I heard the *crack* as her head slammed to one side, and the bones in her neck snapped.

Chapter 54

Sparks flew from the dome as Arial collided, her body held stuck against the bubble for an instant in a scrunched position until her torso caught up, before collapsing as she began to drift downwards, then fell at full speed.

Her hair clouded the blood on her face as she tumbled through the air, her shirt fluttering as wind ripped across it, nothing separating her from the concrete drive below. Her father watched open mouthed before throwing his shoulder against the bubble, staring up as she fell, his fingernails desperately trying to scratch through the force field.

My breath caught in my chest as I watched, my heart stopping, the spectacle washing over me like an Arctic ocean wave. I started to move, but Darian gripped my shoulder, holding me back, and instead I raised my hand, generating a force point just above Arial.

Her head snapped backwards as she slowed, her body curving into a C shape with the low points her hair and her ankles, drifting downwards like a leaf in Autumn, the frozen crowd watching as she slid away from the concrete and to a patch of green just inside the edge of the force field. Gently, she floated the remaining few feet, the blades of grass reaching up to accept her as she settled on them. Her father's eyes widened as he looked to her, then the schoolyard, staring directly to where I was hidden, though I was cloaked by twilight, then flicked back to his daughter.

"Arial!" he shouted as she lay there and my throat tightened. "Arial!"

He turned to Siri, pounding his fist against the bubble.

"You *bitch.* Let me in! That's my *daughter*!"

"Do no such thing; let her crash upon the rock." Siri commanded to the guards, while the Uppers stood still. "Blake, fetch the school nurse."

The Hunter's howls increased in volume, his hands pawing through his typically perfect hair, ripping a clump away as he looked on Arial's body as he saw her chest still, with no breaths to make it rise or fall. Her neck cocked at an angle that should have been impossible, her eyes closed. And he just inches away through the barrier, though it may as well have been the other side of the country.

"SC, there's nothing you can do," hissed Darian in my ear, his fingers tightening as I tried to move forward again. "Move her and the damage gets worse. If it *can* get worse, and you'll just reveal what you can do!"

"She's dying!" I hissed back, breaking free and turning back to Arial, preparing to sprint towards her. But there, just behind The Hunter, the car door opened and a familiar figure leapt outwards, dashing towards the body and pushing him out of the way.

And I froze as I recognized Arial's mother.

Kneeling down, she extended both hands as close as possible to her daughter, her expression locked in concentration. Before her, the wall shimmered, ripples jumping away in every direction, like a glass of water disturbed by a speaker. And a high-pitched noise shrieked as the force field quivered, the sound like a violin bow being drawn across an instrument devoid of any tuning by a skilled hand.

Grey streaks spider-webbed through her hair, displacing the natural color in a rush that left no strands untouched. Wrinkles cut into her forehead and the corners of her eyes, the skin on her arms sagging, one of her hands retreating to clutch her heart. And silver smoke wisped from her mouth and nose, trickling out and *through* the barrier, leaving an impression in the wall for a split second.

The image of an old man's face with sunken eyes, that disappeared as soon as it had appeared, and the smoke flowed around Arial, concentrating in a ring at her neck like a collar, straightening it back into position. It made the flecks of blood that covered her face pop off like scabs, the cuts yielding to fresh skin.

Until Arial's eyelids shot open and she drew a breath so deep her back arched, her fingers clutching the grass underneath her until the knuckles turned white, the blood vessels in her neck standing out against the skin. And her mother collapsed, both her hands now on her heart, her hair not only grey but crinkled, and her entire body shaking.

Chapter 55

The school nurse arrived with a stretcher a minute later, Arial still on her back and dazed, her movements slow and pained. Her father watched as his daughter was strapped down and hoisted upward, Arial raising a hand in a feeble wave as he clutched his wife, who had risen to her feet with his aid. But the grey in her hair and the wrinkles cut into her face remained, her eyes shut tight, and her stance wavering.

"Another example of poor parenting to be documented, driving Arial to near suicide," stated Siri after clearing her throat. "She obviously needs care that only we can provide. *Rehabilitation.*"

"That's *my* daughter," shouted Arial's father. "And we *healed* her! The police will—"

"This isn't an issue for the police; rather, it is under the umbrella of Child Services, Art," interrupted Siri. "Should you choose to have them involved, I would be more than happy to place a few calls for you. Besides, you can always visit your daughter. Simply fill out a visitation form, drop it in our mailbox, and we'll schedule a monitored session shortly."

Siri handed a slip of paper to Peregrine, who teleported outside the bubble for just long enough to tuck the paper into The Hunter's shirt pocket, then disappear within again. Arial's father reached up to grasp the paper, crinkling it through the fabric with clenched fingers, before shredding it.

"Now," continued Siri, her nose high in the air. "If you continue to pose a threat with those officers at your back, I shall consider it a transgression against the agreement between the Police and the Rehabilitation Facilities, especially since this is a personal issue of yours, Art, and *not* one involving the police. Are we understood? You have one minute to depart, which I deem generous."

Siri spun on her heel, the Uppers following her back in the building as The Hunter stood on the other end of the wall, silent tears falling down his now aged wife's face. She took his hand and together they walked back to their car, followed by several police officers, to hold a miniature conference behind the closed doors. From our location, it was too distant to hear, but we could see the shaking of heads. Then we saw the car reverse, but not before The Hunter shouted out the window, throwing the confetti from the paper slip Peregrine had given him against the barrier.

"Don't think you'll keep her! We'll be back!"

Tires screeched on pavement as the cart accelerated away, and the scene returned to that of a normal schoolyard, with dusk finally fallen, and shafts of light from the windows forming long rectangles on the grass. Without the memory, it might have never happened, the slightly depressed grass where Arial had fallen the only testament to her fall. And the twilight progressed as if nothing had happened at all.

"So," said Darian after a moment of silence, dragging his foot against the ground. "Postpone the plan?"

"Yeah," I said, shivering in the sudden cold, staring at the point where Arial had fallen. Where she never would have gotten up had her mother not been so close. And shaking as I remembered how Siri would have just watched her die, and Peregrine just let her fall. How both could have saved her, but neither had moved. "With a few modifications. And we need to act quick - if Siri knows that it wasn't one of the police officers who caught Arial, we might have trouble. Certainly The Hunter knows it wasn't his own men, and he was close enough to feel me - practically looked right at us. But if anything, our plan should work better. Should cause more damage now."

"You okay, SC?" asked Lucio as we walked back to the crawlspace. "Need something to cheer you up? A happy memory? Besides, it looked like she's going to be all right."

"No, Lucio, I want to remember this. I don't want to push it away," I answered, my jaw muscles clenched. "I want it fresh."

I thought of Mason and Mikey from the park, neither of whom had been as lucky as Arial. And I wondered who would be next. Who might be sliding towards a broken and irreparable future with each moment I failed to act.

Darian and Lucio let me walk ahead of them, giving me space as I considered destroying the school in that moment. Of freeing Arial. Of laying waste to what Siri was trying to accomplish.

But that wouldn't help me find my mother. Nor would it help the other students who had fallen under her spell.

I'd wait until tomorrow to act.

"Lucio, Darian, form a wall," I commanded when we arrived, and bent over into the crawlspace. Channeling my anger into a black sphere, I annihilated the opossum carcass with a single swipe, and let the sphere *pop* at the edge of the yard, far enough away to sound like a firecracker.

Chapter 56

"Ready?" I asked Darian, flicking a black sphere into existence as he watched. "Now, your turn."

Biting his lip inside the bathroom stall we had claimed during dinner, he tried the same motion, the door rattling as it felt the gravitational effects but no orb appearing. He frowned, trying again, managing to darken the air above his palm for barely a second before releasing an exasperated sigh.

"Look, it's just not going to work. I can maintain those *things,* but I can't create them. I can't mimic the power that far. You'll just have to feed them to me."

"Well, I can only give you two at a time," I answered. "But that should be more than enough to do the job. Just go heavy on the gravitational sauce afterwards, all right?"

"You got it," he answered and created a force point underneath the toilet paper, unspooling the roll in seconds. "Out of all the powers I've had the chance to use, this has to be one of the most amusing, SC."

I rubbed my eyes as he tried to flush the toilet using only the power, and just managed to make the handle quiver. I was still exhausted from the night before, spent hidden outside the door of the infirmary, listening as the nurse and Siri hovered over Arial.

"A full recovery, it seems, perhaps even more," the nurse said to Siri. "Not even a bruise. Flawless skin, down to the fingernails. If you look, there's not even split ends in her hair. A better job than any healer I've ever met – I bet there's not a single scratch on her."

"I just want to go home," slurred Arial's voice, while Siri spoke up.

"You're in pain, darling; we can't let you move. It's for your own benefit. Hush now, to sleep you go – Nian, up the dosage. I don't want her wandering off in the night."

"Of course, Siri, but rest assured I'll be watching over her personally," said the nurse. "And if I depart, the door will be guarded."

"But—" started Arial, and her voice trailed away, replaced by heavy breathing that I could just barely hear through the door. When Siri's footsteps approached, I ducked into a small side closet to wait until she departed, and listened as the nurse maintained her watch, hoping to hear a second set of snores but instead listening to only the rustling of papers and organizing of medical supplies.

After an hour of waiting, I departed, stealing back along the hallway to return to the Bottom room. My thoughts turned to Arial as I walked, questions filling my mind. Was she truly healed? Had her mother's mending removed Siri's influence from her mind as well? How could I sneak in to speak with her?

When would we kiss?

I stopped, blinking, that last question circling my mind, my cheeks burning in the darkness. Where had *that* come from? I should be thinking instead how to save Arial, how to remove her from Siri.

Or how her body would feel lying against mine.

I blinked again and kept walking, my pace slightly faster. And I thought of us together, somewhere far away from the facility. My hands running through her hair, her whispers in my ear, my fingers running down the curves of her body to be intertwined with hers. The thoughts growing stronger with each step as my breathing shallowed and my pulse quickened, daydreams flashing in front of my eyes in the darkness in vivid detail.

"Just us," Arial's voice lured, so tangible it was indistinguishable from reality. "I've been waiting so long for this."

Pausing, I shook my head, my hand pressing against a classroom door for support. And as I put my weight on my arm, the door gave way, swinging open and slamming into the wall behind as I stumbled into the classroom.

There was a stifled shriek as I jumped back to my feet, my hand searching for the light switch, and hearing a second shriek as I flipped it on. At the back corner of the room, there was a flurry of motion as a blanket whipped through the air, concealing two bodies but not the clothes strewn about the floor in a path between them and the door. Socks and shoes, followed by two pairs of pants and shirts, and finally the undergarments just before the blanket.

"What the hell?" said one of them as my eyes adjusted to the light. "Shut that off; this isn't a peep show!"

"Wha - What?" I said, my mind reeling as the flashes of images of Arial were replaced by shock and anger, and as I recognized the two faces peeking out from under the blanket. Connor, who had sat up and glared, next to a very red Wendy, who was doing her best to conceal herself with the blanket.

"Erm, yes, sorry." I said, backing away. "Though, Connor, you might want to keep it down a little. Up here, that is." I tapped my head and flicked off the light as I felt a flood of embarrassment.

"Will do. No one hears about this, SC, understand?"

"Of course, Connor." I answered, and left the two alone once more in the darkness, feeling relief as I walked away, realizing the visions of Arial had just been from his power. And still rushing back to catch as much sleep as I could in the few hours before dawn would break.

Back in the bathroom stall, I shook my head to clear it of the memory, turning my focus back to Darian as he flicked force points around the enclosure.

"Got the hang of it yet?" I asked, unlocking the stall.

"Enough to matter," he answered. "I'm ready to get out of here. Let's begin."

Chapter 57

"Lucio, is your story straight?" I asked as we weeded the yard after dinner, tossing another patch of crabgrass onto a pile between us and straightening up to stretch my aching back. "We go live in five minutes."

"Down to the details," said Lucio, his eyes still scanning the ground. "As lifelike as I can make it. Any last-minute additions?"

"None," I answered and held out both my palms, generating two dark spheres. "Take these, Darian. Feed them; we're going to want a *bang*. Now, you remember the route?"

"Of course. Stop worrying, SC," he said, dismissing me with a waved hand. "It's pretty simple."

"Just make sure you actually follow it," I lectured, looking him in the eye. "Don't just run off. You won't make it far and the plan will be shot. All right, here's where we split up. Lucio, we'll see you soon."

"Hopefully not both of you!" exclaimed Lucio, and held out a hand. "And, Darian, don't forget about us."

"Of, of course I wouldn't, Lucio," answered Darian, cracking a smile as he grasped it. "You make it too difficult."

They shook, and Lucio started to make his way to the rhododendron tree where I had first met Arial, while Darian and I departed to the front of the school. It was dark enough at this point that the two orbs hovering just under Darian's hands at his sides were not noticeable to the casual observer, though we clung to the side of the school to discourage prying eyes. And as we walked, I could feel their presence growing, their pull increasing, their distortion of space more profound, and Darian's expression deepening in concentration as he worked to keep them under control.

We reached the front of the school just as sweat started to show on his temple, and I generated two more orbs of my own, feeding them with bits of weeds I had carried with me, letting them swell past the size of Darian's in seconds.

"Now or never, SC," said Darian, his voice strained. "I can't hold on to these much longer."

I gazed across the schoolyard, making sure it was empty except for the occasional Bottom intent on finishing their chores, and at the street beyond where the rush hour traffic had long subsided. Drawing in a breath, I reviewed the plan once more, making sure I had forgotten nothing, and nodded to Darian.

"Go."

He accelerated to a full sprint before I finished the word, launching himself towards the school gate, and hurling the two dark spheres in front of him towards the force field. On contact, they shattered the barrier like bowling balls through a thin layer of ice, purple sparks erupting as sheets of the field were dragged into the street and absorbed into the spheres, which continued rocketing upwards at a forty-five-degree angle as Darian crossed the threshold of the rehabilitation facility. He whooped, his steps driven as much by the plan as adrenaline and excitement, and punched a hand into the air as his foot touched down across the border of school property.

He turned back just as the first of the spheres exploded high above behind a building, the boom setting off car alarms in the street below and rattling the facility windows behind me, my chest feeling the wave before my ears heard it. Then the second sphere exploded, the bright flash from this one in clear sight, and the sound slightly louder than the last.

Darian held up a hand as I threw the next two black spheres at him, catching them just as I lost control of them and centering them on his palms. Then he met my stare one last time, nodded, and took off down the street just as an alarm started to blare from within the facility behind me and the front door burst open. The two guards leapt down the steps, hands raised as they frantically reconstructed the barrier, followed shortly by a slew of other shouting instructors and Uppers as I crept around towards the back of the school.

"Which one was it?" I heard Siri scream as bodies swarmed over the lawn, the shield growing purple as it rose into the sky once more, though no answers came. "How many?"

Then their voices were drowned out but another sound was heard, one that grew louder with each passing second. Sirens, accompanied by telltale flashing blue lights on cars that swerved in front of the facility. And just as the doors opened, and police officers started to pour out, there was a third boom in the distance, causing the doors to slam and the cars to peel away in pursuit. I smiled as I watched the blue lights reflecting off the tops of buildings, following the route I had discussed with Darian the night before, and hearing the screech of metal as one of the cars was upended and tossed against the side of one of the buildings. As it descended, it collided with a lamp post, the door ripping off to hang like a Christmas ornament from the peak, swinging almost peacefully as the fight continued below my line of sight.

"*Stop,*" I heard over a loudspeaker, the voice rushed. "*Stop, by the authority of the police, or face –* "

There was a second screech as the speaker cut off, and the squealing of tires as several cars turned. And I pulled my attention away, focusing on rushing to the end of the schoolyard. Where the rhododendron tree stood, and Lucio would be waiting.

Chapter 58

I raced the flashing lights around the schoolyard, watching over my shoulder as the police cars grew louder again, and I saw a jet of fire spiral into the sky. There was a third *boom,* the strongest yet, catching me by surprise and causing me to stumble. I regained balance just as I saw Lucio pressed against the wall, nearly invisible in the darkness, his eye up against a hole just under the rhododendron tree.

There were several reasons we had chosen that tree - for one, I knew the area around it well, and there were few obstacles near the base. Second, an intersection was just behind it, allowing several access points from different directions. And most importantly, the countless leaves and branches served as a dowsing rod to the approaching target.

"This would be *much* easier if I could see right now," said Lucio, his eye pressed against a hole in the fence, and his nose flattened. "You just *had* to choose to do this at night, didn't you?"

"Now you tell me?" I answered, the words intermingled with panting. "You had two days, Lucio!"

"It'll be fine, it'll be fine," Lucio answered, waving a dismissive hand but refusing to break his gaze. "There might just be a few cops with some extra memories floating around. I'll just shotgun blast the group."

"Stealth, Lucio, we can't afford—"

"Jeez, SC, you're easier to set off than a firecracker. Everything is going to be fine. Speaking of," he continued, pointing upwards, "it's time."

Above, the rhododendron rippled, leaves and branches swiveling to point down and right as Lucio stiffened. Sirens still sounded, but they were farther off, crisscrossing through distant streets. And closer was the sound of heavy breathing as Darian arrived on the other side of the wall, a single dark orb still in hand, letting it absorb rays from a nearby streetlight, the leaves angled towards it to indicate its presence.

"And now," whispered Lucio as Darian hid in the tree's shadow, "we wait."

Darian cast a sideways look towards the fence, nodding once, then stilled as the shapes began materializing in the darkness. Five in all, creeping down the street, and spearheaded by a single familiar figure that I could just make out in the darkness.

The Hunter, drawn forward by the scent of my power held in Darian's hand.

"Closer," whispered Lucio as Darian put a hand against the tree and bent over, only half pretending to catch his breath. "That's it, closer."

The four other figures broke away, spreading to form a semicircle that cut off all escape routes from Darian, moving in like a human net. Some of the figures I recognized - the cop I had seen The Hunter speaking to outside my apartment, as well as one that had helped search for me in the public park.

"Almost there," breathed Lucio, both hands pressed against the fence now, his tongue sticking out the side of his mouth. "Almost."

Their party took three more steps in silence, like predators stalking a kill, just as Darian looked up to spot the first among them.

"Got you!" said both Lucio and The Hunter at the same time, just as the hidden officers lunged forward. One, a woman with hair cut just above the ear, performed a chopping motion and the branches above Darian came rushing downwards, growing impossibly fast to wrap around his arms and legs before he could react and swelling to the size of sink pipes. Then they continued down past him to jab into the ground, forming roots that rippled away and locked Darian in place, as additional branches encircled his torso. Bark split off to litter the ground like mulch as the wood expanded, a fresh layer filling in from underneath, and leaving a shell on the ground like a molting insect.

"The Hell?" Darian shouted, losing control of a sphere that spiraled away, whizzing past the officer's ear and taking a chunk of her hair with it as her expression turned to shock and the orb exploded just ten feet beyond. Another officer stepped forward, pointing as a thin tendril of electricity whipped towards Darian, striking him on the right arm and causing the muscles to go limp as the branches continued to constrict. As it made contact, the tendril flashed gold and blue, energy traveling down the beam and fizzing at tight bend points, with small trees of lightning erupting into the air at particularly curved sections.

"Don't resist!" commanded the officer as the tendril reached out again, this time aiming at Darian's other arm, sizzling as it brushed against several leaves and ignited them. "This won't hurt a bit."

"Won't hurt, my ass!" yelled back Darian, tilting his still active hand towards the cop. "But this will!"

Fire erupted from his palm, streaking towards the officer as he jumped to the side, narrowly avoiding flames that started consuming the branches holding Darian. More flames erupted out as Darian directed them around his body using his still functioning hand, and the cop I had seen near the lake stepped forward, basting him with water from a draining pipe with more force than a firehose as The Hunter cursed.

"Damn!" he shouted, kicking the tire of a parked car hard enough to make it rock on its frame. "A damn Mimic!"

Chapter 59

"Where in Hell's name did you pick up that power?" demanded Arial's father as Darian hung sopping wet and limp, stunned up to the neck, and the tree branches wrapped around his limbs and torso the only reason he remained standing. "*Where*?"

"Wouldn't you like to know?" spat Darian, their faces so close they nearly brushed noses. "You'll just throw me back in there like you did it in the first place! In the beginning, you were the ones who framed me. Don't think I have forgotten that! I owe the police nothing."

"You, you idiot," hissed Arial's father. "You think we're letting you back in there?"

"Let me? *Let* me? I have the power of the gods!" cackled Darian. "The strongest I have ever tasted. Maybe now I *want* to go back, what do you say to that?"

"You're not going anywhere until we know where you got that power," The Hunter answered, his face reddening.

"Oh, I'm not, am I? I'd rather go back and ruin them than help you!" Darian retorted, then threw his head backwards, drawing in a deep breath and shouting, "Siri! *Siri*! Right here, come and get me! Come right—"

"Silence!" The Hunter's hand clamped over Darian's jaw, crippling one of the last working muscles in his body. "Bundle him up; we're taking him back for interrogation."

"Ha! You think you can hold me? Hell, you think you can crack me?" came Darian's muffled voice through the hand. "If I can stand up to Siri, I can stand up to anything you throw at me. You're going to have to sweeten the deal."

"And *what*, exactly, *do* you want?" hissed The Hunter as the branches detached themselves from the tree, tightening like a boa constrictor as Darian fell to the ground, and one of the cops hoisted him over his shoulder.

"You know, I'm not too sure about that. Let's see what you have that might convince me. But I'm famished. Maybe I could think of something over dinner. A steak for one. Considering I'm the only one who saw where they are keeping that power, make it good. Maybe I'll even show you what it can do."

"First, where did it come from?" growled The Hunter. "We need to know what we are up against."

"Oh, you want to know that too?" asked Darian, bouncing on the guard's shoulder as they walked away. "*That's* going to cost you lobster too. And the softest bed in the city. I'm not cheap, and these past few weeks have really pissed me off. Thanks again for that, by the way."

They turned down the street corner as Lucio and I watched, then their shadows too disappeared, until the street was silent and empty once more, with little to attest for their presence besides a muddy ground and a slightly larger and unkept rhododendron.

"You caught him, right?" I asked to Lucio when I dared to make a sound again. "The memory has been implanted?"

"As solid as his first kiss," answered Lucio, puckering his lips. "Indistinguishable from reality. I had plenty of time to dull the corners and really root it in there."

"A success all around, then," I said. "Assuming everything goes to plan with Darian, and that—"

Lucio's hand squeezed my wrist and tugged, his other finger across his lips before pointing. There, across the wall and back in the street, something had started to move. Another figure, glinting in the lamplight, that had just rounded the edge of the wall from the direction of the front gate.

Blake.

Without a battle, I'd never seen Blake in full transformation. There had been moments when *parts* of his skin had morphed to diamond, perhaps a finger, or even an entire arm. But here nearly every inch of him sparkled, his movements slightly more robotic than normal, and even his hair taking on the appearance of fiber optic cabling.

"To rip and to shred, that's what I said," he sang, trotting, one of his fingers trailing along and cutting a deep groove into the wall with a similar sound to nails on a chalkboard. "Alive or dead, or just a head."

He stopped under the tree, squinting down both side streets before continuing, his heels clicking against the ground as he moved, his shoes already torn apart by diamond toes and arches. Then he too was gone, moving nearly parallel to the police but not quite in the same direction.

Moments later, Connor appeared from the other end of the wall, then departed in another tangent, his running considerably more labored. And the longer we stood there, the more Uppers that flowed past, scattering through the city, combing the streets, appearing and moving in every direction, searching. Their powers activated and ready to strike, all repeating similar snatches of song to Blake.

"They better be moving fast," said Lucio. "I wouldn't want to get caught by that lot."

"Knowing The Hunter, he'd have been prepared for this. He's had enough time to plan. Besides, he's not moving alone," I answered, stepping back from the wall. "Now let's head back in before they think we are missing too."

Chapter 60

Siri called an emergency meeting in the auditorium just as we returned, an instructor fetching us from the hallway and escorting us in a growing crowd of Averages and Bottoms until we reached the bleachers. And she stood in the center of the floor, a crease formed in her usually flawless suit, and a stray hair escaping her tight bun.

“Tonight,” she started, her voice harsh, “there was a breach of not only our facility, but of our trust. The power used to escape was brought from the outside, smuggled into here, and hidden like a rat beneath our feet. By a traitor.”

She paused, her eyes ice, and looked over us.

“Know that his name is now a curse, that anyone who utters it is worse than the lowest Bottom, not fit to be any of us. And know if anyone aided in his escape, they shall be even lower, should that be possible. That they too will be known as a traitor to us, to their country, and to common good. Now, I ask that anyone who knows the means of how this particular student obtained such a power, step forward now.”

She looked over the bleachers to be met with scared and confused expressions, students actively avoiding her gaze, and my heart quickening as her eyes glossed over mine. And my memory flashed back to when I had discussed the plan with Darian and Lucio at dinner just a few hours before.

“So let me get this straight, the plan is still the same as yesterday before Arial fell,” Lucio had said, his eyebrows scrunched together, looking between me and Darian. “Darian breaks through the wall using your power, which attracts The Hunter since he’s borrowing your power. Next, he lures the hunter away from the facility before doubling back to the rhododendron, where we lie in wait.”

“From there,” interrupted Darian, “Lucio plants a memory inside The Hunter’s head that Peregrine has transported his daughter away for safe keeping, and alludes that the police should stay away, because his project will make them irrelevant. In addition, he alludes that Arial will be kept at the same site as this project.”

“All to be said when he teleported next to her father, which *actually* did happen,” I added. "Remember, let's keep this as close to reality as possible."

"Right," said Lucio, drumming his fingers on the table. "Now, Darian is captured and mentions he knows where the power comes from, and after he is wined and dined, he tells The Hunter that the true wielder is being kept hidden and is the subject of Peregrine's project. Now The Hunter has a double reason to track down Peregrine, wherever he is keeping your mother, and potentially the police backing to do it. All assuming the project is not actually here at the school, of course."

"Correct, and after years of being around my mother, I would have noticed if she was here by her power. Wherever his project is, it's *not* at the school," I answered. "Darian, really make them earn that information. If you make it too easy, they might suspect this is a trap. Remember, make them work for everything - for capturing you and for the information. Don't be afraid to do some costly police damage on your escapade through the city, though I'd avoid injuring anyone. Rest assured they won't harm you, because they care too much about the power they think you have."

"It'll be my pleasure," smiled Darian, cracking his knuckles. "Just name a dollar amount."

"Anyways, what truly matters," I continued, "is that they take you with them because you can identify me. Make sure with absolute certainty you go, and once you do, tell us what happened and where. We'll be waiting. Let's find my mother, and let's hit Siri where it hurts."

Back in the auditorium, not a single person stepped forward to Siri, but a few glanced to me and Lucio. For though none of them had known what had happened, our clique was well known among the others. Naturally, we formed the top suspects.

"Oi, I know what happened," shouted Slugger from the back, as the entire assembly turned. "Lad was spending all his time during chores walking the perimeter. Didn't do shit, worst chores partner ever. Probably picked up the power from some passerby. I'd say good riddance, real dosser he was, had me wrecked picking up his slack."

"Which edge, where was he?" Siri pressed, her expression intent as she walked towards Slugger.

"All round he was. I'd say as soon as he found the power, he probably broke free. Was going on about how he was looking for a digging power for ages. Bet he dug right on through."

"And why didn't you mention this earlier?" demanded Siri, her voice furious.

"We go on picking up leaves every day," complained Slugger, waving a hand. "Then we've got to haul them all the way back to the dumpster. Back and forth, back and forth, 'til we nearly die of boredom. I thought he was just trying to be more efficient like a good citizen by finding a way to bury them instead. Didn't want to waste your valuable time, Miss."

Siri's look lingered on Slugger, as well as the rest of the crowd. But no longer did their gazes linger on us. And together, Lucio and I breathed a sigh of relief.

Chapter 61

"Whatever it is, I'm in. What was that, a practice round?" demanded Slugger as we walked back to our sleeping quarters, his voice too low to be heard by others. "When's the real fun start? I'm always in for a good skirmish."

"The what?" I asked, glancing left and right, making sure no one else was close.

"The big shebang! When we all get outta here, the home run outta the park! I want in, and I deserve it after sticking up to Siri."

"There *is* no big shebang. We had no part in the escape," I answered, speeding up my walk. "Darian acted on his own."

"And my father really did get lost on his way back from a pint," retorted Slugger. "That story would have been far more believable if it was a dozen anyways. He always was plastered."

"Really, I had no part in it, Slugger. You can ask Darian all about it when they catch him again."

"Besides, where the hell did he get a power like that? Did you see it?" continued Slugger, completely ignoring my comment. "Like an Electrospark and a Hurricaner had a baby!"

"Will you shut up!" I hissed back, and he clapped his hands.

"Ha! So you do know something!" he exclaimed, and poked his index finger into my ribcage. "Don't you worry, lad, I'll keep your secret once I find it out!"

He kicked the back of my shoe, and I stumbled forward as he ran down the hall cackling.

"Hey, get back—" I started before I tripped again, my foot held in place by a shoe that now had the mass of several bowling balls, and dragged behind me as my cheek smashed into the cold tile. I jerked my leg forward, but my heel only moved an inch, the shoe dragging laces side down and refusing to release its grip.

"Damn Momentive," I cursed as the mass gradually eroded and my mobility was restored, the feeling like if an overweight adult was slowly shifting his weight away. But by now, Slugger would have made it back to the sleeping quarters, and any talk would be overheard by several pairs of ears loyal to Siri.

And once the lights were out, and I closed my eyes, I found it impossible to sleep. Thoughts of Darian and Arial rolled through my head - wondering the condition that both of them were in, joining the usual thoughts of my mother. As snores started to fill the room, I felt habit takeover, and I crept from the room, slinking down the dark hallways until I was in front of the nurse's office. There, the door was closed, the lights appearing off from the crack under the door, and no sound originating from within.

But in front sat a single guard, his head nodding every few moments, but his chair directly before the door knob. Without waking him up, there would be no entering.

Tiptoeing backwards, I started to make my way back to the sleeping quarters but stopped halfway, taking an abrupt right. I exited the still air of the facility for the breeze outside, shutting the door behind me with a soft click and making my way around the perimeter of the school. Sticking close to the bushes and shadows to keep from being seen, I listened for any sounds besides the noise of faraway traffic and kept a steady pace forward until I reached the far back of the school. And there, feeling my way through the darkness, I found the crawlspace door that Darian, Lucio, and I had entered only a day before.

Slowly, I crept inside, removing a dark sphere I had kept in the pocket above my wrist ever since Arial had fallen in case I needed to make a quick escape. And I let the light play out within the crawlspace, edging my way forward on all fours, avoiding dark puddles and cobwebs that were woven thicker than some of the discount shirts from my childhood. There was no true path and the going was slow - moving too quick would dirty my clothes beyond cleaning, meaning there would be suspicion the next morning.

After several minutes and side tracking around several wooden beams that jutted into the earth with no sense of purpose, I came to what I what I was looking for - six pipes that extended from the ceiling, marking the students' bathroom above, along with a single pipe several feet away that indicated the faculty restroom just across the hall. And there, just a dozen feet to the right, was a smaller pipe - one that would belong to a single sink, and nothing more.

The single sink of the nurse's office, where Arial would be staying.

Orienting myself just next to the pipe, so that I would be under the sink itself, I raised the black orb to the barrier separating the crawlspace from the inside of the school. And I began to feed the orb pieces to the floor above.

Chapter 62

Splinters of wood ripped away from the floor above, disintegrating as they flew into the dark orb, followed by tufts of insulation that streamed into the darkness like a river of cotton candy. Then came more wood, then tile, the orb eating into the ceramic like a drill, microcracks splitting away as the gravity drew the tile into the center.

Fresh air rushed through the hole, just before a torrent of bandage strips and adhesives that scattered through the crawlspace as I guided the sphere in a circle, cutting out a space just large enough for my torso. And above, as the remainder of the material fell to the ground, two doors appeared through the darkness. Tucking the sphere in the pocket above my wrist, I reached upwards, and slowly pushed one open and climbed through the gap, extinguishing the light to be in full darkness.

I held my breath as I entered the room through the cabinet under the sink, the creak of the hinges the only noise besides light breathing, my knees dragging against the cold tile as I inched forwards. Slowly, to minimize the noise, I closed the door, then stood, waiting for my eyes to adjust to the darkness, staring for any shapes that vaguely resembled anything human. Seeing nothing, I released the orb from within the pocket above my wrist, teased out the light, and let it play over the room.

And there I saw her, sleeping the farthest of the three beds and the sole occupant of the room, her chest rising and falling in deep breaths, her hair tousled over half her face, her wrist handcuffed to the metal bed frame, and her clothes the same as when she had fallen. She stirred as the light fell over her face, and I quickly retracted it, my ears too aware of the soft snoring of the guard that had started from outside the door.

"Wha?" Arial slurred, her voice soft in the darkness, the sheets rustling as she shifted. "Who's there?"

I crossed the room in three steps, practically leaping towards her, and dropping my voice to a whisper.

"Shh, Arial, it's SC. Keep your voice down, others will hear. Are you okay?"

"Oh, SC." She giggled, turning in the darkness. "SC the Boreal, what strange dreams I've been having. Show me that light again, will you? It was so beautiful the first time."

"Do you promise to be quiet?"

"Of course, SC. No one can hear us in Dreamland anyways."

I cupped my hands, holding the dark sphere between them, and teased out light that projected onto the ceiling, streams crossing back and forth like shooting stars traveling from wall to wall as if the plaster were the sky.

"I *knew* it was true," Arial breathed. "I *knew* it. How can you do that, SC?"

"Soon, but not yet, I'll tell you, Arial," I answered, keeping her attention on the lights. "But first, how are you? Are you okay? Can you wiggle your fingers?"

"Of course I can," she said, and raised a hand. "See? Why wouldn't I be able to?"

"From your fall, Arial. I was worried," I whispered back. "I wanted to make sure you were healing."

"My fall? What do you mean by - Oh God," she gasped, and I saw one of her hands rush to her neck as the other reached the end of its handcuff restraint. "My mother! Where is she? Oh God, what have I done?"

Tears started streaming down her face as she looked left and right, straining to see through the darkness, and I put my hand on her arm.

"Arial, she's okay, calm down. Quiet, keep quiet, or we'll have trouble!"

"You don't understand, SC. That healing, it's not free - not in the slightest! I've killed her, SC." Her fingers wrapped around mine, squeezing my knuckles so hard they hurt, her nails digging into my palm, and I resisted wrenching my hand away.

"It will be okay, Arial, she'll come back! Just like when her hair turned grey after fixing the cup, when I saw her again, it was gone."

"No, SC, you don't understand," Arial said, her grip growing even tighter. "She can't recover from this. What she gave is gone. Do you know the truth about Menders? About what they really are?"

"What do you mean? They just have the ability to repair, right? That's what makes them Menders!"

"No, it's more than that," she answered, her voice too loud for comfort. "Menders aren't *created* under very specific circumstances, Menders *survive* very specific circumstances. You see, SC, Menders do not fix items for free – they give up energy. That energy has to come from *somewhere*. And at their minute of their birth, Menders cling to life just by their fingertips."

"Yes, I realize that. Then their doctor dies later, which makes them become a Mender."

"No, SC, that part's not true! They're already Menders from the minute of birth, when they are born broken. And the first thing they have to fix are themselves! But as babies on the brink of death, they have no energy to give. So they borrow that energy, or rather take it, from a willing donor. From someone who would give their life to save them. From the doctor, who in the right circumstances, wishes their survival above all else in the world. *That's* why the doctor dies – it doesn't cause a Mender, it's the effect of a Mender! And the Mender carries that energy with them their entire life, surviving off the coattails of their predecessor."

Arial took a deep breath, a fresh set of tears flowing down her face, taking a minute to regain composure before continuing.

"SC, fixing things like a broken cup only takes the temporary energy that is used by everyone on a daily basis, and only lets the life force behind it, that of the doctor, shine through temporarily. But what my mother did for me..." Arial swallowed, fighting to keep speaking. "What she did for me was such an enormous fix that went past it. Just as the doctor gave his life force for her, she gave it up for me. And in doing so, she lost years, *decades*, if she's still alive now. Time that I stole away, that's all my fault."

Chapter 63

I stayed with Arial until she fell back asleep, the time short as the pain medication Siri had placed her on demanded back her consciousness. I wondered if she would remember me in the morning, if the comforting words I had given her after she revealed the nature of her mother's power would remain, or if they would be washed away. And as I climbed back into the cabinet once I was sure she had fallen asleep, placing a pile of towels on top of the opening to seal it, I had one reason to smile.

That her mother's mending had not only repaired her physically, but seemed to reach into her mind as well, pulling away the influence of Siri upon her.

I completed the walk back to the sleeping quarters quickly and in silence, the news of Arial's mother only giving me more reason to hope that my plan had worked. That Darian would be traveling soon with The Hunter to whatever Siri didn't want him to see, together they could expose her, and with her, the facility.

And everything would return to the way it had been before my mother had been taken.

It was Thursday before we received the signal from Darian. And at lunch, Lucio had started to doubt it.

"He's probably gone," Lucio had said, flicking a pea off his plate in an arc aimed for Blake across the room. "He wanted to leave all this time. There's no reason for him to come back."

"He'll make it, Lucio. We had a deal," I answered. "Maybe he won't stay afterwards, but we can at least trust his word until then. And afterwards, where else would he go?"

"Can't say I know, but seems like he always wants to be somewhere else. So just not here, I guess. Besides, *you're* not the one who has to sleep each night with a towel wrapped around his head like a turban to drown out the singing." He sighed and rubbed his temples before continuing. "It won't work much longer, by the way. Barely works now. Every few minutes, I get a stray thought about *wanting to be a good citizen* and it makes me want to puke."

“As long as it keeps it at bay for the next day or two, it's a success. By then, Darian will make it, I promise. And afterwards, maybe we can give him a reason to stay,” I said, my voice far more confident than I felt. “Not just Darian, but you too, Lucio. This will all be for nothing if we just get caught again after and sent to another facility. Hell, if we let other facilities like this exist, we’d be guilty ourselves.”

“So what do you want to do about it?” he asked, leaning forward. "Infiltrate them from the inside too?"

“Let’s focus on scraping this one off the map first, then we’ll make plans for the others. Maybe they are better, but I have a strong feeling it isn’t the case.”

When Darian's signal came, it arrived as a memory, one that flashed into my mind as I walked the inner perimeter of the force field after dinner, performing chores as near as I could to the edge of the facility. Lucio worked the other end, both of us having traded our dinners for the privilege of swapping chores with other students.

The memory was unlike any Lucio had sent - where Lucio’s were carefully crafted and implanted to flow with a stream of consciousness, this was jarring. A single red number that filled my field of vision, with a single word scrawled beneath it in Darian’s handwriting. Flecks of other colors and images floated in the darkness, pieces of intrusive thoughts or emotions from Darian’s own mind. And as it dissipated, it left a searing headache and red stars that crawled across my other memories for several minutes.

3, Tree

The remainder of that night passed at a trickling pace, the chores dragging along slower than I thought possible, and my eyes forced wide open deep into the night. Their lids dragged downwards with the weight of the prior night’s lack of sleep, each blink ascending at a decreased rate, and I wished for power of a Narcolept. The snores and uncomfortable bedding aided my efforts, and taking advantage of the cold floor combined with no pillow, I forced my mind to stay conscious, biting my lip every time I felt a particularly strong wave of drowsiness, pinching my leg or adjusting my breathing to stay alert.

Three was all I had to wait until - three more hours of putting off sleep until I met with Darian, then I could relax for three more hours after that. Perhaps feign sickness in the morning, though I doubted it would excuse me from classes. Under Siri's influence, even those with strong cases of the flu dogged through workouts, the moisture on their skin a mix of sick clamminess and physically induced sweat.

All I had to do was stay awake until three.

And at four, my eyes shot open as I gasped, leaping upwards and rushing out of the room, nearly stubbing my toe on the other sleeping shapes in the darkness. I streaked out the door, soaking my shoes as I splashed through puddles from rain earlier in the night, praying that Darian would still be waiting. And knowing that if he had departed, he had still fulfilled his end of the deal, and he might be gone forever.

I reached the rhododendron in seconds, staring through the fence to see only roots occupying the ground, with no sign of Darian. I cursed, a slight breeze casting the insult back in my face, my eyes watering with a mix of frustration and sheer exhaustion. Then I turned, kicking a rock so it skidded across the lawn and tapped the side of the school, and jumped as I heard a voice from the branches high above.

"You're late!" chastised Darian, leaves shielding his body. "We don't have much time, and there's a lot to tell. Hurry - I'm literally half asleep. And I mean literally."

Chapter 64

Darian groaned as he dropped from a branch high above, shimmying down until he reached the trunk and before jumping the rest of the way to the ground. He rubbed his eyes and yawned, stretching, and squinted at me before walking over.

"Thought the message didn't..." he started, then paused, yawning again and shaking his head. "Didn't get through. Damn, can't clear my head. Listen, SC, if you don't understand any of this, just have me repeat it. Half of my consciousness is still at that hotel they have me holed up at – met a Doubler on the waitstaff a few hours back and picked up the power, so there's another identical me sleeping in the hotel bed. Except I was *supposed* to stay awake, so I'm pretty pissed at other me right now."

"I understand the feeling," I said, thinking back to the reason I had showed up late.

"Yeah, well most Doublers are able to split their body without much consequence, but this one must have been a pretty—" He blinked twice, his eyes moving out of focus, then continued. "Pretty low powered specimen. Only one of my ears works right now, had to leave the functionality of the other one behind. And other me is blind as well. Damn, no wonder the hotel service sucked; guy would have been better off sticking to one body. Probably would've remembered the no onions on the steak. Typical."

"So it worked, then?" I whispered, checking behind me to ensure the schoolyard was still empty. "They bought it?"

"Oh, they bought it, all right. They bought everything. Top notch room, surf and turf, unfortunately the onions, the—"

"Not the hotel or the food – the rest of the plan! My mother! Did you find her?"

"Oh, that," said Darian, waving a hand. "Getting to that now. Yeah, SC, something's up. Something big, though we only caught a whiff. But it definitely smells."

"And?" I asked, leaning forwards.

"Relax, SC, or I'll think you left your patience behind just like I did," continued Darian. "Anyways, here's everything since the start. Ready?"

"Spill," I said. "Let's hear it."

And Darian started, pausing every minute or so to gain composure, and even letting a full snore out twice.

*****

DARIAN

Last I saw you was when I was being carted away, with the tree limbs binding me, and slung over the officer's shoulders. I could've broken free, as you know, but I didn't - like you said, I let them take me. And when the inquisition started, I didn't give up a word to the cops or The Hunter.

At first, I was afraid that they were going to try to use powers against me. But when I threatened to squeal if I ever made my way back to Siri, they backed off real fast. Nothing like arming Siri with a potential abuse case, right? Anyways, I refused to talk, and the only relevant power in the room was a Truther.

After six hours, they let me out of the room, finally agreeing to try to win me over instead of trying to scare me. That was where dinner came in, as well as the room. And this morning, I let them crack me. And this was where Lucio's memories came in useful.

When I spilled that Peregrine had a top secret project in the same place he was keeping Arial, which was where he was keeping your power as well, the Truther verified my statement as accurate. After all, they were my memories, thanks to Lucio. Since all I claimed was that I remembered them, not that they happened, there was no lie to be found. And I claimed that only I would be able to recognize you, since Peregrine had several students loyal to him, but I had been the only one to actually see you use powers. Because you were forbidden to use your powers, none of the other students actually knew you existed.

They left the room then, though I could hear them outside. Talking about how they knew that *something* was going on in the rehabilitation centers, how each year their recruits seemed less skilled than in the past. But none of them knew how to find out what exactly was happening. And none of them wanted to give Siri any means to suspect they were actively investigating - the police were adamant on this, some even suggesting they throw me back onto the streets and deny any interaction ever occurred.

It took them ten minutes to realize, however, that while your power couldn't be traced, Peregrines *could*. And The Hunter verified that, at that moment, he could feel it - a trace, but still something, coming from the distance. Without a warrant, it would be unlawful for the police to track down Peregrine - but they came to the shaky conclusion Hunter was not employed by the police, and what he did without the police's knowledge was his own decision.

So The Hunter came back in the room and managed to bribe me to accompany him on a small trip. Kept promising me more and more if I came with him, and eventually I caved at a semester of college tuition he offered to pay because of *the importance of a proper education to our city's impoverished youth*. Doubt I'll see a dime of that, but anyways, it worked. In an hour, the police removed my handcuffs and discharged me, something they later would chalk up to an accident and allow them to readmit me. Just outside the station, a car pulled up, one that would have appeared to any bystander to be offering me a free ride. Of course, it was a little nicer than any car that I should have stepped into, a *lot* nicer, but the police had given me fresh clothes to replace the uniform I wore. New and provided by The Hunter himself, so I wouldn't stand out as someone of low status as I stepped inside his car.

Then we started driving - and, SC, no wonder Arial wanted to stay at the facility. Riding with that man for over five minutes was unbearable, and we drove thirty. Can't imagine having spent over a decade with him. Sometimes makes you appreciate not having a father of your own.

Anyways, SC, we drove in circles for thirty minutes, not because it was that far away - we could actually walk there from the facility without much difficulty. No, rather it was because The Hunter was lost and couldn't quite catch the full scent, for reasons I found out just afterwards. So remember, if you're ever on the run again, we don't have to put you in another facility to mask your power. There's another way.

We just have to bury you.

Chapter 65

DARIAN

I spent some years growing up in the ghetto, so I felt at home as we investigated. But it became pretty obvious that The Hunter was getting nervous - he has this tic, you know, where he carries a folding comb and runs it through his hair. I swear, once we turned on Crescent Street, he was folding and unfolding it more times than I could count. Anyways, we circled Crescent five or six times, and with a car as nice as his, we got plenty of stares. His hubcaps alone were probably more valuable than anything in that neighborhood.

He insists that we park five blocks away and walk the rest, and he's zigzagging through main streets to avoid any side alleys. Come to think of it, I wouldn't be surprised if he'd had a run in with some of the Crescent Street inhabitants at some point while working with the police, so he was probably worried that one of them would recognize him. They are a really seedy bunch even by my standards - I'd say more people live on the sidewalks of Crescent Street than in the buildings, and they have their own economy based on cigarettes and shopping carts.

The Hunter pulled out a baseball hat and sunglasses when we finally had to turn onto Crescent Street, and he combed out the "hat hair" for a good three minutes when we returned to the parking garage later. Unlike the zigzags when we were in the car, he beelined straight to a gated-off building towards the heart of the street, avoiding a herd of dumpster cats and beggars that started following us.

Not sure if you remember this, SC, but around ten years ago, there was a plan to develop a subway stop on Crescent and a few side streets. Anyways, when the new mayor was elected, the funding was pulled for the project when it was eighty percent complete - apparently, some of the more affluent neighborhoods didn't want *those people* from Crescent having easy transportation into their side of the city, so a few lobbyists managed to nix the completion.

He leads me down into the station, and the first thing I notice is that the lights are on. Strange, since it's supposed to be abandoned, but the escalators were broken, so we walked down them like stairs. A few of the doors had been boarded up, but many of them were smashed through, and in some of the side shops, street merchants had set up small operations moving illegal items. The Hunter and I couldn't have stood out more – with our clothes, it was pretty obvious we didn't belong. So he finds a side hallway and we walk down that, then duck into a maintenance passageway that empties onto the track.

There was never any rail, and the siding isn't finished, but the track is walkable. We took it through the station, ducking low since it was recessed so no one could see us, and the entire time he's moving like an arrow down the track. After a few minutes, he stops, does a three-sixty, and starts poking around the gravel under the track. But there's nothing there, and he's looking more confused. Keeps pacing up and down, muttering how he can feel it, but there's nothing there but dark tunnel and rats.

Eventually, he decides that wherever the power is coming from, it's *not* that tunnel, but rather somewhere close. So he decides he's going to check that and see what else might be next door – something like a basement or a sewer system, since he knows someone at the city permit office who has access to the blueprints of the infrastructure under the city. Based on how this city is run, I doubt he'll have much luck, and he didn't look happy either. I'd thought I'd heard some profanities on the streets, but that man knows how to *curse*. Eventually, he gives up, and we backtrack, being careful not to be seen.

But here's where it gets interesting, SC.

When I mimic powers, I get a sense of how strong they are based on how many I can carry at once. If there's a stronger power, it takes up more space inside me, and pushes the others out. Things like Lucio's or The Hunter's powers take up almost no space, since those are more skill-based, and much harder for me to replicate. But high power Flamethrowers, Electrosparks, Hurricaners, or anything that really has *oomph* to it weighs me down. Typically, they're easy to absorb as well, since they're practically spilling over the edges of their wielders.

The powers I hold degrade over time and I'd been looking to refresh some of my powers in case things got ugly again at the police station. And that's when I noticed that one of the people we passed in the station used a spark from his finger to light a cigarette. So I picked the power up, and I'll be damned if it wasn't the strongest Electrospark I ever felt. And I kept doing it - anyone we passed that showed any power I absorbed, and each time there was the same result.

That station, SC, is crawling with high powered Specials like it has an infestation, dressed like they're beggars or gang members. *Something's* up, and there's enough energy bottled up in there to turn that station to dust several times over, or blow it up to your birthplace.

Chapter 66

"Darian," I said, the words coming slow as he finished his story. "What was at the end of that tunnel if you kept going?"

"Eh, nothing," Darian answered, waving a hand, and squinting at me with one eye. "Just looked pretty dark and kept going. Nothing interesting, at least."

"But did you check?" I pressed, my breath quickening.

"Check for what? Looked empty from where I stood, couldn't really see much. No reason to keep moving. We were busy; you can't expect us to check *everywhere*."

I laughed, and he yawned before speaking again, his voice irritated. "What's so funny? We didn't find anything."

"Oh, but you did!" I exclaimed, a smile wide on my face. "Because for me, you finding nothing where there *should* be something is better than finding something where there should be nothing!"

"I'm not following, SC. Break it down for me, I'm only half listening."

"Get some sleep, Darian, and touch base with us soon. I'll explain later. But what matters is we know where my mother is. Now all we have to do is fetch her," I bit my lip to stop it from quivering with excitement and paced, my mind racing with possibilities.

"You wouldn't stand a shot down there, SC. Even with a power like yours, you're sorely outmatched. It'd be like walking into a tsunami."

"We'll see. I've got an idea – I need to sleep on it, but I think it will work. Are you sure you weren't seen going down the tunnel, by the way?"

"Certain," he answered. "At least from what I could tell. Unless there was someone invisible or something, but typically, I notice those powers if they're around me long enough."

"Good," I answered. "Then surprise is on our side. And Darian, make sure you keep The Hunter busy. Drop some hints or say you know more than you're letting on. The last thing we need is for him to make it on the school grounds through legal action on his own. We only need a few days. Wait here, by the way – I'll fetch Lucio; you'll need to scrub the Siri from his head."

"You wanted in?" I asked, sidling up to Slugger the next day as he washed the dishes after dinner, picking up a rag to dry and stack the plates beside him. Cleaning the Upper plates came first, and the amount left over on them was more than what had started on the Bottoms'. The amount of waste was almost enough to dampen my mood.

"Well, *technically*, I want out of here, lad. I'm knackered," he answered, turning his face away as he hit the garbage disposal button and a small geyser of water erupted in the sink. "But yes, I do. You have a new plan? Hopefully, your noodle came up with something better than the last, since only one of ya actually made it."

"I do, but you've got a pretty strong role in it. I'll need full commitment." I dropped the dish I was drying on top of the pile, the *clank* adding weight to the response.

"Look, if you can get me over that wall, I'm all business. I'll miss the dishes dearly, truly I enjoy being manky, but I think I'll make it on the outside." He stopped washing, turning to face me, his eyebrows raised.

"It's more than just getting over that wall," I answered. "If you're joining us, you're not just getting out. You're sticking it to the people who got you in here, and it's going to be dangerous. Real dangerous."

"Oh no, you're going to sweeten the deal with revenge?" he said and threw his hands up in mock dismay. "SC, shut up ya stook; now I'm doubling down. How do we begin?"

"Well, for starters, I'm going to need you to be an asshole. Like, even more of one than normal. Smartass levels will have to be off the charts."

Slugger laughed and rolled his eyes, then stopped when he saw my face remained serious, and that I waited for an answer.

"Lad, in Ireland, there's a breed of dog called the setter. You know what a setter does? It's bred generation by generation for a single specific purpose in hunting, for fowling. Each time it's bred, the best of the past generation are matched up, over and over, until what's left is tip top. The best genetics, all geared towards a specific purpose."

Slugger puffed up his chest and raised his chin, then continued.

"See me? I'm like the setter, but my lineage trait is jackasses. You couldn't have picked a better man. I'm bred for it, and I consider it an art."

I hid a smile, fighting to keep my face businesslike, then made my final request.

"Perfect. And two more things, Slugger. I'm going to need you to stop being a Bottom. Think you can win your next match?"

"I've challenged Brianna, should be over real quick." He snapped his fingers. "Not like last time. No cheating this time around, and she can't just blow me out of the ring. Does this mean I'm actually going to be able to get a night's sleep in this hell hole?"

"Actually," I answered and paused. "You're going to get less of it. A *lot* less of it."

Chapter 67

"We're planning on staying Bottoms?" complained Lucio as we prepared for bed. The next day was the tournament, and the other students had serious expressions on their faces, working to finish chores early and catch as much sleep as possible, knowing that a good fight could completely flip their quality of life by providing warm dinners and a reasonable sleep schedule. And that a bad fight would erode the already microscopic amount of hope they had left.

"That's right," I answered. "But not for much longer. Think you can you manage that?"

"Since you don't expect me to win a fight tomorrow, I'm all game!" responded Lucio through a foam of toothpaste, flecks of it flying onto the mirror. "Because after this, I'll be wiped. We'll be lucky if I can stand."

"Just do what you can, and remember, you don't have to clean them as much as you did for Darian and me. We just need some original thoughts flowing through their heads again, just enough to peek through. Enough to make Siri nervous, and to force her hand."

"I won't have to fix any Uppers, right?" Lucio asked. "Siri has personal conversations with them. Trying to clean their minds would be worse than a ballpark restroom neglected all season."

"No, not yet, at least. Just Bottoms for now. I remember when you did it to me, though - it was pretty unpleasant. Can you do it while they're sleeping?" I frowned, hoping that this minor detail I had overlooked would not have significance.

"As long as you only need a light brushing, and not a full sweep, it shouldn't be a problem. Mind you, not easy, but after doing this for the last few weeks, I know where the sensitive areas are. Besides, I'm much better than when we started. This place may suck, and Darian might not agree with this statement, but I think I've actually learned something. And for that, I commend them!"

He rinsed and we made our way to the sleeping quarters, watching as the students drifted off into fitful sleep. Some had their eyes closed to focus as Instructor Cane had told them - planning each of their moves, running through potential scenarios, imagining the reactions of their opponents and then their own counter reactions. Repeating over and over again in their minds that they were better than their opponent - that if they couldn't overpower them, they would outsmart them, and if they couldn't outsmart them, they would try harder than them. But soon their chests eventually began to fall with the telltale steady rhythm of deep sleep, and in the darkness, Lucio, Slugger, and I stood and crept towards the back of the room.

"Look, like I said, I *think* I can do this without waking them," whispered Lucio, rubbing an eye. "But in case I'm wrong, I'll need you to restrain them. If everyone wakes up, the plan's out the window, got it?"

"Understood," responded Slugger, squinting in the darkness. "And I can help by making their clothes heavier, which will help keep them passed out. What's the point of this, if they're going to just fall under Siri's spell again later tonight?"

"Siri doesn't sing the night before fights," I said, then glanced towards the door. "And anyways, once Lucio starts tidying a mind, it's easier for him to do it a second time. Even if she were to sing again, we would have the upper hand."

"Just as it's easier for Siri to rope them back in when bits of song are still echoing around their cranial chambers," added Lucio. "All right, let's get started. It's going to be a long night. Especially if I have to do this all again tomorrow."

"Do it well enough this time, and you won't," I answered. "But my bet is on day three, she cracks."

"Her and me both," sighed Lucio, bending over one of the sleeping bodies.

Slugger ran his fingers around the outer layer of their clothes and the breathing became slower, the wrinkles in the fabric disappearing as it stretched downwards. As I held my hand a few inches above the student's mouth in case they awakened, Lucio started.

From the outside, there was little to see. Every few seconds, the student's face would flicker with an emotion, or they would draw a sharp breath, but Lucio would take a step backwards, waiting for them to make a full recovery, then start again. Pushing them right against the edge of awakening but never past it, though once or twice, we had to wait a full five minutes for deep sleep to resume.

"All right," he concluded, his voice strained, a bead of sweat dripping down his nose to splash on the concrete floor. "That's one. Best I can do, SC, before I start tugging at some deep memory roots. And now," he continued, glancing around the room where the rest of the bodies waited, the corners of his mouth turning to a frown. "Only one dungeon left of Sleeping Beauties to go."

Chapter 68

"Halfway there," groaned Lucio as he straightened up over the most recent sleeping body. "You promised me a break, SC. Let's take it."

"Sure, it's about time Slugger and I moved on," I answered, stretching and yawning. "You have what I asked you for, Slugger?"

"Oh, I do," he answered, smiling. "Stashed it outside, right where it belongs. Now let's put it where it doesn't."

Seconds later, we were outside, creeping back towards the outside crawlspace, until Slugger threw open the door and pulled out a shoebox taped along the seam and several small holes poked into the top. He shook it lightly, just enough so that I could hear small objects sliding around within, followed by a chorus of chirping and buzzing that lingered as we walked back towards the door. We waited a moment for the contents to settle before we re-entered the facility, moving slowly on a path that I hadn't taken since I had been an Average.

Half the night had passed when we arrived at the door into the Average rooms, and I opened it slowly, putting pressure against the frame to prevent it from creaking. Tiptoeing past each of the dorms, Slugger cracked open the box and gave it a hearty shake inside each of the doors, loosing a generous amount of the crawling, chirping, and flying contents into each. While the rooms were not tiny, they were small enough that the creepers would be noticed quickly. And Slugger aimed for the beds.

"I aimed for a good mix," said Slugger as we returned to Lucio. "Some bumblebees, *lots* of ants, centipedes, crickets, katydids, and generally any other sort of nuisance. Almost had a mouse, but they're better fed than the Bottoms, took off before I could get my hands around it. That crawlspace was a goldmine for the things. And it doesn't matter if they don't affect the entire dorm - they just have to affect one of the lads, and they'll wake the rest right on up."

"That's the plan," I responded, entering the Bottom sleeping chamber. "I don't want any of them catching a wink of sleep. Now, Lucio, ready to start back up?"

"Ready as I'll ever be, SC," came the voice from a figure crouched against the wall as he stirred. "Drying my power up like a raisin."

"Just make sure you save enough to wake up in the morning," I answered, and we started again, working our way through the remaining bodies and finishing without delay. Then we settled down to pass out, taking advantage of the few hours left until daybreak. And in my sleep, a dream began. One discussed by Lucio and me several hours before, featuring the means that each the Bottoms had to be promoted. And one that Lucio projected over the sleeping room like one of his movies, infecting the minds of everyone present with the same memory.

"Now listen up!" shouted Instructor Cane in the dream, jabbing a finger towards me. "Look here, of all the Bottoms, I know you've got a damn good shot at becoming an Average. That's right, you in particular. Hell," he said, with a trace of pride in his eye. "You might just ascend the entire way to Upper."

He paused, wiping away a tear, then continued.

"Now, remember, have faith in yourself. Remember the moves that I taught you. Remember your confidence, your strategy, and the weakness of your opponent. Walk into that arena knowing that you are the stronger player. That you are the winner. *I* know you are, but do *you*?

"So say goodbye to dishes and shit sleeping conditions. Say farewell to meals that barely fend away the pangs of hunger for an hour. And fight for all you're worth. This is survival, and I know you're ready. *I* know you'll win, that you're better, no matter what they say.

"So go out there," he said, placing a hand on my shoulder, and squeezing it with reassurance. "And prove to me that you're the warrior I've trained you to be."

In my sleep, I smiled, along with the other Bottom students. And when we awoke the next day, there was a sense of purpose to each of them, a source of motivation that had not been there the night before. A sense of excitement rather than dread. A belief that, even as a Bottom, they might just win. That they were worth far more than the label Siri had placed upon them.

We gathered in the second gym after breakfast, staring at the bracket posted on the wall, with energy from the dream still coursing through our bodies with each heartbeat. The Uppers arrived afterward, making their way to the cushioned seats, and looking at us down their long noses. And the Averages followed them into the room, with bags under their eyes and feet dragging on the ground, and several covered in red bumps that had not been present the prior day.

Anticipation filled the room as Siri and the instructors arrived last. And as Siri picked up the microphone, the Bottoms held their collective breaths.

"Time to prove yourself once more," she announced, standing at the center of the arena. "You know the rules, and you know the challenge placed before you. And you know the consequences of inferiority, and the rewards of supremacy."

She scanned the crowd, and rose the microphone back to her lips to speak once more.

"Time to prove to me what you're worth."

Chapter 69

"Time to stop with all the chores!" shouted Anna, a low powered Laseret as she pointed a finger at Siri that made a red dot appear on her blue suit, then immediately clapped a hand over her mouth. A smoldering spot the size of a cigarette burn remained just above one of Siri's buttons, which was near the full extent of Anna's power. Shock streaked across Siri's face to match the stammering Anna, and the auditorium held its breath.

"I'm - I'm sorry," managed Anna, tears brimming as she bit down on her lip. "I didn't mean, I don't know what happened, I didn't—"

"Match one," interrupted Siri, partially recovering but still appearing as if she had been slapped, and ignoring Anna's words. "Fighters report to the judge table."

No one stood as Siri backed away, her gaze lingering on Anna with eyes once solid steel but now shaken. Instead the silence descended like a blanket, holding the crowd still, and insulating any action.

"Match one!" snapped Siri, command returning to her voice. "*Now.*"

After the first week when several Bottoms fought each other before making their way into the Average bracket, the Bottoms had coordinated who they would challenge prior to submissions. And now, that meant that no Bottoms versus Bottoms fights would occur, and their bracket would be skipped entirely.

Anthony descended the steps to be met by Lola the Transient, her soles absorbing the sound of the loose wood planks, and her figure catching little attention. Eyes tended to look through Lola - not just for her small stature, or her tendency to avoid social contact, but for the appearance of her skin as well. Those parts that were visible were slightly transparent, taking on the hue of the objects behind her, almost as if she were a chameleon.

I'd been surprised to see Lola among the bottoms - with an immunity to the effects of a wide array of high power types, Transients typically floated towards positions at the top of society as surely as their wallets weighed them downwards. Their ability to walk unfazed through the hottest fires, or the coldest nights, or even a hurricane as if it were a cloudy day earned them their nickname as *Ghosts*, as energy simply passed through them. For the highest powered, it was as if they were not there at all.

I remembered Lola's aptitude test given by Instructor Linns, and how pain had flashed across her face when he held any flame larger than a lighter's lowest setting under her outstretched hand. And even Linns found it difficult to hide his disappointment when he demonstrated that Transients with brighter shadows were the strongest, and Lola's proved near indistinguishable from any of ours.

But while Lola's powers were ill suited towards any attacks of heavy substance, there was at least one material that they made her invulnerable against.

Air. Or more suitably, wind.

When Siri started the match, Lola walked forwards with steps timed as carefully as a metronome, her skin sliding into a more transparent state. She sank into the earth nearly to her ankles, or rather the dirt sank into *her*, as no footsteps followed behind. Anthony smiled from the other end of the arena, conjuring up his strongest blast of air, and following the same tactic that had won his match against Slugger - to blow her out of the ring.

The torrent struck Lola head on, her clothes flapping while her hair remained perfectly still, and from my seat, I could see the majority of her clothes had been turned into mesh. Hundreds of tiny holes peppered the garments, letting the wind pass through with minimal effect. And at Anthony's second but more powerful strike, her feet only paused for a half beat.

"Gives me the creeps," commented Lucio, watching as Lola reached Anthony. "That's one reason I don't want to visit the mountains, SC. Dozens of those ghosts crawling over the peaks, blending in with the mist. Hell, I heard a story once there's entire villages up there you can't even see, because they're so powerful, you can't interact with them. What's worse, *they* can't interact with *you*."

"Oi, what if they're here right now, just watching us?" added Slugger from behind us.

"Slugger, does your power give you the ability for making conversations heavy too?" snapped Lucio as he shivered. "And here we go, looks like that's point one!"

Lola reared back for a punch, and her hand was stopped well before the disbelieving Anthony by a guard's force field. But her fist slid through it, and the second guard raised his hand to generate another field, which slowed her fingers but stopped short of halting it. A third force field generated just in front of Anthony's nose and stopped her short, though by this point her momentum, was so little, it would have just brushed against the tip.

"Spoiled the fun; they should've let that one through. He deserves a black eye for the way he scrapped," complained Slugger as the buzzer sounded.

"That'd be much more than a black eye," I answered, watching as Lola's arm retracted. "We're talking severe internal damage. I bet her knuckles would have passed through his nose as if it wasn't there. Makes you wonder, Lucio, if one of your village people could punch straight through you to come out the other side."

Lucio shivered again before responding. "Doesn't matter, SC, if they punch through me, they won't interact with anything."

"Won't interact *much* with anything," I corrected as the match below continued. "But I bet you there's still enough force in that hit to scramble your insides like soup. Probably wouldn't even feel anything. You'd just notice once your kidneys and liver put in their two weeks' notice."

Chapter 70

Anthony fell without scoring a single point - each time Lola approached, no amount of wind could sway her, and two weeks of learning martial arts with Instructor Cane had trained her well enough to avoid any of the clumsy punches he lobbed in her direction. Five minutes later, Anthony sat several rows ahead of us, several feet away from any of the other Bottoms and taking care to avoid looking at any of them. Refusing to admit that he now was one of them.

The next few Bottom matches were close, but each time, the Bottoms prevailed. With the advantage of choosing their opponents, as well as the fitful night of sleep that dulled the Averages' reaction times, their chances of winning were severely improved. Averages steadily trickled into the bleachers to join Anthony or take solidarity in other unoccupied regions, and the curse words soon became as ubiquitous as the hushed conversations in the stands.

"Well, here I go, lads," said Slugger when Siri called match five. "Don't have too much fun without me, will ya? And SC, let me know when we're ready to go."

"Will do. And, Slugger, no more than three hours a night, understood?"

"Oi, I got you. Just hurry up, won't ya? Half the appeal of being an Average is scoring a damn mattress. Shame I can't even take advantage of it."

Then Slugger descended, his match against Brianna beginning nearly as soon as he stepped in the arena. It was mercilessly quick, with none of the bravado of when he had faced Anthony. Picking up the same pylon, he defeated Brianna before she could approach close enough for contact, even tapping her ten feet upwards like a pop fly when she tried to jump him.

He nodded to us as he made his way to the Average bleachers, while a dejected Brianna resumed her position as Bottom. Several more matches passed, the outcomes still favoring Bottoms, until EVERY Bottom except Lucio and me had been replaced. Like Lucio's match the week before, we had both let our opponents win, but had each scored two points and had chosen opponents from the upper end of the Average pool to make it believable.

"I'd call that a success," remarked Lucio as the Average versus Average matches began, "Are you sure it was a good idea to stay Bottoms, though?"

"Positive," I answered. "We need to cycle through as many students as possible, and it's much easier once everyone is in the same room. This way, we can control it. And, Lucio, save some energy for tonight. We'll need one Upper as well."

"Not a good idea, SC. It's going to get ugly."

"It's necessary," I said, turning to face him. "We need to create an outbreak, a viral infection. And the only way we can do that is if it's at all levels."

"As long as I get the sleep you're taking from Slugger, I'm in," he answered. "Think you can get him to do my chores at night?"

"Might as well," I said, cracking a smile as I looked towards Slugger. "SOMETHING'S gotta keep him up!"

We paid little attention to the remainder of the matches, Lucio and I taking turns napping between bouts, nudging each other if Siri's stare turned our way. But she seemed too preoccupied to notice us - at the start of the matches, loud conversations had broken out among the Bottoms that Lucio had cleansed. And now, those Bottoms were among the Averages still under Siri's control, expanding the disorder across two - thirds of the bleachers. Bleachers that just the week before had been silent with every match, just like they had been likely every year since Siri started her rehabilitation facilities.

Her stare flickered back and forth between pockets of the outbursts, trying to track their origin so she could silence it with song. But with today being a tournament day, any song would affect the matches. And more importantly, if she used her power now, she might not find the source.

"Stop, now, or be demoted to Bottom once more!" she nearly shouted when Slugger and a few other fresh Averages broke into laughter. Her voice had an edge to it - not the hard edge of ice that was typical, but now something more shrill.

Slugger rolled his eyes and turned back to the arena. But Siri's expression froze when she saw that not ONLY Slugger rolled his eyes, but also the students around him. Students who, only yesterday, would have been terrified to take an extra breath without her permission.

"Let's go already," Anna had complained during a particularly long match, as Siri bristled.

"Bullshit!" shouted another Average after a near tie was decided on a technicality.

"Just stomp him, Wendy. Your feet are big enough!" jeered Slugger during the final Average to Upper match, and Wendy's face turned bright red. A few rows over from where Connor sat, several racial insults geared particularly at the Irish were hurled back at him, while Siri took a seat behind the judges' table. And now, the surprise of the initial outburst over, she watched the crowd carefully, trying to trace the origins backwards, a task nearly impossible after the dispersal of the Bottoms.

And a task that would prove even more difficult the next day.

Chapter 71

"That's it. If I do another, I'll be spent. Let's move on." Lucio held his hand against the wall, his outline just distinguishable in the darkness and his breathing coming heavy. Around us, the fresh Bottoms slept, though they slept more fitfully than the batch the night before. The air was thick with increased groaning, while stirring, tossing, and turning occurred throughout the night. And with increased care, Lucio had entered the minds of each, removing the song from Siri and planting a fresh memory.

The memory was unique to each individual, but each concerned Siri. In one, an image of Siri spitting in their food before dumping it into the trash, then sending the student to bed teary eyed and homesick. In another, mocking a student in front of the entire auditorium for the shape of his ears, until the rest of the students joined in laughing. Every time, the memory was personalized, Lucio rooting the memory to match the target's own personality. The first student was known to seek the largest portions in the cafeteria, and Blake had once made fun of the second student's ears until they could no longer be found in the same room together.

But no matter what the imagery, they shared a common goal - to breed resentment.

"Look, in the real world, these students would be angry at having lost their match. They would lash out, a little disrespect would be expected," I had said to Lucio as we prepared for the coming long night. "But in *Siri's* world, that doesn't happen. They should bow their heads and continue moving forward like good little citizens, perhaps losing hope but never *dreaming* of lashing out. It's time to give her a dose of reality. It's time to make her panic."

That night, Lucio had completed half of the Bottoms, adding to the new Averages that he had completed the night before. And now, we had one student left to turn. One who would solidify the doubt in Siri's mind that *something* had gone drastically wrong in the academy. One who would be impossible to ignore.

An Upper.

We knew where their rooms were from the time we spent cleaning their bathrooms, and we knew who slept where from fetching their laundry. And now we crept out of the Bottoms' sleeping area, then climbed the stairs to the Upper rooms, taking care to keep our hands off the creaking hand rail.

"Which one are you thinking?" whispered Lucio when we reached the top of the stairs but before we entered their hallway.

"Let's try Connor first," I said after a moment of thought. "If we turn him, then others might pick up on his emotions and create more panic."

"Deal," answered Lucio. "Just know if he wets his bed during the procedure, we'll have a *hell* of a mess to clean up tomorrow. The entire Upper floor would be dripping. And, SC, this won't be easy. I'm not sure how much I can clear away. These Uppers, their minds have been affected deeper than any of the other students'."

"At the very least, just piss him off, then," I responded. "Siri will already be suspicious. We just need to cement doubt in her mind."

We opened the door to the Upper hallway and slid inside, walking to Connor's room at the far left, and pausing just before the door. But before opening it, Lucio placed a hand against my chest and hissed a single word.

"Listen!"

Raising an eyebrow, and my feet glued to their position, I followed Lucio's other finger as he pointed down the hallway. There, at the end beyond all the Upper rooms, a door was cracked open. The week before, I had tried that doorknob out of curiosity during chores. But I had found it locked, made a mental note to return and investigate, and had deprioritized looking into it after Darian escaped. Since the door was rickety, not the type to use if you were hiding something significant, the thought had slipped my mind.

For a moment, all was silent. Then I heard the sound that had stopped Lucio, a voice that descended from the spiral staircase I could see just through the crack, accompanied by the faint glow of moonlight.

Siri's voice.

"Damn, I'm starting to think she sleeps less than we do," I muttered and started towards the door.

"What the *hell* are you doing?" Lucio demanded and pulled my arm backwards, "If she sees you, the entire plan will be ruined."

"If she sees me, it will only further convince her that this school is out of her control," I responded. "Besides, every clue I've gotten so far has been from being in places I don't belong. Who *knows* what she's doing up there."

"Probably just hypnotizing some Upper," Lucio said, still attempting to drag me backwards but following. "Like she does every night."

"Then it would pay to hear what she says, wouldn't it? We'll get the scoop straight from the source."

We reached the door and I pushed it open further to fully reveal stairs. To my relief, they were stone, meaning that they would make no creaking noises, and that I could continue to approach. For at the bottom, few of Siri's words were distinguishable, and the ones that were shed no light on her conversation.

As I climbed, reaching near the top of the stairs but not daring to look over the edge, I heard my first sentence in her seductive voice, just as a blast of fresh air hit my face.

"Go on, go on," she crooned, the voice spooling down towards me. "It won't hurt but for a second. Jump."

Chapter 72

"Just a single step," Siri continued, the her breath just barely carrying her voice. "No, no powers now. You needn't worry about that. Just a step."

"But—" came a slurred voice that lost itself before the word had even finished. "But—"

"But nothing," Siri interrupted, eager. "Sweet nothing. Go on, just a bit closer. Let your toes curl over the edge."

Lucio and I were crouched just where we could see shadows dancing on the ceiling, but neither of the bodies that they represented were visible. And from our position, crouched just low enough on the stone stairs to be hidden at the back of the room, we could see the shadows looked away from us.

Holding my breath, and moving so slowly that my muscles quivered with the effort of holding the position, I rose until just my eyes peered over the ledge, my pupils level with the floor. And I stifled a gasp.

The room itself was small, the size of a study with a stack of old boxes piled in the corner to store teaching materials. Siri sat in an old rocking chair at the center, tilted so far forward that it rested against its curved points, her elbows on her knees and her fingers steepled between. Her eyes were alight and pupils wide, so intent upon the scene before her that I could have walked directly across her gaze. She bit the tip of her tongue as the figure before her bent beneath her command, her ankles bouncing with anticipation.

The figure stood in an arched window, his head barely brushing the top of the opening and his hands at his sides while he balanced on the thin frame. He wavered with each of Siri's words, edging forwards, his knees shaking and jaw clenched. Moonlight silhouetted him as a light breeze ruffled his shirt, and I caught a glimpse of his face as he leaned backwards to compensate for the shuffling of his feet forwards until only his heels remained perched on the frame.

Blake.

"Go on," whispered Siri, relishing the words, her hands now clasped across her knees as her voice took on a musical quality. "Just a bit farther. Take the step, right foot first. So easy, and you want to so bad. Don't you want to make me happy, to be THE BEST student? My best student?"

For a second, I almost echoed her words as Blake lifted a heavy ankle, stepping forward into nothingness. Without his power activated, he was defenseless, and the fall of three stories would leave his face in a far more agreeable condition than the sneer that constantly occupied it. A tear slid down his cheek as his weight slid forward and his fall began, a slow tilt that started him in a dive and ensured his nose would reach the ground first.

"Yes," whispered Siri as he started to lose control, her bottom lip quivering. "Oh yes, dash yourself upon the shore. Do it for me, give yourself up for me."

Blake's other heel started to lose its grip as panic combined with guilt surged through me. And I realized that he was prepared to commit, to follow Siri's words over the edge and into nothingness. He would die if I did nothing, if I just watched. And even Blake didn't deserve that fate.

I raised a hand, preparing to yank him back inside the building with a force point, just as Siri's sharp voice rang out.

"Stop! Catch yourself!"

Blake's hands shot backwards without a second bidding, the fingertips just barely catching the sides of the window as they turned to diamond. He nearly slipped once as he propelled himself backwards, catching himself just in time to regain balance. His chest heaved as he recovered, then jumped backwards off the ledge, hugging the window frame as his feet met the floor, his face a pale white. As his hands left the frame, they revealed hundreds of fingernail marks in the wood, deep gauges that could only have occurred as a result of his diamond power.

"So close," Siri said, twirling her hair. "Oh so close, but not quite there! You didn't. I know you would have. YOU know you would have, for me."

She laughed as Blake shrank backwards, trying to become one with the shadows.

"But you didn't. I took care of you, Blake, just like I always do. And I always will. Now that's enough fun for today - go on, time for you to retire. Without any memory of this in the morning, of course. You did well, Blake, you pleased me. Just like you will again."

A half smile formed across Blake's face, Siri's words pushing it upwards and the events of the last few minutes weighing it down, forgotten tracks of tears still streaking down his cheeks. I ducked away as he turned to walk back to the stairs, descending in silence, and following Lucio as he threw open the door to Connor's room below. We slipped inside, frozen until we heard Blake's door click shut, and then Siri lock the far door moments later before leaving the Upper hallway.

In the darkness, I could just make out the whites of Lucio's eyes, and could tell the words were building inside him to near overfill about what had just transpired. But I shook my head, nudging him in the direction of Connor, whose snores created their own Gregorian chant.

Chapter 73

"Seriously, it was sadistic," said Lucio to Slugger as we waited in line for lunch, his face still stuck in the horrified expression it had adopted since the night before. "Psychotic. I've never seen anything like it. Explains a lot, though, if that's where she gets her kicks."

"Oi, yeah it does," mumbled Slugger, the dark rings under his eyes more prominent than ever, and his attention wandering.

"No, man, you don't get it," exclaimed Lucio, throwing open his hands for emphasis. "It was absolutely insane, like—"

"Aye now, I get it. Your lad SC here just has me on night watch. You're practically speaking gibberish, not that it's much different from normal." He yawned, tapping his foot as the line slid forward a single person, then halted again.

"Apparently, night watch makes you into a total prick as well, then!"

"Nah, lad, I've always been that." He craned his head, looking to where the front of the line was loading up their trays. "Speaking of pricks, looks like it's an optimal time to put my abilities to good use. You two better prepare yourselves because this is going to be some real craic."

Slugger stepped to the left and out of the line to where he had a clear line of sight to the front, and raised his voice just as the line shifted again, and the next person started loading up their food.

"Oi, Wendy!" he shouted just as she reached for an apple, then changed her mind and took the one next to it. "Think you can speed it up a bit, or is that too much cardio for your fat ass? We're hungry back here, and frankly, you could do with a smaller lunch. Back home, we had potato famines for the likes of you."

"You, you—" Wendy stuttered, whipping around as a few in the line smirked, particularly those Lucio had worked on the night before. "You jackass!"

She threw the apple at him, but it missed, sailing a few feet to the right and bouncing off the shoulder of an instructor across the room. Slugger laughed, widening his stance and throwing back his shoulders before retorting.

"A few more minutes outside a day might fix that aiming problem of yours. Want to try again? I made myself a bigger target, but not as big as you're used to, though."

He winked, nodding at Connor, who was now walking over from the Upper table, just as Wendy's face turned a deeper shade of red than the next apple that found her hand. More laughs erupted along the length of the line but were extinguished out like a campfire in a tidal wave as Connor reached the group.

"What the *hell* was that about, Slugger?" demanded Connor, and the smiles as laughing faces around him hardened to snarls.

"Just speaking the truth, big guy," answered Slugger. "You got a problem with that? Too bad I haven't challenged you yet in the Arena, or I'd have your position by now."

For a second, the old Connor shone through as his mouth fell open – the Connor from before he had been an Upper, when he struggled in the outdoor exercises, from before Siri's song had instilled enough pretentious ego to answer Slugger with aggression. The Connor that would rather back down than maintain confrontation.

"Lucio, a little help?" I whispered, nudging him in the ribs as the conversation stalled.

"Already on it," he whispered back, his eyes on Connor. "I'll push him right over the edge."

A moment later, Connor puffed out his chest, and his voice turned to a shout as his fingers clenched. His eyes narrowed, the vein in his neck throbbed, and I heard his knuckles crack.

"I'm sick of your attitude, and your remarks." Connor took a step forward, shielding Wendy behind him, while Slugger held his ground. "And I'm done with ignoring it, *especially* when it's coming from someone who was recently a filthy Bottom. Time to put you in your place."

"Damn, what'd you show him?" I hissed to Lucio, and we stepped backwards to avoid the brunt of Connor's power as I felt anger wash over me.

"Heh, he thinks Slugger hooked up with Wendy before he did. Nothing like a little jealousy to spur him forward."

Before Connor, Slugger raised his hands and curled them into fists, hopping back and forth as he punched air.

"Bring it, big boy! Put 'em up if you're gonna protect your wagon!"

Connor lumbered forwards, but before he had the chance to strike, Wendy threw another apple, this time hitting Slugger square in the chest. Connor hesitated, his face still seething, while the students around him with trays looked down at their food. Then the first plate was launched, a combination of spaghetti and meat sauce that splattered down the front of Slugger's shirt and rained down onto the floor. The second plate followed shortly, then a third, this one coming from a maniacally laughing Lucio, who whipped it off the nearest table. It missed, landing among the crowd by Connor, and fueling the pulsing anger that emanated from him.

Though Slugger was still at the center of the brawl, side arguments fueled by Connor's power broke out in a wide radius around the duo, spurring on the chaos until pockets of food fighting filled the entire lunch room. Those whose minds had been cleaned by Lucio were the most eager, with little left internally to remind them to be *good citizens*, while many of the Uppers looked on in horror before trying to stop the escalation. Their interaction, however, only added more food to be thrown as they brought the fullest plates to the fray, providing more ammunition for those already knee deep in meat sauce.

"*Halt*!" commanded a voice from the entranceway of the cafeteria. "*Stop!*"

Even without the usual singsong quality, the words chilled the room, freezing students in various positions of the assault. Siri looked over them, her eyes livid, her blue suit the only piece of clothing not tainted by the remnants of the lunch.

"He started it," shouted Connor, pointing to Slugger, who was now little more than a mountain of spaghetti. "He made us—"

"*Dare* you speak out of turn to me?" demanded Siri. "Dare any of you to shame yourselves like this? Have you forgotten your reformation?"

She turned to the instructor who had fetched her, the one who Wendy's apple had first struck, his face white as her words struck him like a whip.

"I want a full assembly called. It's time to put an end to this. Ensure *every* student is there, perform a full count. Bottoms, Averages, Uppers, I want them all. *Now*."

"And so," I whispered as she stalked from the room and the instructors began to herd us together, "we begin."

Chapter 74

The instructors corralled us towards the auditorium in three lines, each carrying a clipboard with names and marking them off as we passed by, checking for each student. All but three were present. Arial, who received a check mark despite her absence, and was being fetched from the nurse's room to join us. Mason, whose name had been whited out long ago. And Darian, which the instructors had not yet removed, but had a single line through the lettering.

Adrenaline flooded through me as we walked and as I reviewed what was about to happen, thinking back to when Lucio had first scrubbed my mind, and he had made a comment that stuck with me ever since about Siri's power. A comment that formed the foundation of our plan.

From what I can tell, she could enchant someone in a single session, but it would be dangerous. Basically, she would have to rip open their subconscious, and at that point, she would have far less control of the outcome. It's much safer to gradually take root.

And now that we had forced her hand, I twisted my fingers for luck, praying that Lucio was right. Knowing that as we entered that auditorium, and the instructors filed us into the bleachers, that I had one chance to turn the facility into my greatest weapon and asset. I nodded to Slugger from where he sat across from us, wisely having chosen an aisle seat nearest the door, and he winked back. Thanks to him, we had convinced Siri that the only way to ensure the entire school was under her control was to see it with her own eyes. To ensure no one escaped her power by being personally present.

Slugger looked exhausted, his eyes barely open, but we would only need him for a few minutes more. Out of everyone in attendance, he was the only one I could trust with what had to happen next. For in his exhausted state, understanding the words of Siri's song would be near impossible.

"You ready for this?" I asked Lucio as the last of the students ushered in.

"Ready as I'll ever be," he answered. "It's either freedom or I become one of Siri's minions now. Can't say I'm happy with those odds. Hell, I'd rather bet on an ass at a horse race than this."

"I'm just hoping we can shake it off," I responded. "What's your take on that? Once we're under, is there no coming back?"

"If she does it right, she'll be stripping us down to our subconscious first. Classic mental technique - lure the victim into a state of security, *then* set your agenda. With Siri, she has enough experience to know the ins and outs of mental gymnastics. Otherwise, if she attempts to rush the job, she'll risk her commands not taking root or eroding away too quickly. So long as we escape *before* she gets to the actual brainwashing part, we're home free! I'm more worried about how fast Slugger can run."

"If we're anywhere as near disoriented as the first time I went under, he might have to slow down on purpose," I answered. "Besides, you've seen him fight. He's crafty enough to hold his own."

"Fine," Lucio said and pulled a face as Siri entered and walked towards the center of the room. "And when this is over, SC, don't just disappear on me. I have nowhere to call home."

"When this is over, Lucio, that will change."

I patted his shoulder, then watched as the auditorium doors shut and were locked as each of the instructors departed, leaving us alone with Siri. In the pocket above my wrist, I already had two black orbs generated but hidden. And I stared at the spot where I would throw them, repeating the location over and over in my mind, knowing it would take every ounce of mental strength I had to use them.

State champions, state champions, state champions.

Those words would form my target, and I knew I must not forget them.

Below, Siri began to sing, spinning in a circle, her voice loud enough to fill the auditorium without a microphone. Each of the words stuck heavier than before, lulling us into a trance, like a heavy lead blanket placed over reality. I smiled as I drifted away, and I realized that perhaps I had been wrong this entire time. That perhaps all I had to do to be happy was listen to Siri sing forever. That her voice not only made my problems seem minuscule, but removed them entirely. Like turning off a horror movie.

Good citizens, good girls and good boys,
Let your stress fade away,
Listen now, my pride, my joys,

Forever here you'll stay.

Siri continued to sing, her meaning lost as I was lulled under. And my smile grew deeper, more content, more relaxed.

Ball's in your court, Slugger, I thought, the words coming slow as I looked towards him, half forgetting why my heart was still pumping so fast.

And I saw that he had fallen asleep.

Chapter 75

Wake up, I thought, my inner voice screaming. *Wake up!*

But the thoughts faded as Siri's voice continued, removing any concern that they carried with them. And even if they *had* mattered, and I had wanted to move, I wouldn't have been able. It felt as if my mind had sunk deep within itself, that the part that controlled muscles was far away, unreachable. That if Siri kept singing forever, I doubted I'd ever be able to raise my consciousness enough to move a finger – and if she left me in that state, I doubt I would ever have escaped without outside interference.

The same feeling flooded through the rest of the auditorium – from Bottom to Upper, all gathered in one place as Siri attempted to sweep any thoughts of rebellion away from us.

As the minutes rolled by, I forgot why I was staring at Slugger – and in part, I looked through him, and not quite at him. He looked as peaceful as I felt, his breath coming and going slowly, his head tilted back. But then Siri's voice changed its tone, wrapping up the first part of her procedure to expose the subconscious and preparing for the second part. To plant the seeds of obedience.

And when it morphed, Slugger stirred, opening one eye. Then he jumped to his feet, shaking his head, and his expression panicked.

"Damn!" he shouted, the words distant, Siri's voice faltering from shock. "Damn, what was it? What was I supposed to say?" He paused, thinking, casting his gaze around the auditorium for inspiration. But besides him, the entire school was stone, their eyes straight ahead, their expressions unchanging, as if he were a ghost.

"*To your seats, and back to sleep!*" sang Siri, her voice increasing in volume and determination, her stare focusing on Slugger. His face scrunched in annoyance and he shook his head, inserting his pinky into his ear and twisting as if to remove a lingering bit of earwax.

"Oi, stop that racket. And that's it!" He hit himself on the head, laughing. "Almost forgot. Wendy waddles!"

He scanned the crowd, then found Wendy, though she gave no inkling of having heard him.

"Wendy," he yelled, jumping down from one bleacher to the next, being sure to stomp with each change of level. His own voice took on a mocking songlike quality as he pointed a finger at her. "Waddles! Wendy waddles, like a walrus!"

"I—" started Wendy, drawing a sharp breath like she had risen out of frigid water and her voice slurred, but Siri's song cut her off. And Siri walked towards Slugger, removing a small metal baton she kept on the inside of her suit, her voice growing louder and more commanding. More desperate.

"Wendy Waddles like a fat Walrus!" belched Slugger as he darted away from Siri and danced towards Wendy, reaching out to give her a small pinch on the cheek, "The fattest one I ever did see!"

"I do *not* Waddle!" screamed Wendy, shooting upwards, her fingers curled and voice so sharp it pierced through Siri's command. It knocked the song construction down like house of cards, shattering Siri's progress. She stomped her foot, narrowly missing Slugger's toes, and the auditorium floor rebounded in a wave away from her. Wood splintered and cracked at the crests and troughs, utterly destroying the finish. The reverberation shook the bleachers like an earthquake, knocking over dazed students still partially eroded to their subconscious in a mess of tangled limbs.

Wendy stomped again, her face furious, bouncing the bodies of confused students a foot in the air as she rounded on Slugger a second time. In this state, straight out of Siri's hypnosis, she lacked any ability to govern herself. She *felt*, not capable of thought, moving and acting on instinct. Like an animal.

Behind her, a figure stood from the mess of bodies and howled, his eyes bloodshot and teeth showing in a snarl. Raw rage rolled over me as Connor leapt towards Wendy, a boiling emotion that erupted from me as my voice matched his, my vocal cords burning as I roared, the blood vessels feeding my muscles popping as I flexed. As I rose to my feet, I felt the sheer power for destruction at my fingertips, my vision laser focused upon the object of my hate that continued to taunt Wendy.

The ferocity infected the auditorium, intoxicating the other students as Connor's power flooded forwards again, turning them all towards Slugger. Alone, he stood against the mob, Siri fallen near his feet from where Wendy's power had knocked her over, his chest puffed out and fists raised in defiance.

"Oi, ya pissed?" taunted Slugger to him. "Come and get me, then. Let's scrap!"

Connor and the crowd started forwards in a rush, and my anger congealed in the black orb that rushed to my palm, ripping away at the edges of my shirt and whistling as wind rushed into it. I aimed as Slugger started to run towards the wall of the gym, leaping over the fragments of wood flooring that had popped loose, cornering himself as the rabid students rushed in a horde from all sides. I threw the orb as hard as I could, a voice jumping into my head just before I released, speaking the words I had repeated just before succumbing to Siri's voice. The words that reminded me of the plan. Not destroying my anger, but directing it.

State champions.

Just before I released the orb, I tilted it slightly to the right, curving mere feet from Slugger's body to intercept the *State Champions* banner hanging from the auditorium wall, carving a hole directly through the names of the team members who had earned the honor years before. Cinderblocks gave way as I propelled the orb forwards, powering it to pull the wall inwards until it caved in, leaving a hole the size of a door that Slugger leapt through before the dust had a chance to settle, tossing loose sections of wall behind him as if they were made of marshmallow. And through the dust were rays of sunlight stretching inside, illuminating the path to freedom.

Brianna reached the hole first just as the black orb exploded, blowing her backwards and into the crowd as the rest of the stampede arrived, each trying to fit through the hole at once with Connor at their center. The wall formed a bottleneck that only allowed a few through at once, giving Slugger a few precious seconds head start before their powers enlarged the passageway, a torrent of wind from Anthony clearing the dust while Miles pounded away at the outer edges.

With Connor farther away across the room, my emotions dulled - though still present, I now felt enough control to hold myself back from joining the rush. Knowing the plan had helped - without the knowledge of what was going to happen beforehand, I surely would be among them, rushing along as a slave to impulse. Following anger instead of rationality.

Instead, I walked away from them towards the far corner of the auditorium. And I began to carve another hole through to the outside.

Chapter 76

"Take me with you!" shouted a voice behind me as I broke through to outside. "I can catch him!"

I whipped around to see Arial still handcuffed to the wheeled nurse bed where the instructors had dragged her prior to Siri's singing. She strained against the metal links as she rose into the air, dragging the bed underneath her at a crawling rate as the legs skittered across the floor. Her eyes were crazed with the same infectious anger that had possessed the other students, but due to her constrained angle from the handcuffs, her power was at only partial capacity.

"I can catch him!" she repeated in a hiss. "I just need to be free! Help me, SC."

"And that," I said, walking over to her, "is *precisely* why I can't let you go. Sorry, Arial, you need to stay here."

I took off my belt as I walked, then looped it around the leg of her bed before running it through a metal grommet on the bleachers. Out of reach, it would stop her from following, effectively tethering her to a foot radius of where she was now attached to the thin bed frame.

"You jerk!" she said, writhing in an attempt to escape, swiping at me and catching my shirt before wrapping the fabric twice around her wrist to yank me towards her. I stumbled, prying her fingers away as my knees knocked against the bed frame and she collapsed onto the mattress, unable to keep flying at that angle. I succeeded in breaking her grip just as her fingers latched onto my own, interlacing, as she pulled me closer.

For a moment, we stared at each other, the rational region of our minds still slow to regenerate after Siri's song. Our emotions jumbled, her mouth slightly open as she hesitated, my heartbeat accelerating. I felt myself drawn forward, the plan forgotten, just as I heard a crash from outside followed by a chorus of angry shrieks.

"I - I'll be back, I promise," I stuttered, turning towards the sound and breaking my gaze. "Soon, this will all be over."

I pulled her fingers away, leaving her wide eyed and shouting, and returned to my fresh hole in the corner of the auditorium to jump out into the afternoon sun. I blinked as my feet hit grass, the brightness temporarily blinding me, my pupils shrinking just in time to see Slugger whipping around the corner to my left, barreling along at full speed towards the front of the school. He burst out laughing as he passed me, smacking my shoulder with enough force to spin me in place and face the stream of students forty feet behind him.

"Oi, the hunt is on!" he whooped, running backwards to goad the others. "Slugger rounds second and is picking up speed! He's halfway home, and the other team is too fat to follow!" Then he kept sprinting directly towards the gate of the school, where the force field met the gate. A few seconds later, the front runners of the crowd started whizzing past me, their powers activated but still too distant to utilize them accurately. All except for Anna, who spewed lasers from her fingers with each step aimed at Slugger, each striking him in the back. But by the time the light covered the gap, the colored dots were too diluted and fuzzy to cause anything more than slight warmth.

I felt the rage surge up in me again as Connor neared, his weight keeping him in the middle of the pack, though his power was spurring them forward. I reached into the pocket above my wrist to remove the second black orb I had prepared, launching it high into the sky before I started to run with the group, blending in among them.

The orb connected with the top of the force field dome high above us, ripping a hole into the apex and reeling the remainder in like a sheet thrown into the sky as purple sparks fluttered down the entire length. They leapt like flames from the ground as the force field disconnected, tatters of it splitting away to dissolve in air, and Slugger leapt over the remains with a triumphant jeer.

"And he's out of the park!" he bellowed, pausing just an instant to rip the facility's brick mailbox from the ground and launching it towards the forerunners of the pack. They scattered as it gouged the earth, spraying dirt and bricks in its wake as Slugger cackled. Then he started sprinting again, pausing only to scatter massive objects behind him, leaving a trail of garbage bins, air conditioning units, and motorcycles for the rest of the students to dodge.

Josh the flamethrower launched an arc of fire to clear the debris but succeeded only in heating the asphalt to melting temperatures, widening Slugger's lead as the road gripped our shoes. And now the rest of the objects were no longer simple obstacles, but red -, hot flaming barriers to our path.

"Going to have to try harder than that!" Slugger yelled over his shoulder and lobbed a portable toilet from a construction site towards Josh, the plastic box splitting to shower him in blue liquid. "Seems to me like I'm beating you all at once! I should be the only Upper of the lot!"

The he reached an intersection and turned, weaving among the light midday traffic as sirens started to sound in the distance. Heading deeper into the city.

Directly towards Crescent Street.

Chapter 77

Shop owners gawked and passerby fled as the solo escapee darted down the street like a pinball, tossing anything from flowerpots to manhole covers over his shoulder at the growing horde following him. In return, they scarred the street, unleashing fire, cars, and other projectiles in his direction, though he continually danced out of their reach. Fortunately for Slugger, he did not have to outrun *all* the students chasing him - rather, he only had to outrun Connor. Anyone who rushed too far ahead left the radius of Connor's power and forgot the purpose of why they were running, and all those next to Connor were too far from Slugger to inflict damage.

Several students were fully powered. Blake dazzled like a diamond, his skin throwing rainbow patterns over the others. Waves of heat ebbed and flowed from Fino, forcing a ring of space to form around him as the other runners avoided becoming burnt. And Wendy carved a fresh rut into the road with each step, creating countless potholes that would surely take months to be filled under the city budget.

Spewing fire hydrants, shattered windows, and uplifted trees were left behind with bewildered citizens. In the distance, sirens sounded, followed by the flashing of blue lights playing against the windows of skyscrapers and reflecting into the street.

Slugger rushed past light after light of intersections, pulling the crowd behind him, taunting them with every chance. In minutes, we were at Crescent Street, the homeless scattering before the rampage, leaving behind mounds of blankets and smashed bottles on the sidewalks while the doors of the building lining the street slammed shut. He whooped as he zigzagged, stopping at the entrance of the abandoned subway station, then turning back and searching through the crowd, his chest heaving. Then his eyes found Connor and he bent over, pulling down his pants to moon us before taking a celebratory jump worthy of a ballet audition into the station.

I felt a new surge of hate well up within me as Connor shouted profanities, spurring us forward, and we flooded into the station like bees into a hive just in time to see Slugger taking the escalator stairs two at a time. Down we followed, our voices echoing off the barren walls, the lights above us flickering. The floor was scuffed and unkempt, litter covering it like autumn leaves, fast food wrappers a primary offender around trash bins that had never been emptied.

The station seemed to suck us in like a vacuum, pulling us deeper as we nearly fell through the levels. I recounted the route that Darian had taken, the one I had relayed to Slugger, instructing him to avoid the maintenance tunnel and take the main path to the terminal. To ensure that we would arrive at the bottom using the quickest route possible, and that there would be no opportunity for him to be cornered, even if that meant we would be spotted.

But the hallways were nearly deserted, the sentries likely fleeing to alert the guards below.

The ceiling arched high overhead as we broke into the terminal, sculpted concrete decorated with a carved map of stops that the finished subway would have taken, including one just outside my old apartment. Windowless, no natural light entered the vault, the only illumination originating from the florescent lights high above that dangled from swaying chains bolted to the ceiling. Graffiti covered adverts that spanned the walls, and only the shell was left of ticketing machines looted long ago in hopes of finding spare change.

The subway track flowed through the center of the station, dividing it like a river and disappearing in a tunnel at one end. Separating the flood of students from the tunnel were fifteen figures, each with their shoulders squared against us and dressed in the ragged clothes of the homeless. But their eyes were too alert, their stances too confident, and their frames too muscular to fit the demographic. And each displayed a characteristic of a Special, something that would never be found in the city slums.

Frost covered the ground in a radius around one, his bright blue eyes as cold as the icicles growing along his fingers, his breath visible as he exhaled. Three dust tornadoes swirled around another, gaining speed and size as he watched us with a cocky grin. Other displays of power were exhibited down their line, from balls of white hot fire to electricity that crackled eagerly to be released.

"Halt!" shouted one of them, the Electrospark, a spray of lightning erupting from his hand to catch our attention. We hesitated as he continued to speak, as I recognized him as the same man who had taken my mother from our apartment under the guise of the police.

"Turn back! This is our territory, and you see us as we are – high powered Specials. You will go no farther, whether you turn back now or we stop you with force. Deadly force."

The horde of students hesitated, spilling over one another as they waited for a decision. A decision none, in their reduced state, could make. One that I made for them.

"They're protecting him!" I shouted, pointing behind the line to where Slugger had just crawled out of the track behind the guards, his laugh magnified in the space of the chamber. The line of guards whipped around at the sound, while Connor's power provided the goading to spearhead the students forward, their logic forgotten as emotion took control once more.

In my hand, I held a dark orb that I had prepared on the trip into the station, helping it grow by feeding it as we descended. And I threw it ahead of us, releasing it just as the high powered Specials turned back to face us, and letting it explode in a violent combination of light and sound mere feet in front of the Electrospark.

Chapter 78

The explosion blew the Electrospark backwards fifteen feet while scattering his companions, their faces shell shocked and eyes blinking away the flash. They struck out blindly, slashing out with their powers as their vision returned, two of them incapacitating each other with misdirected blows. But Siri's training had prepared the students well, and those without protective powers wove among the mayhem, diving for cover as arcs of fire and lightning spewed over the station.

From behind trash cans, the doors of side hallways, and benches, the students returned blasts of their own powers, counteracting the guards through their sheer numbers. Anthony conjured a bellowing wind that swept away fire before it had a chance to reach any of the students, redirecting it upwards to splash on the ceiling and rain down along the edges of the station. Blake charged forward in full diamond form at the Electrospark, absorbing bolts of lightning that fizzled through his feet into the ground, slashing and advancing at a pace too quick to allow for a planned counterstrike.

After disappearing for a few moments, Miles returned with arms laden down with unused cinderblocks from the incomplete construction of the station, then started lobbing them like hail, preventing the enemy from creating any organized front as they continually skirted the artillery fire. Taking cover on opposite corners of the students, Josh and Fino combined forces to dampen the effect of the Blizzarder, negating the icy projectiles and arctic wind that threatened instant frostbite.

Had the guards been prepared, the students would have had no chance fighting against them. But the combination of my exploding orb and their expectation that the students would back down left them in complete disarray.

After only a minute of fighting, the guards retreated to find cover, driving Blake back to the ranks of the students with the use of tornadoes combined with fire, the heat and force giving him no option but to flee. The tornadoes raced across the gap between the two forces, spewing black smoke that formed a deceptive haze to turn bodies into shadows. With the weaving fire tornadoes, lightning that crackled through the darkness, and needle - like ice shards that descended in volleys, no student dared cross the center. In return, no guard jumped the gap across their defense, instead forcing a stalemate.

But there was another force that kept the two sides separated, warping any powers that came too close to the students. Through the smog, I directed my dark orbs, their explosions pushing against any advance, preventing both the students and guards from moving due to a fear of the unknown power. For if either side gained ground, it would only endanger the students. And this was a battle that did not need to be won, but only prolonged.

I maintained my position until I heard shouting coming from the above levels and saw the first of the police poke his head through an opening, then immediately swear and fall back as a fireball singed away half his thick dark mustache. Launching two more particularly large black orbs into the center of the fray, I dashed sideways as they erupted, darting down onto the track just as more of the police arrived on the scene. With the distraction at its peak, I sprinted down the track towards the tunnel at the end, keeping my head low to stay hidden.

Slugger appeared at the entrance, slack - jawed as he watched the scene unfold, and I kept running past him, stopping only for a moment to speak.

"If you see anyone come this way," I said, panting. "Give me notice. I don't know what I'm going to find down here and the last thing I need is someone sneaking up behind me. And if the fight starts to die down, stir it back up. Don't let the students become any more endangered, though. We want them in foxholes."

"Sure thing, boss," said Slugger, and whistled. "They say Troy was fought over Helen, but *damn*. To think I started all this by calling one girlfriend a wagon."

He smiled, then nodded appreciatively as I started into the tunnel, speaking a final sentence.

"Empowering is what that is."

Chapter 79

I spooled light outwards from a dark sphere as I ran, the rays dancing across unfinished concrete and gravel. Ahead, the long shadows of rats scurried in search of dark corners and crevices, their squeaks echoing as a herald to my arrival. Every fifty feet, the roof leaked, droplets or streams of murky water saturating my hair when I failed to avoid them, and leaving mud - colored trails along my shirt. Drafts passed by me in a rush, carrying with them whiffs of familiar scents - mildew, sewer, and stale air.

Even with my light, it was impossible to see far ahead, the path blocked by turns of the tunnel and overlaid with sheets of cobwebs. I squinted, wondering *what* exactly I was looking for and realizing I had no inkling what awaited me at the end of the tunnel. Only the unknown.

Perhaps there were more high powered Specials waiting for me in a trap, already alerted by their cohorts in the station and ready to spring the instant that I appeared. Their powers might turn me to ash and bone before I could react, and I would never see my mother again. Or perhaps they were working on Peregrine's project and, *whatever* it was, I doubted that it would play to my advantage.

But I noticed no aspect alien to the subway as I trotted - rather, there seemed to be nothing particularly spectacular about any of the features, my eyes gliding over them as if they were a blank canvas. It was a familiar feeling, like an old smell or hearing an old tune played from years past. And I realized that I did not need to sense anything at all.

Rather, in sensing nothing, I had found everything.

I nearly kept running through the next station as I exited the tunnel, my eyes straight ahead, my brain not comprehending the change in scenery as the roof and walls expanded upwards or the empty train car I edged around. After all, there was nothing special about the opening, nothing that I was looking for here. Except for a single name, shouted by a voice that shattered the illusion around me, and hurled my mind into the current setting.

"Star Child!"

I knew it was her before I turned – to her child, the call of a mother is unforgettable, impossible to erase from the soul. While faces can be forgotten without pictures, and personalities altered in retrospect when reviewing fond memories, that voice never changes within memory. I slid to a stop, gravel skidding before me to form a mound and kicking a thick layer of rock dust into the air that surged into my nostrils. To my right, the ledge of the platform occurred just above shoulder height, and I searched over it for the origin of the voice.

She was at the far end of the platform, near the entrance and exits, had they existed. For the doorways had been filled with cement, cutting off any access to the station except through the tunnel that I had just taken, including the exit tunnel at the opposite end of the station.

She had lost weight since I had seen her last, her cheeks hollow, the mass instead migrating upwards to fill the bags under her eyes. And one of those eyes was bruised, the green and purple remains left over from a black eye forming a crude circle, accented by scratch marks that grazed across her jawline. Her clothing was ripped along some of the weaker seams, my fists closing when I realized that she was still wearing the same clothes as the day she had left. A fresh tearstain formed across her shirt as a she pinched her lips together in an effort to keep them from trembling, and when she stood, I saw a chain link drag across the ground to her right wrist.

"Mother!" I shouted, vaulting up the edge of the platform, renewed energy powering my sprint. With each step, I caught more details about her appearance that made the muscles in my jaw clench – that a host of other cuts and bruises occupied her skin. That her hair, usually kept and neat, stranded in multiple directions from lack of care. And that the shackle around her wrist had cut into the skin, dried blood fusing to the metal to give it the appearance of rust.

We embraced, my face digging into her shoulder as she held me close. And for a moment, I was no longer the leader of a small rebellion, or a student at the rehabilitation facility, or a Special with an unknown power. Rather, I was a child again, and nothing more.

"You shouldn't have come, Star Child," she said, her voice soft as I looked over her shoulder and saw a long table on the platform with the space around it shimmering. And not only did I *see* it, but I *felt* it. "You should have stayed hidden."

"Yes, boy," said a voice behind us as we stiffened. "You really should have."

Chapter 80

I whipped around to see Peregrine alone on the platform, ten feet away, his chin tilted as he stared, his eyebrows raised.

"I should have noticed the resemblance," he remarked, studying us. "The facial features are quite similar. Not that you can notice much about your mother at all, but that's why I brought her here, isn't it? And I suppose that makes me directly responsible for bringing you to the academy as well, by effectively orphaning you."

"What are you doing with her?" I demanded, stepping forwards as my mother's hand restrained my shoulder. "Why did you take her from me in the first place?"

I stopped myself as my fists clenched tighter and black orbs threatened to spring into existence. First, I had to extract more information from him, to find out who might pursue us if we escaped. And second, though Peregrine was a seasoned fighter, there was one advantage that I possessed over him. A lesson from Instructor Linns when I had just started at the facility.

The strongest power is the unknown power.

"Boy, I wouldn't have taken her from you if I knew you existed; rather, I would have taken you *with* her. She hid you well. But it was necessary, absolutely necessary to steal her for her abilities. She's incredibly unique - I could not have picked a better candidate if I tried."

"So you shackled and beat her?" I shouted, watching as he walked in an arc around us but maintained his distance.

Peregrine shrugged, his expression unchanging.

"She's a Snuffer, and Snuffers' powers are saturate. They emulate nature. The opossum plays dead when it is afraid, the hedgehog balls up, the chameleon blends with its surroundings. Pain and fear drive a Snuffer's power." He frowned, looking over my mother. "If your mother had cooperated, we wouldn't have had to rely upon such methods. But the risk of discovery was too great. So we activated her powers ourselves."

"By torturing her?!"

"By stimulating her abilities, boy." His tone was corrective, as if he were teaching a lesson, "SC, we would never cause anything permanent. No, we need her too much for that. But now that you are here, why hurt her at all? There's no greater fear to a mother than the harm of her child - by keeping you here, I maximize her powers without laying a finger on her again. Think on that, SC - stay here with us, and you will be remembered when this is all over. When our side has won the war on the horizon."

"And is that side Siri's side? How many have died at the rehabilitation facilities over the years, and how many now live as your slaves? Why would I *ever* join her, or you, after what you've done?"

"Because, SC, we're going to win. No price is too steep for that!" A smile widened across his lips as he spoke, and his eyes glinted. "Ask any war general. Besides, we have already won, because my project is practically complete. My weapon, the ultimate advantage."

"Who are you even fighting against?" I asked, watching as he continued to walk so we now faced the table we had seen earlier, with the shimmering air above it, "And you can't force students to fight against their will just to win a war."

"Is that not what you just did tonight, SC? Are you not any better than us, after leading the charge of your friends without their consent, after you somehow managed to shake off Siri's influence?" He tilted his head, his eyes scrutinizing me, and continued, "But I'll let you answer that one on your own. You'll have plenty of time to think on it down here. I've fought many wars, and I know the nature of people. Those in power act like we do, using others for their own gain, pitting them against each other. Sacrificing lives for trivial matters, whether the motive be for minute differences in opinion or ownership. And I, along with many others, came to a simple conclusion - that the only way to eliminate those who do not deserve power is to unify under a common front. To have one last war, a terrible war against *all*, against the police, our government, corruption. To command afterwards. A war won with my weapon, which brings us back to why you should consider fighting alongside us, and why your mother is so necessary."

He gestured, then held up three fingers.

"Optimal because, first, she has the power of a Snuffer, which was required to hide the weapon."

He ticked down a finger, and continued.

"Second, because of her past profession. A nurse, particularly a delivery nurse, someone with experience in the field. That could enter that role again."

His second finger collapsed, until only one was left.

"And third, because she has seen the insides of the space station high above us. And she can direct me there."

Chapter 81

"Let him walk," insisted my mother behind me. "Let him go, and I'll cooperate."

"Unfortunately, we can't do that. Not anymore," answered Peregrine, "He knows where the weapon is located, and I *can't* move it, considering it's woven into existence itself. Besides, he may be interested in working with us if he comes to his senses. He's clever; we could use someone like him. The problem with leading an army of drones is none of them seem to have good ideas."

"And what, exactly, does this weapon do?" I asked as Peregrine walked towards the table. I followed at a distance, my stomach turning as I came closer, the space before me disorienting. It was as if the entire room was tilting, or that I walked on uneven ground. Like standing on a ship in the center of a storm, as invisible waves fought underneath the deck.

"Something you can appreciate with your telekinetic power. Your mother must have travelled quite far to be able to gift that to you. It's something I wouldn't expect to see from one born in the city. As a maid, I can hardly believe she would have the funds to purchase a birthing slot in a Special hospital. No, if I had to guess, you were born illegally, SC."

"Perhaps, but you can't prove that. You don't know anything about my birth." I protested.

"Exactly!" he exclaimed, and clapped as if to capture the words in midair, "And even if I did, the documents could be forged, the officials paid off. But here, SC, is the great equalizer. It's well known that powers are influenced by the location of birth - the data collected over centuries demonstrates this fact. And it's been proven that environmental factors drive power type - even in the coldest locations, if a child is born near a roaring fire, there is a chance they may become a Furnace. But until now, it was unpredictable, the chances were low, and often there were ill side effects like a reduced power. But now, that's all changed."

He placed his hands on the table, one of his rings clanging against the metal, and continued to speak.

"It took years to build, *years*. And only someone like me could have done it, with strong teleportation powers like myself. And even then, I spent decades learning how to make it permanent."

He paused for a moment, staring around himself, his eyes bright with admiration.

"Come inside, SC. See what I've created. What I've done."

"Don't get closer," warned my mother, and Peregrine shrugged.

"With my teleportation powers, he's already as close as he can be. If I was going to kill him, I would have done so already. Let's go, SC – consider this another lesson, perhaps our final one. Careful, walk just over that strip of tape on the ground. Don't take another path."

He pointed to a two - foot - long stripe of blue at the edge of the table, and I stepped forwards slowly, nausea growing with each movement. I blinked as the world compressed, stepping over the line, feeling as if someone were stepping on my chest. Peregrine backed away as I entered, leaving me in what I saw was not mere open space as it appeared from the outside, but rather a small room. One surrounded by windows ten feet tall, except for the space with the masking tape, which formed a doorway back into the subway.

There were eight windows in all, shaped like an octagon around me, each of them displaying different scenes. Different portals into worlds beyond.

To my left, I saw a desert, the wind blowing sand in whirling gusts, the blistering sun far overhead making the air above the ground dance. The dunes stretched as far as I could see, and from the position of the sun, I could tell that it was far earlier in the day than our current location.

A forest occupied the adjacent pane, the sound of hooting monkeys and the chirping of tropical birds coming through the window, accompanied by the sickly sweet smell of wildflowers. Bugs whipped past, buzzing along their path and stopping occasionally to investigate blooms. Here, it was early morning or twilight, the heavily shadowed area barely lit.

Next, there was a wall of water, dark shapes moving in and out of layers of seaweed. The plants swayed with the current and the wall of water bulged slightly, as if threatening to enter our enclosure. A school of bright fish darted by, their scales each from a different part of the rainbow, and their eyes alarmed as they saw us staring back at them. And at the ground inside the enclosure, a small pile of them lay dead, their fins coated with frost.

Each of the other windows portrayed scenes just as exotic - from an active volcano to a peak of a mountain, each an entry into a location far away, perhaps on the other side of the world. Each with their own distinct flavor, feeling alien so close to one another, as if they were warring for the nature of the room. All except for the final panel, one unfinished, which fuzzed with rushing images too quick to recognize in a blur of static.

"Amazing, isn't it? Well worth the years of effort, and beyond what even I thought I could do. Something I once thought impossible," whispered Peregrine, his voice close to my ear. "Something to change the world forever. Watch now, as we travel to the Pacific."

Chapter 82

Peregrine stiffened as he closed his eyes, the muscles on his forearms bulging outwards, his lips pursed and his fingers gripping the edge of the table. And the world around me shifted, the space stretching and constricting in a dizzying fashion, making it difficult for me to stand.

"Enter," started Peregrine as the window that was the desert flashed to ocean water, the pane with the forest following.

"The," he continued, the next three windows switching.

"Pacific," he finished, just as the last two panels flashed to underwater ocean, and I stared, the hair on my back prickling. It was as if we were in a glass room twenty feet below the surface, surrounded by coral, the light a dancing blue and the air even cooled by the water. And it felt as if any second a flood would come rushing in to make us part of the scenery.

"The trick is in the elevation changes," he boasted as I gritted my teeth, focusing on holding back my churning stomach, "That's what holds the water back. You see, we are at a higher altitude than the water - for it to enter this enclosure, it would have to climb to our elevation. That takes a heap of energy - enough, as you see below, to suck all the heat out of particularly determined fish."

"So this," I said, the pieces coming together in my mind. "You built all this as a portable location chamber. So that whoever is born here, on this table, can have any power their parents desire."

"Any power *I* desire," he corrected. "Just think, an army of any power type, no matter how exotic, at my hands. They're born here in secret, then deployed to our schools, under our influence. No longer do we need to accept the scraps that the police send to us off the streets. Now the rehabilitation centers can manufacture their own powers at will. The strongest powers and it would be years before anyone knew. And if they ever found our secret, it would be years to develop their own portals - simply making one portal stable enough to exist takes *months*. Along with a high powered Teleporter, which are quite rare."

"So my mother, you wanted her to deliver their children? So that, from the moment they entered the world, they are your high powered slaves?"

"So that the moment they enter the world, they are our soldiers. They are good citizens. Just imagine, SC - we can create powers completely currently unknown to man! Even I cannot teleport as far as these portals stretch, but when I create a portal, there's no limit to how far it can go since I create it piece by piece. There's an entire network of portal connections I have created, and it can only expand."

"So what? Why don't you just transport the mother to the locations instead of using this device?"

"Because they're protected and regulated. Use your imagination, boy! Think why I chose your mother! We can stretch the bounds of human exploration! With your mother's help, I can create a tunnel to rooms in the space station once she describes them. Or even farther - imagine a child born on the moon! A child born at the core of the Earth! What a wonder that would be, and who *knows* what the powers would look like."

"Who knows," I answered, rolling my eyes. "That truly would be a mystery."

"Are you being sarcastic with me, boy?" Peregrine asked, an edge in his voice.

"Absolutely not."

"Then take this room right now. Someone born in this environment would be the equivalent of being born on a submarine. It could produce an Aquatic, a Waver, or countless other marine powers. And they would be strong, stronger than any born above water on a ship. Not only does this increase variety, but also potency."

"What if it doesn't work? What if you've done all this for nothing."

"It will, but even if it fails, we still have the rehabilitation centers. There is a movement, SC. *Thousands* of us. Siri and I are only a small part of the machine - soon, very soon, the cause will emerge across the globe. The cause for a perfect world. To *rehabilitate* the *entire* world."

"And you're asking me to be a piece of it? To join?"

"Yes, and very near the top of the chain! What do you think, SC? To turn this down would be ignoring the greatest opportunity of your life," he said, spreading his arms wide, a maniacal smile playing across his lips.

In response, the nausea from his portals welled upwards inside of me, and I released my willpower as it surged. Leaning over, I vomited over his medical table, shaking as I retched, and backed out of the portal room.

Chapter 83

"I'll take that as a no," intoned Peregrine, his face darkening as he followed me through the exit. "Fortunately, the area is not yet sterile. Think, SC, about what I'm offering you. And realize that I cannot let you leave. Stay here through your own will or through mine."

"Then I can only thank you for the classes on fighting," I responded, widening my stance. The hair on the back of my neck pricked as he studied me, and my senses heightened, particularly those waiting for the ripping of space prior to teleportation.

"You realize this is foolishness, madness," he said, his eyes cold. The eyes of someone unfazed by death, who had seen it many times before. Who had caused it many times before. "I've seen your skill, I've watched you train for a paltry few weeks. At your power level, I could reach in to crush your very heart."

He extended his hand with a grasping motion, the fingers curling to point the nails inwards in a gnarled ball.

"Then you should try!" I shouted, and reached out with a force point to the lights high above, dragging a swinging fluorescent down with enough force to snap the dual chains fastening it to the concrete. The fixture and tube fell with an acceleration several times that of gravity, slamming into the ground in an explosion of white powder and glass where Peregrine had stood just a moment prior, just before he materialized five feet to the right.

"You don't stand a chance, boy. Stand down," commanded Peregrine, dusting off particles from his coat with the nonchalant back of his hand. "It's only murder if the subject is innocent, and you have used up your first warning."

"Then make this my second!" I yelled, dragging an advertising board that had been leaning against the wall towards him in a swipe that covered the length of the station, air *whooshing* away like the swing of a baseball bat. But Peregrine simply sidestepped, not away from the board, but rather *through* it, disappearing just before it reached him and materializing on the other side.

Confidence surged within me, for neither time had I intended to actually hit him. Rather, I wanted to test that I could feel him ripping through space just before he moved. And each time, I *felt* it just before he flickered away.

For a moment, I considered launching a black sphere at him in a direct strike. I knew he couldn't feel space like me. If that was among his talents, he would have known that I was an imposter far before now. He would have sensed my power was not, in fact, telekinetic. And without that sense, he might have no time to move. The sphere would leave a hole in his chest the size of a bowling ball, and the battle would be over before he would have a chance to attack.

But if the sphere missed, my power would be revealed. Peregrine would be more cautious, would anticipate the unknown in his attacks. And if he did win the battle, instead of killing me, he would bring me back to Siri. With my power revealed, perhaps I would become just as strong of a weapon for them as the device Peregrine had built.

"Your mistake, boy," Peregrine said, his lip curling, twitching his mustache. "But I won't kill you here. No, instead of taking your heart, all I shall do is disconnect a single vertebra. Cripple you beyond the help of most healers, make you watch all that you turned down come to fruition. And turn you into the wedge that will make your mother cooperate."

"No, don't!" cried my mother behind me as Peregrine extended his hand once more, and I felt space open just before his fingers and at the small of my back, the seam of reality splitting with reluctance. Then he pushed his hand through, his expression triumphant as his fingers disappeared into nothingness. For a moment he was still, the expression on his face frozen, while I felt a mounting pressure build just above my hips. Then his eyebrows raised in disbelief as I continued to stand, my head cocked to the side, feeling his fingers trying to ram through the barrier.

Without my intervention of creating a tiny force point just where he tried to break through, effectively trapping his fingers, he might have accomplished the task. Peregrine *had* mentioned that higher powers possessed auras more difficult to penetrate. Maybe mine would have stopped him. But my mobility was not something I was willing to chance.

"Was that supposed to hurt?" I asked, my voice level, "Or are you trying to tickle me, Peregrine? After creating all these portals, maybe your power is exhausted. Or maybe, you've underestimated my abilities!"

To punctuate the last sentence, I raised my hands, calling forth the strongest force points I could muster. As I pulled the empty train car from the subway track up into the air and hurling it at Peregrine, sparks erupted as it bounced, the metal screeching as it peeled back and grated against the floor. His expression still shocked, Peregrine failed to teleport before the car and he collided.

Chapter 84

The roof of the car drove into his shoulder with the unstoppable mass of several tons, sending him skittering backwards on his heels until his instinct kicked in. He teleported away as the car continued on its kamikaze path towards the wall, the metal wailing as air RUSHED out from the closing gap. And without powers, Peregrine would have been in that gap only moments later, crushed and the fight finished.

Instead, he scowled, evaluating the damage of his torn sleeve before nodding his head in approval.

"If nothing else, we taught you the element of surprise," he sighed. "Just another trait that will go to no use. But you're out of your league, boy. *Far* out of your league."

The punch came out of nowhere, the space ripping open just right of my head as Peregrine led his teleport with a fist. Two knuckles caught me across the face as he stepped through the void, my vision flashing as I reeled backward. Then he was through the other side, teleporting away in an instant, both the entrance and exit rips in space appearing too quick for me to react. I sprawled backwards, launched by the force of the collision and rolling against the concrete.

Blood dripped from my nose as I climbed to my feet, stars flashing across my vision and lacerations digging into my forearm. But Peregrine was already thirty feet out of reach, casually leaning against the side of the station, his eyes on me like a snake watching prey.

"It's no fair fight," he said. "No way for you to win. This is a game for me, SC. I only have to invoke the lowest extents of my power."

Provoke him until he makes a mistake, I thought, *Make him too confident. Time it just right.*

"You're still no match for me!" I shouted, raising my hand to whip a stream of gravel from the track. The stones curled in midair, a band of rock cascading as hail in a strike where Peregrine stood. He sidestepped, not even bothering to teleport as the projectiles missed him and scattered about the station, bouncing in every direction as they met the wall and floor.

"Inexperienced *and* incompetent," commented Peregrine, disapproving. "With many more lessons to be learned."

This time, I caught the rip in space as he stepped through, his left hand gripping my shoulder as his right dug into my gut. I doubled over, coughing and gasping as a second impact followed the first. My hands gripped my knees as I sputtered, Peregrine already departed out of reach once more as I lashed outwards, kicking only air where he had been moments before.

"I do believe pain is the best teacher." He laughed, now at the other end of the station, his voice echoing. "And maybe, with time, you will learn from it."

He teleported again, only ten feet away and directly facing me. From behind me, I could hear my mother screaming, shouting curses at him that I pushed into the background while I concentrated, as I focused my attention away from the throbbing side of my face, and my breath that came too shallow, and the blood that was seeping through my clothes. Becoming aware of all that was around us that could be sensed by my power.

There was his machine, a twisted knot at the center of the station, with tunneled stands that travelled through the air away from it in all direction. There were the rips in space he had recently closed, like wounds still healing, steaming as they faded away. And there were smaller sensations, such as the feeling of the earth bending space around it, a light ever present touch that was always in the background. Far away, I also felt reverberations from the raging battle in the last station, the distant ripples of thick packets of energy being released so quickly they warped space itself.

"One last time I offer you," Peregrine said as I stared, waiting on the balls of my feet, reaching out with my power to feel the space between us. He held up a single finger and leaned forward as he spoke, like a parent to a disobedient toddler. "One last courtesy. Choose."

"Never!" I shouted back, my voice coming out barely as a wheeze.

"Then your lesson in pain has only just begun, boy!"

His eyes flashed as he lunged forward, and I tensed, knowing I would only have one chance. There, just milliseconds later, I felt it start to form, the rip in space that preceded his teleports. And right as his body started to cross through the tunnel in space, I struck, putting all my power behind a single blow.

Chapter 85

The space behind Peregrine collapsed with a force so violent that the station shook, the force point I generated by him so powerful that it pulled in objects from far edges of the track. To Peregrine, the point would be indistinguishable from gravity. And now, he was already moving through the rip in space, propelled forwards by his own power, climbing out of a gravitational energy well with no way to pay the debt.

Cold exploded in front of me as he stepped through, his eyes widening in shock as frost leapt across the tips of his hair, and his breath billowed in front of him like a miniature cloud. Snowflakes flurried out from the rip in space as if an arctic blizzard were on the other side, partially obscuring him as I aimed my punch directly into his lower chest. In his unexpected environment, the blow caught him defenseless and his expression flickered to confusion, then panic, and he initiated the logical course of action for a seasoned soldier in an unpredictable situation.

Retreat, reassess the situation, and return to attack.

Two dark orbs appeared in my hands by the time he opened the second rip in space, his steps slow as frostbite bit him down to the bone. And as he stepped through once more to escape, I yanked the space around the orbs downwards, pulling him as hard as possible towards me while still letting him flee, creating a second gravitational debt that he would have to climb out of to teleport.

What came out the other end of the portal was not Peregrine - no, the figure that materialized on the other end of the room was solid ice, the skin cracking as moisture flash froze within cells, the muscles refusing to obey commands as energy fled them. Moisture from the damp underground air rapidly joined him as his knees buckled, covering his exterior in a layer of white that hissed like dry ice. Then he fell backwards, his limbs locked in position as he rocked on his back and stared at the ceiling, his temperature as cold as liquid nitrogen.

I walked to him with caution, still nursing the injuries that he had given me, and stared down at what remained. Through the layer of ice, his eyes were frozen and still. His face was a shade of blue, his expression locked and his chest unmoving.

"The trick is in elevation changes," I whispered as a chunk of ice fell from his hair and skittered across the ground. "You said it yourself, Peregrine. And you gave me no choice."

I turned back to the machine he had created, the monstrosity intended to generate an army of super - soldiers to obey him. And I realized that it would be no small feat to destroy it. The strands of ripped space surrounded it like bits of spider webs and knocking them down at once would only tangle the web together, twisting and folding space rather than smoothing it out once more. I would have to return later, after the battle was over, when I would be at full strength and my injuries would be healed, and when I would have hours to work. The portals still showed the Pacific, the azure ocean waving through the small doorway to the room, the dark shapes in the depths hiding just out of sight.

But now, it was time for one more shape to join them.

I had to wrap my shirt around my hands to lift Peregrine, his skin still too cold for me to touch. Even then, I could only drag him, leaving behind a trail of white that led to the entrance of his contraption.

"You made this to bring people into this world," I said, pulling him up onto the metal table at the center. "It's fitting, then, that it delivers you from it."

I pushed, the legs of the table screeching as they moved, as if Peregrine himself were resisting his fate. Then the lip of the metal met the border on one of the portals and pushed into it, the Pacific absorbing the edge of the table with greedy tendrils of water. The table continued sliding as if it were moving downhill, pulling itself through, tipping into the depths, taking its payload, Peregrine, with it as the last portion passed through and was now only visible from my side of the barrier.

Together, they sank, Peregrine weighed down by his boots and the undercurrent of the falling table. And around them swam the same bright school of fish as before, darting in and out with curiosity to view their new visitor. Swirling around him, but gradually leaving in a flurry of color that travelled towards the surface, forgetting the faceless shape as it sought the ocean floor.

Chapter 86

"I had to," I mumbled, my hands shaking as I looked back to the portals. I sat next to my mother, my breath coming in shallow gasps. In my lap was the chain that had shackled her moments before, the metal links in the center freshly vaporized by one of my dark spheres.

A dark sphere that sickened me to look at. The same that had brought Peregrine to his death.

"SC, how did he die?" she asked, her voice soft as tears welled in my eyes. Now the police had a true reason to find me. Now I was no longer innocent.

"I froze him," I started, swallowing. "I killed him by using—"

"No, SC," she said, using the edge of her shirt to brush away the blood on my face, the fabric stinging as it met open cuts. "What was he doing when he died? What action was he taking?"

"He was teleporting to hit me, to punch me again. And it was either I attack, or I be killed. It still doesn't feel right, though. Not at all." I shook my head as I tried to use the words as a flimsy shield.

"Tell me, SC," she continued, running a hand through my hair. "If he never teleported to attack you, would your attack have worked? Would he still be alive right now, and speaking?"

"He would. Without jumping, my power would have had no effect."

"Then to me, it sounds like he decided his own fate," she comforted, embracing me with both arms. "Through his own actions, he died from a force of nature. As surely as looking over the edge of a cliff and walking into nothingness. And even if you *had* taken his life directly, SC, there are many that he has already stolen. Plus many more to come. Mine, yours, your classmates."

She stood, taking my arm, and started to walk towards the subway tunnel, continuing to speak.

"You prevented that, SC. Remember that Peregrine brought this on himself."

"That doesn't make it much easier," I said as our footsteps echoed in the cavern. "It does a bit, but not much."

"And it shouldn't. If it were easy for you, I'd be worried. Do not take it lightly," she said, though her brow was already creased. "But given the chance, I would have done the same. You saved me, SC. You made the right but difficult decision."

We reached the track and climbed down into it, my mother sighing as she dropped over the edge. We stared into the dark tunnel, pausing, blinking.

"Is there another way out?" I asked, casting my gaze over the station. "Things aren't going to be calm on the other end, and I'd rather approach from above."

"All the exits are filled with cement," she answered. "I nearly escaped once, but the only path is through this tunnel. And before I could take it, they found me - took them three days of searching while I hid in plain sight, but Peregrine had the tunnel boarded up until I was shackled again."

"Then the tunnel it is," I said, and we stepped forward together.

After the last few weeks, it felt strange to fall into the rhythm of footsteps with my mother, for her cadence to lead my walk. I'd grown used to setting my own pace, to choosing my own path. The world had forced me to learn to move on my own, to make my own decisions.

And now, shadowing someone again was strange, almost awkward. As if the muscle memory no longer existed and was now replaced by something else, something stronger.

"What happened, SC?" asked my mother as we moved. "Ever since the apartment. Did they harm you?"

"A *lot* happened," I sighed, my thoughts racing, unsure where to start, "but I came out okay. And now, everything can go back to normal. We can move back home - wait, *can* we move back home?"

I'd never actually planned farther than rescuing my mother - everything afterward seemed secondary. Something that *she* would be able to figure out once we had reunited.

"We're not going to be able to, are we?" I asked, my voice deflated.

"Most likely not, SC. But home is not simply the apartment we left a few weeks ago. Home is where we make it. Where we're together. And with my ability to keep you hidden, that can be many places."

As we retraced my steps, the tunnel turned to reveal a dull pinprick of light far ahead. And with the light, I heard the sounds of fighting, battle cries accompanied by crashing and explosions. Indications that my friends were fighting.

"I have to go!" I said, turning to my mother. "Home might be more than just the two of us! Don't leave the tunnel."

"SC, wait—" she shouted, but I had already started sprinting, leaving her behind in the darkness. Ahead, my friends were still in potential danger. Danger that I had brought them into.

And now, I would need to help them escape.

Chapter 87

I exploded from the tunnel at full speed, two black orbs hovering just above my palms, and leapt up onto the platform. Smoke still obscured the scene in a thick haze, but I could see the guards lined on one end, their powers still fully activated. And on the other, crouched for cover but holding ground, were the police and students.

Neither side was moving - both held back, tentative, as two figures stood in the middle between them, their arms outstretched against both sides. The guards from the rehabilitation facility, with thick glowing force fields generating from the palms, stronger than any I had seen them use before, and splitting the fight down the center, preventing either side from mounting an attack.

"Stand down." The voice came from within the mist, a slight singsong quality to it that I knew all too well. "What has happened today is the business of the rehabilitation facility alone. We shall cover all costs for damages and assure you nothing of this nature shall ever occur again, as testified by our unblemished track record prior to today."

Siri's typically spotless suit was covered in dust, a hole the size of a baseball singed into the side, and an entire collar missing. Her hair, usually restricted to allow no strands freedom, was frazzled and unkempt. And her voice was low, dangerous.

"Neither the police nor I can ignore what transpired in the last hour," came another voice, one that made me bite my lip. The Hunter. And far closer to me in the smoke than Siri. "Perhaps we can ignore the outbreak, but there is something far more sinister occurring. The rehabilitation facilities are *not* authorized to hold a militia. And worse, they appear to have been attacking *children* before we intervened."

"The business of the rehabilitation facilities is beyond the police, and this was simply a training exercise gone awry," Siri retorted, her voice low, almost a growl. "We have a balance, Art. A delicate one. Lives will be lost if it is toppled. Do you really want to be responsible for that? Just to try to prove a point that doesn't exist?"

"If it's not extinguished now, it will only grow worse," said The Hunter. "The wound cannot be allowed to fester. What are you hiding, Siri? What is it that you don't want the police to know?"

"I assure you, nothing of consequence," she answered, throwing her arms wide. "Nothing of interest, and nothing of any danger. As I said, simply a training exercise some of the students took slightly too seriously."

"Unless you are harboring a rare and strong power," accused The Hunter. "I can feel it here now; I know it exists. I am absolutely sure that it is not documented. But I don't know what it can do, and that makes it extremely dangerous."

"Rare powers?" Siri threw her head back and laughed. "Art, *you* and the police supply my feed stock. Any of my students must come through you. You likely know their abilities better than I do! Back at the facility, I will throw my doors open to you and your team for a full inspection. But now, I repeat, stand down. This goes deeper than you know, higher than you know. You will deeply regret any action you take."

"Defy me—" started The Hunter, shrill, but I saw an officer rush forward to take his arm. Roland, the same officer who had investigated my apartment with him hissed into his ear, his voice low enough to be missed by Siri but making it to my position.

"Take the offer, Art. We'll investigate the facility and you can search as long as you want. I'll station officers to monitor the subway until this time. This isn't worth losing lives on a theory, and she won't go down without a fight."

"We have them under our thumb," hissed back The Hunter. "It's our best chance in years. Letting them go and giving them time to cover their tracks would be insane."

"These are *my* officers, and therefore *my* decision to make," said Roland. "Whatever happened here can technically be explained away. The risk of finding nothing is too great. I need something concrete, Art. Proof of an act of aggression against *us*, not within her own program."

"Then what I do after this, I do without the knowledge of the police."

The Hunter's eyes blazed as he looked upwards and met Siri's triumphant gaze, preparing to concede when they were so close to discovering the secret in the tunnel. Giving away their opportunity to interrogate the confused students who still couldn't quite remember *why* they were fighting. He drew a sharp breath and cracked his neck, the words coming slow but firm.

"Tomorrow morning, be prepared for a complete search," he said, and I stiffened in disbelief, knowing that now was when I needed the police most and realizing I might be able to give them the boost that they needed. "If we find but one shred of evidence—"

As he spoke, I fed the black spheres in my hands, urging them to grow larger.

"One stray hair—"

I started to run towards the dual forcefields, cocking my right hand backwards to throw.

"Or *any* reason to investigate further, we—"

I shouted as I released the orb, the gravity around it sucking the dust out of the air in its trajectory until it collided with the force fields. I shouted as the explosion rocked the chamber, my voice the sole noise in the stunned silence.

"I am the rare power! I am her weapon, created by the facility to destroy those who oppose her, and I will protect Siri with my life!"

I threw the second orb at a shocked Roland, aiming to just barely miss him and cut a long gouge through the floor. The Hunter jumped backwards, his eyes locking on mine, his expression greedy as I shouted a final sentence.

"Prepare to die at her hand! The war begins now!"

Chapter 88

"Treason!" shouted The Hunter, throwing a hand forwards. "We arrest you for treason!"

Roland hesitated but his officers had already started moving forward, carried more by instinct than orders.

"Formation!" he cried. "Formation, unified phalanx!"

Two officers darted to the front, raising their hands as Siri screeched and an assault of powers began. Fire and ice tornadoes whipped across the station towards them, screaming across the concrete floor with alarming speed. But the two front officers flourished their hands, redirecting the energy back towards their opponents with a power that could only mean they were Bouncers, boomeranging any projectiles back towards the enemy. The other officers fell into a V-formation behind them, while those that had projectile-based powers occupied the outer layer to return fire on Siri's thugs. Protected on the inner layer were officers with close combat powers, and I recognized Ulrich, the officer with super strength who had forced me into his car several weeks before at the gas station. At the center of it all was Roland, his hands conducting movements like a composer, the reactions to his motions too quick to be natural.

But before I could admire the cooperation of the police, more pressing matters forced me into action. For while Siri and the police opposed each other, *both* Siri and the police opposed me.

Fatal forms of destruction rained down towards me from Siri's side, the powers intended to cause as much damage as possible as she looked on with rage. And from the police, powers intended to stun like the electric tentacle that had struck Darian emerged. Even more dangerous were the students, half of them remembering their allegiance to Siri to strike at me, while the other half following the police for the same effect.

I dove back into the recessed subway track as an arc of fire singed my hair. Several cinder blocks followed, shattering against the wall to shower me in chunks of concrete. Creating two black spheres, I positioned them in front of me to absorb the blows, pulling in anything that came close enough to strike me as a shield. But maintaining them eliminated my line of sight to the battle, as well as preventing me from forming an offensive.

"Oi, SC, mission accomplished?" came a voice from behind me and I turned to see Slugger strolling down the track, holding a piece of steel plating the size of a large shed as if it were made of paper as his own personal shield. "Time to brawl? How about we stir the pot and empty the dugouts?"

"Slugger, get the students out of here!" I answered just as Miles flung a piece piping ripped from the tunnel wall at me, parts of the metal making it between my spheres and whizzing past my neck. "Some of them are starting to attack the police, and I need their firepower off me!"

"Aye, coach, clearing the benches of the third string!" he answered and popped over the edge of the subway track before shouting in the direction of the students. "Oi, remember me, ya loons? Wendy waddles, Wendy waddles, yada yada yada, let's go!"

Winking at me, he whispered before sprinting away, "Too easy, SC. It's almost as if they couldn't think for themselves, eh? Likely due to the sad state of our academic system these days. The taxpayers would be so disappointed."

In a wave, the students turned to face him, their faces popping out of cubbyholes and hideaways like curious meerkats. Then Connor emerged, his expression furious and contagious. They leapt forwards in a stream, forgetting the battle as they remembered their initial purpose, rushing after Slugger as he disappeared cackling in a side tunnel. Funneling through the opening in pursuit, their cries drowned out by the sounds of the battle, and though they were numerous, it was impossible to tell if *all* of them escaped.

Turning back towards Siri's men, I narrowly avoided a fire tornado deflected by one of the Bouncers that careened down the track, evaporating into wispy sparks just thirty feet away. I sighed in relief, then frowned, realizing that the heat not only still remained but seemed to be increasing, as if the tornado was getting *closer* instead of disappearing. And was coming from the opposite direction.

"Hey, SC!" I heard from behind me in Lucio's voice. "Just snapped out of zombie mode! Whew, I'm exhausted. Being that pissed really takes it out of you!"

I held up a hand as I looked down the track, feeling another wave of heat and seeing a smoldering shadow appear. Behind me, I heard Lucio's footsteps approaching, his voice sill light.

"Don't tell me you're loony, SC! You would think that you'd be happy to see me, you know, alive! Maybe you should—" He stopped as he caught sight of who I was looking at and cursed. As we both realized that not *all* the other students had followed Slugger back to the surface.

Fino had remained behind.

Chapter 89

Another heat wave emanated from Fino as his face turned a deeper shade of red, and Lucio crouched behind me.

"I can't touch his mind at all," Lucio cried. "There's little to no rational thought going on in there, just rage. I could broadcast him a memory of frolicking puppies and he'd torch them into chicken nuggets."

"Shouldn't be a problem this time," I answered, remembering my initial match with Fino, when I had been unable to use my power because it had been a secret. But now, the odds of the match had changed.

"What's wrong here, Fino, lose sight of your friends?" I taunted, luring him forwards. "Even becoming an Upper didn't score you any of those, did it?"

This time, the heat wave was scorching as he shook, and I raised a dark sphere between us, letting it absorb the energy. With it as an obstacle, Fino would be unable to cross. And so long as I continued to provoke him, he'd eventually wear down, spent as his Furnace power consumed all his energy.

"Come on, Fino, is that all you've got? Are you scared of a round two?"

Enough heat poured forwards to turn the rails of the subway a glowing red and make the walls chip, but the black sphere held, stopping the heat like a cork in a bottle. And Fino shouted with frustration as the sphere stopped him too, pulling at him from several feet away as he stopped, realizing even in his enraged state that the orb was a danger that would have to be destroyed before moving forwards.

And Fino attempted just that.

Wave after wave crashed forwards as I realized that he was no longer a danger but rather a benefit - with Fino outpouring energy, no one would safely be able to approach from his direction. So long as he was pinned down, he formed a human shield. In a way, he was fighting *for* me.

"How long do you think he can keep this up?" asked Lucio, sweating. "And what's the plan? Are we jetting soon? I'd prefer *not* to be thrown back in handcuffs."

"Looks like the police are winning, so we should be good to go. Then we'll come back to find my mother after everything cools down. The police are after me too, so if we stay too long, they'll become a problem," I answered, watching as Roland directed two of his officers to absorb a stunned guard into the police cluster like an amoeba, handcuffs rapidly following as they left him paralyzed and facedown on the ground.

"Where are we going to be hiding out, then?" Lucio asked, ducking as debris rained down from the ceiling and the police captured another guard. "They'll be running a comb through this place finer than The Hunter uses for his hair once this is over."

"Once this is over, I wouldn't worry. Until then, we'll be wanting to watch the exits," I said, focusing on the dark orb that had started to grow heavy as it absorbed more of the surroundings. "My mother has a way of avoiding being found. Now that the police have reason to arrest her, the *last* thing we want is Siri escaping."

"Oh, that would be the *last* thing you would want, wouldn't it?" laughed a voice from above, and I turned to see Siri staring over the edge. Soot covered her right cheek while a crooked smile spread across her lips, one that failed to reach her eyes, which had narrowed to thin slits. Chills ran down my spine as she spoke again, her voice filled with relish. "And the *last* thing I would want would be for you to escape the police as well. If we go down, shan't we go down together?"

Then she started to sing, directing the words at both Lucio and me.

You've come so far, and now you'll rest,
SC, let your power turn lame,
Lucio, of your spirit we shall now put to test,
Its strength against the flame.

Calm washed over me with Siri's words, and my hands grew heavy. Ahead, the black orb started to shrink, throwing off rays of colors as I released my hold upon it. The colors danced along the subway track, peaceful in their arcs. Lucio sidled beside me, continuing forwards as I heard familiar laughter in the background.

Lucio stepped forwards again, staggering as his toes dragged and left tracks in the cement, the strength of the orb diminishing along with its size. And the heat surged forwards, bypassing the shield, hearing the buttons on my shirt until they burned into my chest.

Lucio cried out, shaking, but continued to glide ahead into the wave of heat, his shoes starting to smoke as their soles melted. Then he shouted again, the pain apparent as he took another step.

And I released my grip on the sphere entirely.

Chapter 90

Lucio screamed as he raised a hand, extending a finger towards Fino as the skin around his nail crackled, yet still edging closer. I felt another wave of serenity wash over me as I heard song in the background, paired with another feeling. One of pride.

Never before had the song been directed so strongly towards me, never before had I been the subject of its poetry. And now it vibrated through my entire existence - not background music but rather the focal theme. As if my own soul were singing with it, rejoicing with it. Becoming it.

My voice joined Lucio's as fire singed my eyebrows, a triumphant shout erupting from deep in my lungs as we fulfilled our purpose. I prepared to dash forward, casting myself among the fire, fulfilling the song.

My leg muscles tensed, a smile forming across my face, just as the singing morphed to a yowl, the sound like a cornered alley cat. The song dissipated as the illusion shattered, and Lucio jumped backwards, holding his hand and whimpering. I scrambled after him, forgetting about the dark sphere as it exploded, the recessed subway track carrying the full force of the blast towards Fino like a rifle barrel. He flew backwards, collapsing thirty feet away as the final energy behind his heat sputtered out, his skin pale white and calm, his breaths ragged.

But his gasps were not the only I heard as I turned and saw Siri fallen across the track, her eyes wide and unfocused as she stared upwards, a hand clasped across her lower chest. She struggled to breathe, the wind knocked out of her by the fall from the platform above. Without breath, there was no song. And without her song, my thoughts were clear.

Above her, Arial floated, the pair of handcuffs still dangling from her wrist, her shoulder still lowered from where she had crashed into Siri at full speed. From the end of her handcuffs hung a piece of the bed's headboard, the cheap meal connection unscrewed at the joint and ripped from the frame.

She glared as she looked at me, her eyes still as ablaze as when I had last seen her in the gym.

"Don't you *ever* leave me behind again," she barked, slightly tilted from weight of the headboard. "It almost cost you your life!"

"And mine!" started Lucio, cradling his hand, his voice pained. "Might do you a little good to listen to the lady next time, SC!"

"Get down here!" I shouted in response, realizing that she was hovering in the direct line of fire from the battle above.

"Or *what*, SC?" she sputtered. "Are you going to lie again, or leave again, or—"

"Or you might get hit!" I retorted, leaping up to grab her hand and pulling her towards the ground. "It's a battlefield up there!"

"Not *anymore*, it isn't," she said. "The police are just finishing up now, everyone is stunned and handcuffed. They've got a Healer working on two of them who took some nasty frostbite. And there's a few students down there that they're caring for too. But they didn't notice *this one* sneaking away," she said, nodding towards Siri.

"It's a good thing you did," I answered, looking at the tar tracks Lucio's shoes had left on the ground. "I don't think we would have made it much longer, Arial. Thank you."

I squeezed her hand and she blushed, her eyes meeting mine from underneath her brunette hair. She leaned forwards slightly, her pupils dilating and eyelids blinking.

"In case you two have forgotten," started Lucio from behind us, clearing his throat and pointing to Siri where she lay, "there's a murderer who will literally do us in as soon as she finds her voice on the ground here."

He bent over and took off his shoe, then wriggled his toes as he took off a sock and pulled away his shoelaces.

"If you ask me, it's time she put a sock in it!"

He bent over Siri, lashing one of the shoelaces around her wrists with no resistance in her stunned state. The knot was amateur but enough to hold for a few minutes, and he balled his sock up before pushing it into her mouth, looping the other shoelace around her head once to hold it in place.

"There. Bad breath is the best thing to leave that mouth in weeks, so I'd say the look suits you, Siri," he said when he finished, admiring his handiwork as she started to recover, her eyes flitting between us.

"We'll need the police here now, before she has a chance to work her way out of that," I said as she started to struggle. "I'll lure them in."

"No, SC, this one's on me," responded Arial, putting her hand on my chest and raising to shout over the edge of the platform, her voice high and distressed "Daddy! Daddy, I found one!"

"*Arial*?" came the shocked cry of The Hunter from the end of the station as she dropped back onto the track.

"I'll need to be going," I said as she took my hand once more and pulled me closer.

"I know, but not just yet," she answered and moved inwards, her lips brushing against mine for an instant in time that seemed to pause the actions around us. They were soft, softer than I would have expected, and my hand instinctively glided upwards to rest on her cheek. And for a moment, I forgot the rest of the world existed, that a battle was finishing around us, that there were others on the track.

Then she pulled away as I stood still, less thoughts occupying my brain than when Siri had exercised control over me, my mouth still parted.

"SC, let's roll! No more handcuffs, remember?" Lucio interrupted, pulling a face as he tugged at my elbow, and my feet started to move, though my stare still tracked Arial.

"See-see you soon," I stammered, starting to run.

"You better," she answered, watching me leave. "Don't give me an excuse to be more angry with you next time."

Chapter 91

"Back to the tunnel!" I said to Lucio as we raced along the track. "Now that we have Siri, there's no reason to guard the exit. Let's get my mother, then get out of here!"

We dashed into the tunnel and I turned left and right, looking for my mother and trying to feel the presence of her power.

"SC!" she shouted, her voice distant from behind us at the entrance from where we had just run. "Here! Where are you!"

"Deeper!" I shouted back, seeing her silhouetted against the edge. "Come on in! And you weren't supposed to leave!"

"The last thing a mother would do after losing her child is let him run back to the wolves," she lectured, coming towards us. "I searched for you outside and found nothing, but then saw you return. Of course, no one paid me any mind."

She waved as she walked, and behind her, I saw something glinting at the edge of the tunnel that caught my eye. A quick flash that made me squint, like a mirror catching sunlight, or a piece of glass splitting light. Or a diamond.

Blake stalked my mother from fifty feet behind, his entire power activated, practically glowing as he walked. He dragged a finger along the side of the tunnel, sparks flying off the wall as it dug in up to the knuckle. Rainbows danced around him as the light in the tunnel grew more dim, and he shouted, his voice carrying clear along the tube.

"I saw what you did, SC! I saw what you did to Siri, and I don't know how, but I know you're behind all this! You and your friend Slugger, and you're both going to pay!"

He started walking faster, and I remembered how he had appeared the night he had searched for Darian, his clothes and shoes shredded by his power. There, between him and me, walked my mother. Even if he touched her by accident, his sharp edges would still cut through her skin with ease. And if he had seen her, it would be a far more dangerous position.

"Stop! Let's have the arena match that was denied to me now!" I shouted back and started forward. "I challenge you to a fight in the station!"

"No chance. I'm not letting you try any tricks!" he said and increased his speed to a run. I cursed, trying to think of options. In ten seconds, he and my mother would intersect—if I threw a dark sphere at him, there was no guarantee it wouldn't harm her in the narrow tunnel. He was too far for a force point to pull him backwards, and trying to collapse the tunnel between them could destroy enough of the structure to kill everyone inside.

To reduce the distance, I rushed towards them, feeling out with my power for when I would be able to accurately and safely use it. But the farther I reached out, the more it became muddled. In the distance, I could feel lines extending like a spider web from Peregrine's machine, forming distracting warpages of space that ran around me like conduit.

Then Blake was ten feet away from my mother as she pressed herself against the wall, and I prepared to strike. I snapped my fingers in the motion to create a black orb, but as it sprang to life, Peregrine's lines around me shifted, dancing in alignment to the new factor. In some areas they stretched, the space itself almost seeming to elongate, and in other areas they compressed, giving my vision the illusion of a funhouse mirror.

I pushed my control over them - here, where the space itself was not ripped but merely tunneled, moving the lines came naturally. Instinctually, I pinched them together, flipping them inside out just like the pocket in space above my wrist where I kept spare spheres. They obeyed, looping in a circle around the space between Blake and my mother, then rapidly constricting like the neck of a balloon.

For an instant, the world turned upside down as if I were looking at my reflection in a spoon, and as the lines collapsed, so too did the cross section of the tunnel. Brinks on the walls stretched inwards, elongating from several inches to several feet, reaching towards the center like dozens of fingers. Then they met just before Blake, leaving what felt like a knot in space itself, the walls tucking in upon themselves to form a wall that appeared impossible.

Sensing out with my power, I knew what I had created - a curling in of matter, a region impossible to cross because the very fabric of space itself was tied together. Even if Blake managed to cut through the bricks, he would only loop inwards on himself, finding himself turned around to face where he had already been.

It was a cork in a wine bottle, an impassable barrier for him. And judging by the curses that reverberated through the brick, his mind had also reached that conclusion.

Chapter 92

We await the official police press conference, but our several witnesses have agreed to share their accounts of the events under Crescent Street. *Continued on Page 4.*

I flipped the newspaper to the center and continued reading the article, taking a moment to view the photograph of the subway entrance with a trail of thick black smoke pouring from the door. As the police had dragged out Siri's guards, one of the Flamethrowers had managed to lash out a last time with enough heat to catch a plastic trash bin on fire, providing the press with the perfect photo opportunity.

Select students were available for interview following the events on Crescent. With the closure of the rehabilitation facility until further notice, approximately half of the students were entered into the care of the local government and denied comment. Those with living guardians were returned to their families and provided breaking information, though still traumatized.

"It all happened so fast," states Anthony Weezer, age sixteen, who suffered minor injuries from the conflict. "One moment we were in class, the next we were in the station. I don't really remember how we got there, just that we had to fight. That much was important; there's nothing more I wanted more than fighting. But I'm not sure who, or why."

Anthony was unavailable for further questioning in his state, but student Josh Harper shed light upon inner workings of the rehabilitation facility.

"We fought because we were told, because that's how we were supposed to be good students. If you didn't fight, you scrubbed toilets and ate less, since you were a burden."

The facility is under additional scrutiny as approximately ten of its students have entered counseling due to an extreme allegiance or form of Stockholm syndrome to the headmistress, Siri Cerena. Upon her arrest, several engaged the police in physical combat, demanding her release. None of these ten have regained independence since separation from the facility, and all have been deemed a danger to themselves without restraint. One such student, Blake Rockwell, suffered from hallucinations and visions of grandeur following the event, leading to the drug testing of all involved students.

Several students remain missing and are actively being sought by the police, though until an official statement is released many of the names have remained private. One student, Mason Florence, has been identified as missing from the facility for over a week from their internal paperwork and is considered a separate case.

Siri Cerena will be transferred to a high security prison without bail until her court date. From the public records, Siri is a Special possessing a low powered version of Teaching Aid, allowing her to ingrain lessons into the minds of her students. After her father's death via automobile accident two decades prior, Siri herself was an orphan to the state, and is quoted to have joined the rehabilitation program to "improve the country through a strong citizen base." Additional interviews with students are expected to shed further light upon both her intentions and actions.

Several suspects have been taken into custody, though many instructors at the facility are currently at large. Additional details are to emerge tonight providing their descriptions, and any leads regarding their whereabouts should be immediately reported into the provided hotline below.

I finished reading and frowned as Lucio appeared with Slugger, each carrying two armfuls of groceries. We were underground in the station with Peregrine's teleportation machine, though in the past week, the appearance had changed significantly. Each of us owned a tent spread out across the floor and a small kitchen was erected near the center, complete with a foldable pantry and a cupboard made from a repurposed filing cabinet.

"I'll tell you, SC, I don't think I'll ever get used to walking through the entrances you created," said Lucio, setting down the groceries. "Feels like my insides are being squeezed out every time! One of these days, I might actually get stuck."

"You'll be getting stuck because ye ate all the granola bars," complained Slugger, dropping his groceries as well. "But I like the entrances. No one getting through those in a hurry, that's for sure."

"I didn't eat the bars, I swear!" countered Lucio. "I don't even *like* granola! Besides, we have *plenty* of money now that we're selling the construction materials down here. I should be able to eat all the ones I want!"

They continued to bicker and I cracked a smile, looking back towards the way they had come. The first day after we decided to return to the station, I'd cut several holes in the cemented doors towards the surface, then had turned space inwards on itself in the same fashion that kept Blake out. After some trial and error, Lucio had discovered that the barriers were not entirely impermeable - at the corners, each had a small *crease* in space. And by walking into the corner *just* right, nose first and spinning twice, the traveler would pop out the other side unharmed.

"Well, if you didn't eat it, I suppose they're just disappearing into thin air!" retorted Slugger. "You could at least have given me a memory of eating them, then I'd at least have some enjoyment!"

"Enough," silenced my mother as she took the groceries. It had been her idea to return - with her power, she had already proven the area could be hidden. And for the next few weeks, or until Siri was sentenced, it would be too dangerous to live above ground. Even the trips to the grocery and salvage yard only occurred after dark, and my mother had insisted upon accompanying us with her powers. "Lucio, start cutting tomatoes. Slugger, you're on salad dressing; it won't make itself. And SC, start cleaning. This kitchen is certainly dirty enough to warrant it."

Chapter 93

I pulled my hood up around my ears as I walked, letting the long shadow from the nearby street lamp obscure my features. I shivered, the cool breeze kicking up advertisement fliers that had been tucked into mailboxes and swirling them down the deserted street. Above, the moon offered little illumination. It was better that way.

Only a few weeks had passed since I had last walked down this street, measured in time. But measured in other ways, it had been far longer. Measured in experiences, in memories. In new friends and fiends. In learning that the world extended far beyond the four walls of my mother's apartment and the occasional glimpse at an academy I had once considered magical. And realizing I could help direct that world for better or for worse far more than I had ever imagined.

The ornate decorations that surrounded each of the houses seemed less impressive now, less flashy and rather just another part of the background. I counted addresses while I watched for others in the night – but at two in the morning, my only company was the occasional stray cat and hooting owl. I stopped when I reached a house with a lavish fountain sporting a family crest, accompanied by a lawn so verdant it looked painted.

I stood on the curb, the tips of my shoes just touching the grass, and raised my right hand, shaking a dark sphere out from the pocket above my wrist. It glided forwards, coming to rest at the top of the fountain, drawing the water upwards but not pulling hard enough to absorb anything more than mist. The crest almost looked better elongated – less confined, the water free from the grasp of gravity.

In less than a minute, the door creaked open, and the man I was waiting for stepped out, peering at me across the fountain water from his porch. For a moment, we were both silent, waiting, the tension palpable, the only sound the trickling of water between us, cascading on marble that had lost its luster over time and appeared grey in the night.

"I assume you are not here for dinner," said The Hunter, his voice different from how it had been just a few days before. Thinner, the words with a slightly more wheezy quality than his usual sharp and polished tone. As I squinted through the darkness, I saw other differences becoming apparent - silver streaks ran through his once black hair, and where it had once been uniform, it now receded above his brow in thinned patches. Fresh creases cut into the skin on his forehead, and his eyes had turned dull, more sunken.

"Not this time," I answered, unmoving.

"Then what is it you want? I could have the police here in minutes. Quite audacious for you to show your face."

"And your family is in that house, which I could destroy in seconds," I answered, letting the black orb on the fountain swell to punctuate my sentence. "No, I came here for something else. A truce."

"A truce? A truce?!" He laughed, the sound eerie in the deserted neighborhood. "You cost me ten years, you threaten my household, and you come looking for a truce? To think this all could have been prevented if I had recognized you for what you were when you were at my very table."

"And if it had been prevented, the rehabilitation facility would still stand. Those students would be slaves."

"Yes, *those* students. *Those* students who never had an impact on me and never will again," he sneered, his lip curling. "You'll learn there will always be an equivalency of them in your life, always people you can help, or you can ignore and never experience their existence again. Eventually, you'll learn that they don't matter. That no matter what you do, they will always be there. *Always.*"

I shivered at his words, staring down at the fountain. And I continued to speak, ignoring his statement. Wondering if Mikey the homeless man from the park would have shouted *True* afterwards.

"Regardless, it does neither of us good to continue this game. There's more like Siri out there - we can't waste time fighting each other when there is a larger enemy."

"But I thought you were on her side?" he mocked, then held up a hand to silence me, "Rhetorical question, boy. I do admit it was clever of you, that trick in the station. And though you may have some of the officers fooled, in hindsight, it is *very* apparent. There are those who would not have been deceived so easily. Perhaps I was never deceived at all."

He paused, looking down at his hands, studying the fresh wrinkles that had claimed them, and continued to speak.

"*Whatever* it is you are, I agree to this truce so long as you do not give me reason to find you. That you swear you do not aid those behind Siri. Realize that she is only the surface - with each layer, it stagnates, it rots. I've seen it from experience. And know that should your motives ever change," his voice dropped low, almost to a growl, "I can find you, and I *will* find you."

"I swear," I answered, holding a hand over my heart and starting to back away, "if anything, I plan on destroying them, not helping them."

"I've heard that promise enough times to hold my doubts. Those two actions are more intertwined than you can imagine." He paused and cast his gaze back to the orb floating above the fountain. Suppressed curiosity flickered across his face, and for a second, I saw the same Hunter that had sprinted from his house to discover an unknown power on the streets. A man driven with the obsession of a collector.

"This much you owe me," he said. "*What* are you?"

"Something out of this world," I answered and returned back to the street. I nodded back, both to him and to the face of his wife that peered through the curtains, now ten years younger than I had last seen her.

And to the girl who floated just above his roof, hidden from his sight, who had convinced me to return. And who was the reason I would continue to return.

Chapter 94

I sighed in the station, staring at the multiple facets from within Peregrine's teleportation machine. I had hoped that, with his death, the power that held it together would fade. That like an abandoned car left to rust, it would crumble over time, removing my need to dismantle it. Reaching forwards with my power, I felt the seams of space ripped wide open by the portals, pulling the bucket at my side closer in case I would need to use it. Earlier that day, when I had initially probed the machine, it had come in useful twice.

"SC, do you have a moment?" asked Lucio, jolting me out of my concentration as my eyelids shot upwards. In front of me, the portal flickered, shooting through several landscapes before returning to static as I pulled away. In that second, I caught sight of snow, of a busy city street, and a wall of thick mist.

Don't sneak up on me like that, Lucio," I managed as my stomach clenched. "Next time, the results might be messier."

"Sorry, SC," he said, the usual play in his voice missing. Facing him, I saw he wore one of the backpacks that we had purchased for moving groceries. And that his tent was strapped to the outside, folded and held together with cord. "I figured I'd want to say goodbye, though."

"Goodbye?! What do you mean by that?" I asked as he shuffled a foot against the ground.

"Well, I just, I don't want to be a burden, SC. I'm not part of your family. I don't want to be an outsider here."

"Lucio, don't be ridiculous. You *are* part of this family, and the last thing I would want is for you to leave."

Tears welled up in his eyes as he clutched the shoulder straps, and he bit his lip.

"You – you mean that?"

"I do, Lucio, and you aren't going anywhere. We're in this together now. No matter how deep it goes. Brothers."

He leapt forward, throwing a hug around me and wiping a tear away behind my back.

"I've never heard that before, SC, not from someone who meant it. I've never known how it would feel."

"Now you do," I said as he stepped away. "And don't forget that. You belong here and nowhere else."

He dropped the pack on the ground, removing the tent along with several other possessions he had packed. Then he squinted at Peregrine's machine, his eyebrows scrunched together.

"In this together, you say?" he asked. "What exactly do you mean by that?"

"From what I can gather, there's a whole group of people like Siri out there. Someone has to stop them, and it seems like no one else is trying. I won't force anyone to fight, but—"

"But you won't have to," Lucio completed for me. "I'm in. Heh, us versus the world. Plus Slugger. And maybe more. A whole alliance, a rebellion! I'd say it was grassroots, but I think we're a little deeper than that." He tapped the floor and looked towards the station roof, which was still underground.

"We'll need all the help we can get. If there's one thing I know, it's that this won't be easy," I said.

"And we'll need all the tools we can get too!" Lucio exclaimed, his voice growing excited as he took my arm and pulled it away from the machine. "Whoever is behind Siri, what if they're global? What if they aren't just in this city?"

He looked over the machine, nodding, "The *last* thing we would want to do is dismantle our ability to appear in dozens of locations at a moment's notice. SC, this might have been their greatest weapon. But now, for a completely different reason, it's *ours*."

I hesitated, then nodded, moving away from the machine. No matter its purpose when it had been created, Lucio was right - dismantling it would be destroying a valuable resource.

I looked over the station, with room for countless more tents. Over Slugger and my mother playing cards at a small table, the beginnings of a team. A small team now, but one that could grow, that could have a tremendous impact. One that maybe Darian would join, wherever he was, when we established contact with him again.

And somewhere above us, there were dozens of students recently released from the rehabilitation facility. Students whose minds Lucio could scrub of remainders of Siri's influence from, who might be motivated to join us. To rebel.

To fight back.

END OF BOOK 1

For more stories by Leonard Petracci, or to find out when book 2 of Star Child will be released, sign up for his mailing list on Amazon.

Contact Leonard at

LeonardPetracci@gmail.com

Made in the USA
Monee, IL
20 June 2020

34093935R00173